A TALE OF THE
FRENCH AND INDIAN WAR

THE BORDER COVENANT

HUGH C. GRIFFITH

TATE PUBLISHING & *Enterprises*

Published by Tate Publishing & Enterprises, LLC
127 E. Trade Center Terrace | Mustang, Oklahoma 73064 USA
1.888.361.9473 | www.tatepublishing.com

Tate Publishing is committed to excellence in the publishing industry. The company reflects the philosophy established by the founders, based on Psalm 68:11,
"The Lord gave the word and great was the company of those who published it."

Published in the United States of America

ISBN: 978-1-61739-114-9
1. Fiction, Historical
2. Fiction, War & Military
10.10.18

THE BORDER
COVENANT

DEDICATION

This novel is the result of a boy's imagination, inspired by the history of his homeland, in the countryside of New England. Growing up in upstate New York and Vermont, Hugh Griffith read the "Leatherstocking Saga" by James Fenimore Cooper, including *The Last of the Mohicans.* His quest to understand the creation of his great and beautiful country led to a long study of Francis Parkman. A career in academics beginning at Union College in Schenectady honed his skills, but he never lost his boyhood love for his heroes Major Robert Rogers and the characters of *The Last of the Mohicans* fame, penned by James Fenimore Cooper. In *The Border Covenant,* a struggle for survival in the New World is shared by the men and women, native and new, who loved their country and fought and died side by side as brothers for the cause of good as they saw it. God bless all who are now laid to rest, both the author and the beloved subjects of his book, who were caught up in a magnificent but terrible struggle in the long history of the formation of their new country.

TABLE OF CONTENTS

MAP OF NORTH AMERICA IN 1759

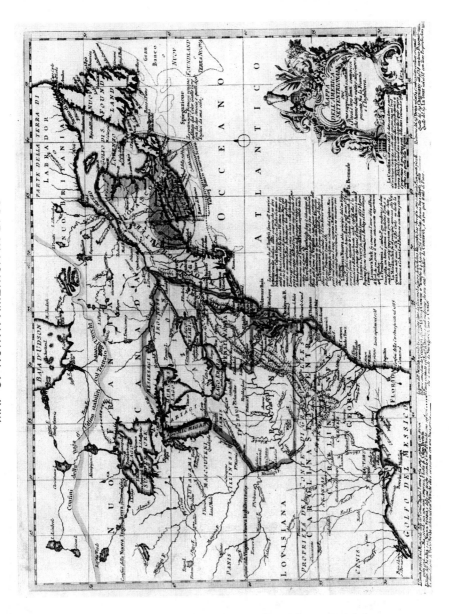

PLAN OF THE ISLE-AUX-NOIX DEFENSES NEAR MONTREAL

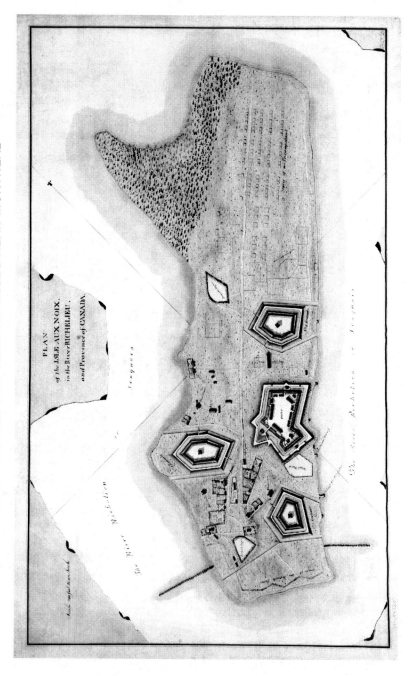

PLANS FOR THE SECOND BATTLE AT FORT TICONDEROGA
DRAWN BY WILLIAM BRASIER IN MAY 1759

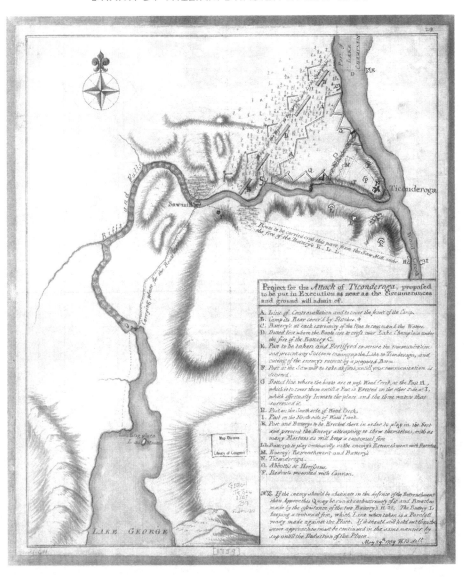

MAP OF LAKE GEORGE AND LAKE CHAMPLAIN DRAWN BY WILLIAM BRASIER IN 1762

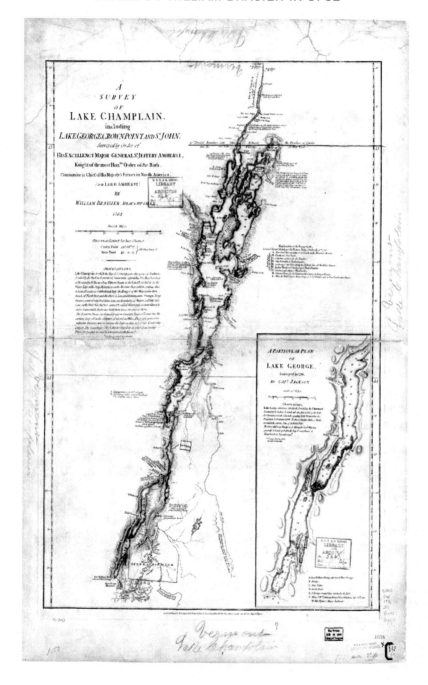

A VIEW OF QUEBEC IN 1759

INTRODUCTION

The story you are about to read is set in the historical background of the French and Indian War, fought from 1756 to 1763 over the control of New England and French Canada, protected by the mighty Fortress of Louisbourg at the mouth of the St. Lawrence Seaway on Cape Breton Island. Tens of thousands of soldiers and their Indian allies clashed, and thousands died on all sides in an era when it was common for boys as young as fourteen to fight.

The French cities of Montreal and Quebec were already old and established. Quebec was at this time a sparkling fragment of the reign of Louis XV, in the words of Francis Parkman in his book *Montcalm and Wolfe.* The colonists of New England were hardy settlers, without the refinement of the French Court, to put it mildly, and the contrast of the emerging American nation with the settled culture of France transported to the New World is remarkable. Roger's Rangers fought on snowshoes in the dead of winter, on ice skates, in boats, in swamps, and in deep woodlands in the heart of hostile Indian Territory. They fought with musket, knife, and hatchet. But they were not undisciplined; they followed Rogers' Rules of Ranging and trained with live

15

fire. They were the first *special forces* created entirely out of the American heartland at the time, defending their homes against what they saw as terrorist raids by the French and the Indians. Sadly, their losses many times were over 50 percent, and yet they fought on throughout the seven-year long war.

The Border Covenant is a story about those colonists, ordinary men and boys like young Tom Evans, and Native Americans who were fighting for home and family against those who they thought would destroy everything they lived and dreamed for. In another twist of history, they both admired and disliked the ordered display of the British regular army, and many see the fragility of this alliance as a seed for the American Revolution to happen less than fifteen years after the end of this novel. In a word, men like Johnathan Evans and his young nephew Tom in this story were the first true patriots, and they foreshadowed the War of Independence.

1

VICTORY AT TICONDEROGA

I n the drama of the forest, darkness is often the essential condition of the action. Without darkness, the actors do not come together, the forces in conflict do not meet, the mood is not sustained.

In the drama about to begin, the actors had already gathered under the dark curtain that descended upon Mt. Defiance. Each player, clothed in a costume designed for that larger drama, within which forest tragedy is only a pageant, went about his own business, as blind as any Oedipus to the real nature of the part he played.

At this moment, a young actor was busily working at his craft as he matched curiosities with a spring squirrel who had flattened himself out upon the branch of an oak tree to observe the strange creatures below him. In both boy and squirrel, instinct worked silently, honing upon their curiosities the sharp edge of survival. Suddenly the squirrel, in his three-month innocence, scurried nervously to the other side of the thick trunk. Young Tom Evans stepped automatically to his right, raising his eyes to the higher branches on the far side of the oak in time to catch the patch of gray that fled down a limb to become an indistinguishable part of the forest's shadowy form. The boy laughed silently. He had added another level to his understanding of the first axiom of forest warfare: do not move if you would not be seen.

The boy's two companions had not observed the lesson taught by the forest, though they were, themselves, headmasters in the school of survival. They stood motionless, two indiscernible and inseparable details of the mountain, looking down upon Fort Carillon and the waters of Lake Champlain. One of the men grew weary of watching.

"Lookee there, Toe-lee-ma," he said, turning to his comrade. "No smoke stands up from the kitchens. Looks like Hebecourt ain't plannin' to feed his men supper. Likely as not, they'll spend their eatin' time rowin' up to Crown Point."

"The walls are as bare as autumn limbs," replied the comrade. "The French will all sleep tonight at Pointe à la Chevalure." The man dressed in ranger green turned his gaze back to the fort. His eyes swept over the unguarded walls and came to rest on the breastwork beyond.

There were no French regulars there now; there was no abatis heavy with the broken bodies of British troops impaled on the sharpened points of its heavy boughs. The litter of the previous summer was gone, and British regulars looked confidently over the breastwork at the silent fort.

"Well," said the ranger, "might jest as well call Tom and report in. Ain't gonna be no fight over Ticonderoga this year."

"Damn," he said, feeling his gut tighten in sudden anger. "Damn fool Abercrombie. A battery planted right here on Rattlesnake Hill would hev scoured the inside of that breastwork with round shot from end to end. Could hev hit the fort right in the breadbasket too!"

The ranger captain turned to his companion. "Fort Ti's there for the takin'," Toe-lee-ma," he said. "If Amherst don't stop to build *six* new forts and a navy, we kin push clear to Canada an' mebbe end this war before the snow sets in."

The Indian gazed down upon Lake Champlain. "General Amherst studies the trees that surround his army to make certain that the army is surrounded by trees," he said. "Let us pray that the gods hold back the winter." The men turned expectantly toward the sound of Tom's footsteps, but in their eyes gleamed the open-minded curiosity engendered by countless perilous surprises.

"Now, Tom, where hev you been all this time?" said Johnathan Evans, grinning. "It'll be too dark to read sign by the time we get down to the lake, an' besides, Major Rogers is waitin' for us. Don't you know there's a war on, lad?"

"Gosh, Uncle John," replied the boy, "I was jest wanderin' 'round, lookin' at some of the scars this old mountain has from last year's battle, an' then this little squirrel moved on a branch right over my head."

"All right, lad," interrupted Uncle John. "You kin tell us about yer squirrel while we get ourselves down to the landin' place. We've spent too much time here as it is, tho' that's really my doin', not yers."

With that, the ranger led the small party down Rattlesnake Hill. Tom was still talking about his discoveries on the mountainside when Uncle John interrupted him again, this time with a hand signal. Tom and Toe-lee-ma blended into nearby trees as Captain Evans stepped from the trail and was lost from view. For some time, there was no sound in the darkened forest but the breathing of the wind, and then a faint whistle pitched just above the wind's sigh detached the Indian and the boy from the shadows and sent them down the trail at a rapid pace.

Tom tried to run in Toe-lee-ma's footsteps as they fled through the deepening darkness. The path began to flatten out as they approached the lake before the Indian slackened his pace and finally stopped.

"Some sounds of the forest are hollow sounds," he said. "Your uncle has heard such sounds. Not much time will pass before he comes to tell us what it meant. We must go slowly now and find the ranger Major's sentry."

Tom recognized the importance of Toe-lee-ma's warning. Whatever Rogers's mission was, it would be conducted from beginning to end under ranger rules. The forest would take on new eyes and ears; purposeful, expert, vigilant. The Indian and the boy moved so their bodies caught the darkness, and when they moved it was as if the soft wind caused the brush tops to wave gentle shadows to the ground. Tension gathered inside Tom until he could feel his pulse beating against his stomach. Then, in the same instant, he saw a tiny spot of light and heard Toe-lee-ma's soft signal call. The answering call came at once, and Tom stepped with Toe-lee-ma from the densest part of the darkness to the path upon which one of Rogers's rangers now stood. He watched the starlight on the waters of Lake Champlain as his companion and the ranger exchanged information.

"There is time, then, to wait for Captain Evans," Toe-lee-ma said. "Major Rogers may wish to hear him before he puts his boats upon the water."

"Likely he will," replied the ranger. "Don't seem to be no hurry to cut the log boom now, anyhow. Even if we saw through an' our boats git by, don't appear likely they's gonna be any movement downstream tonight. We should've cut the damn thing three days ago, afore Bourlemaque took most of the garrison and run away." The ranger paused briefly. "Well," he continued, "a little bit's better than nothin' at all. At least we'll have Frenchie's ear."

Tom's ear caught the cautious, muffled sounds of men attempting to move in absolute secrecy under conditions which prevent absolutes. His eyes strained to pick up a shape that would give meaning to the sounds. Finally, some of the shadows on the beach assumed the form of two lines. Tom's eyes followed them, then moved ahead to the denser, blacker patch of floating darkness toward which they moved.

"Boats! They're loading boats!" The idea settled into certainty, and Tom felt the surge of satisfaction that comes to every solver of puzzles, but the solution was, after all, a simple one, and Tom's satisfaction was not allowed to outlast its proper time. A familiar whisper interrupted his reverie and signaled the return of Captain Evans.

"Where's the Major at?" asked the whisper. "I surely hope I haven't held him up any."

"He's on the beach. Finishin' up the loadin'," answered the sentry. "I'd say yer timin's jest about perfect."

"Well, I'm sure glad o' that," replied Johnathan Evans. "I don't want to be the man to hold up Robert Rogers."

As they hurried to the lake, all the pieces of Tom's puzzle came together. The patch of floating darkness became a *bateaux*, and the shadowy shapes now hunkered down on its flat bottom, shoulders and rifle barrels rising above its sides.

A little farther out on the lake, Tom could see two whaleboats, each carrying its compliment of rangers, rifles, and saws to cut through the timbers of the log boom the French had constructed to keep the British ships from getting downstream.

They stopped in front of a large, powerful, heavy-faced man who was issuing orders to an older man as tall as he, but so sparsely put together that he could be described as emaciated.

"We'll go as usual, Matty," he said quietly. "Single file, no noise, straight to the east side of the lake. I'll lead in the *bateaux*. Put Isaiah in charge of the first whaleboat, and you take the second. Make sure every man is ready when we get near the east shore. If there's any trouble, that's where it'll come."

There was neither exchange of salutes nor words. Both Robert Rogers and his men knew when form counted and when it did not. Each man simply turned his own way.

"Glad you could make it, Johnny," Major Rogers said. "We probably won't do much but sweat over our saws, but I always feel better with eyes like yours and Toe-lee-ma's watchin' out for me. Did you see anything movin' on the mountainside?"

"Wasn't till we were comin' back to Champlain," replied Captain Evans, "that I heard somethin' I shouldn't have. I turned back up trail till I found some sign. Appears like we jest missed runnin' into some St. Francis Abenaki. Prob'ly part of a scouting party sent out to see if Amherst was goin' to put a battery on the hill. Since they didn't see nothin', my guess is they're on their way back to Crown Point, er mebbe they were just hopin' fer a scalp er two to take back to St. Francis. They can see how the French are in a bad way, and they don't have much stomach for what's commin'."

"Well then, we'd better get started," said Major Rogers. "You know how sudden this lake can turn on you." Then, as if he had an afterthought, he nodded toward Tom. "We'll set the boy in the middle of the boat. Be a good experience for him." Tom sat dutifully in the middle of the *bateaux*, his spirits considerably dampened by Rogers's protective act.

As the *bateaux* traversed the lake in uneventful silence, Tom began to feel the effects of the long day on Rattlesnake Hill. Young eyes grown weary with straining after sun and shade began to close. Darkness had settled heavily down on Lake Champlain. Even experienced, untired eyes looked carelessly out at the night. All had forgotten that the theater of forest warfare is a chaotic theater, a theater with a falling curtain that perversely calls the actors to a performance that is extemporaneous from beginning to end. There are no acts, only scenes, and the best players are those whose instincts unerringly fit their actions to the moment's demand. It is a play for players only, and the single measure of success is survival. The forgetfulness did not last long. Chaos erupted on the western shore, splitting the darkness with a violent flash. The main bastion of Fort Ticonderoga blew sky-high; debris fell with clatter and a splash on lake and shore. Cannons, left overloaded and primed, roared insanely and burst. Flames from the burning fort illuminated the lake, revealing the French fleeing downstream under the cover of the explosion.

Instantly Tom's eyes were wide open, but the details exposed by the light glinting over the lake came too suddenly for comprehension. He knew he was not having a nightmare, but he felt as if he were witnessing some inexplicable natural catastrophe. Major Robert Rogers was the first to understand. "Hebecourt *is* runnin' downstream to Crown Point," he shouted. "Turn these boats around and get after him. I want every man with an oar to bend it to the breaking point. The rest of you, pick a target. Shoot as soon as you're certain of your man."

Rogers's rangers whipped the waters of Lake Champlain furiously. Tom could see the men in Matty's whaleboat kneeling, shoulders bent against the butts of their rifles. He could hear Rogers's voice thundering over the waves. "Get those baggage boats. I want those powder barrels. C'mon, boys, let's get after 'em."

A nightmare began on Lake Champlain, but it *was* a French nightmare. It began with a sound like the snapping of a tree limb breaking under the weight of winter snow. There was a sharp, agonized cry and the flat smack of a rigid back smashing down upon the waters, followed by a series of cracking sounds and the resultant cries of agony. For the French, the cleverly planned and confidently executed retreat suddenly lost its rationale. They reacted in fragmented terror, beating the waves in all directions of the compass. A baggage boat with still rowers and unguided oars drifted toward the eastern shore, followed and then outdistanced by the flailing crews of livelier craft. A few boats pulled straight for the deserted fort, as if the holocaust of their own making would protect them still, while others fled straight north toward Crown Point.

As ranger oars steadied the motion of the *bateaux*, they stared in amazement at the boat which bore down upon them. Tom tried to find the right place for his rifle in the line of fire that slanted toward the enemy.

"Are those fools tryin' to ram us?" he heard a voice cry out.

"No," he heard Rogers's reply. "They're just gonna pass by close enough so their muskets are as good as our rifles. They hope to cripple us with a good volley and escape into the darkness, come to a forty-five degree angle, and put our stern even with their bow. If they veer east, we'll broadside 'em, and if they come at us, we'll get 'em on both sides. We'll fire from stern to bow; adjust your targets accordin' to the line of their veer. C'mon, get the boat around. Get it around!"

Tom found himself unwilling to take his eyes off the French lieutenant, who had hoped to pass his own boat paralleled to the ranger's *bateaux*. The Frenchman screamed a command. The boat turned, and the lieutenant came straight at Tom. The line of fire had been determined. The boy felt a strange comfort in his newfound certainty. Circumstances had worked out his target.

On the Frenchman came. Tom could see the pistol in his hand. No thoughts crossed the boy's mind. He fixed his eyes upon the dark spot that marked the middle of the man's chest and waited, watching the spot rush at him.

Suddenly, unaccountably, the spot jumped backward. At nearly the same instant, Tom heard the sharp crack of the ranger rifles and saw the flash of the Frenchman's pistol. A hammer smashed into his head and sent him spinning over the side of the *bateaux*. He felt the searing agony burning along the hairline until the waters of Lake Champlain closed over him.

For Tom, the nightmare on the lake had ended. The scene went on without him until each actor had played his part. It ended as it began, in disoriented confusion, with the French fleeing downstream. The rangers would estimate the cost in actors to the French and total their own losses as soon as the scene closed. The morning sun would reveal on the east shore ten boats with considerable baggage, fifty barrels of powder, and a large quantity of ball. The scene had been mostly spectacle. In the general scheme of things, it had been of no importance.

Major Rogers stood in the bow of the *bateaux* as it approached the landing place. His heavy face was faintly marked with the pleasure he had taken in playing his part. He spoke over his shoulder to Captain Evans.

"Like to have you come with me when I make my report to Amherst, Johnny," he said. "You know as well as I do the French can't hold out at Crown Point. They'll blow that up too, and maybe try to hold us back at Isle-Aux-Noix."

A small, abrupt shudder ran through the *bateaux* and its occupants as its prow ground into the sand of the beach. Young Tom Evans, lying on his back on the bottom of the boat, felt again the hammer that had smashed into his head. He threw out an arm to keep himself from falling. A sense of wetness, of dampness, overwhelmed him, and he wondered why the pain in his head did not wash away.

Captain Evans, kneeling expectantly beside his nephew, gently grasped the flailing arm. "All right, lad. All right now, boy. It's all right now," he said. "Tomorrow mornin' you won't hev nothin' to show for this night's work 'cept a crease along the hairline … an' mebbe a little headache. Nothin' a good breakfast won't cure."

Still kneeling, he spoke again, this time to Robert Rogers. "Major, are you certain you want me to go with you? That's all right, of course. We could see that when we pulled him out of the lake; still, Frenchy did get a piece of the temple, an' they's some sign o' shock left. Mebbe I ought to stay with him till he gets his bearings straight."

"Well, Johnny," replied Major Rogers, "you do what you think best, but you know how careful these British generals are. Even if we convince Amherst we can keep the French runnin' till they hit Canada, he won't move till he's mapped out a full campaign from Ti to Montreal. Mebbe between the two of us, we can shorten his planning some."

"All right then, Major," said Uncle John, glancing at his Indian comrade. "Toe-lee-ma kin fix what ails Tom better than I kin anyhow."

The Indian nodded assent. "There is a medicine," he said. "The boy will sleep without dreams."

Uncle John and Major Rogers stepped from the *bateaux* and hurried up the slope, past the deserted fort, until they reached the heights of Carillon. They paused before Montcalm's battle lines of '58, looking at the abatis of felled trees that had sheltered the French from the charges of Abercrombie's gallant soldiers. In the memories of both ranger officers burned the picture of men marching against a forest that looked like it had been laid flat by a hurricane, marching as if they crossed the open plains of Europe, only to be torn to pieces by grape shot and musket balls as they struggled through the forest entanglements.

Absorbed in private grieves, neither man spoke until the sentry posted in front of Amherst's headquarters challenged them.

"Major Rogers and Captain Evans to see General Amherst," answered Rogers.

"Yes sir," replied the soldier. "You're to go right in. Captain Langley is waiting for you in the office on your left."

"Captain Langley?" muttered Rogers as he stepped past the sentry. "Who in hell is Captain Langley?"

Rogers got his answer instantly. As soon as he set foot inside headquarters, a cheerful voice called out to him.

"Major Rogers? In here, sir. Great pleasure, sir. Great pleasure, I assure you!"

Rogers moved instinctively toward the abrupt movement that caught his eye, but the movement had ceased before he could step through the office door. He focused incredulous eyes on a uniform starched until it looked like it was all corners and edges, a uniform frozen in the stiffest, most ludicrous parade ground salute he had ever seen.

My God, thought Rogers. *He looks like he just sat to have his portrait painted. What is he doing here?*

As the shock caused by the figure that posed before him passed away, Rogers felt laughter start to shake his muscular frame. Quickly he returned the salute, concealing his amusement in the action.

Still, the figure did not move. Robert Rogers began to feel something like panic flood in on him.

Lord, oh Lord, he thought. *What does he want me to do?*

Then, behind him, he heard something move. Johnathan Evans, whose sense of the fitness of things had been as disoriented as his own, had also returned Langley's salute.

The young British captain brought his arm down smartly to his side, and Rogers realized that the entire encounter had not lasted three seconds. Now that the spell had been broken, once again he became master of the situation.

"This is Captain Evans," he said quietly. "We're here to report to General Amherst."

"Yes, of course, of course," said Langley. "Pleasure, sir. Pleasure indeed. Captain Langley, here. Henry Langley. But then you know that anyway, don't you?" Wide, honest blue eyes reflected open respect and admiration. "I've just come up, you know. Heard your names at every party I went to. Incredible adventures. Simply incredible. Know it's silly of me, but I can't help wishing I could join you fellows." Embarrassment tinged the young man's face with a becoming blush that suited his open nature. With obvious effort, he looked straight into Rogers's eyes. "Excuse me, Major. Know I'm an *ass.* Don't mean to be, though. I'll get right to business. Sorry General Amherst can't be here. Too busy, but he asked me to take your report and give you these orders. Don't know what's in 'e m, of course, but there's one envelope for you and one for Captain Evans."

Rogers returned the young man's gaze. *There's a man inside all that starch,* he thought. *I've seen this type of English boy before. They sound ridiculous and they look soft, but they've got steel inside 'em.*

"I'm happy to hear the rangers are so well thought of in Albany, Captain, though I suspect you might have missed a few comments not designed for ears as fair and open as yours. If you can get me a regular report form, I'll just fill it out and leave it here until I can talk to General Amherst."

Langley called out an order and a report clerk appeared, paper in hand.

"Give that form to Major Rogers, will you, Corporal? Major, your orders; Captain Evans, yours," he said, handing the rangers the envelopes which bore their names. Except for the stiff newness of the uniform and the honesty that permanently resided in those wide eyes, there was no trace left of the exuberant boy who had, minutes earlier, greeted them with a hero's welcome.

"One more thing, Captain," said Rogers. "Do you have any idea when we can get to talk to the general?"

"No, sir, I don't." replied Langley. "We had three French deserters come in just before the fort blew, and they turned out to be typically French—they talked so much and so fast we can't tell which part of their lies we can depend upon, but I can tell you this: General Amherst has already sent the chief engineer to inspect Ticonderoga with an eye to rebuilding it, and runners to Crown Point to alert our scouting parties there."

"Thank you, Captain," said Rogers, turning to leave. "And Captain, I think you'll get the action you're looking for. It's a long, hard journey from Ticonderoga to Montreal."

Rogers had his envelope open before he left the room. He paused before the writing desk in the hall, scanning the last few lines.

"Well Johnny," he said, "we won't find anything out tonight. I've been ordered to encamp at the sawmill to guard against enemy flying parties. I sort of thought I might be sent to Crown Point, but that'll probably come tomorrow. Whatever happens, I'd guess you won't be comin' with me."

"No, not this time," said Johnathan Evans disgustedly. "I'm bein' sent back to the border to tell the folks that Ti has fallen and recruit anybody I can get for a campaign against Montreal. For certain, it's work that's not much to my likin'!"

"Still, it's work that has to be done, John, and you'll do it quicker and better than anyone else could. I'm not so sure I like the feel of it though. I hope Amherst isn't going to set us to watchin' and buildin till it's too late to do anything else."

Both men simultaneously extended their hands. They knew that the uncertainties that lay ahead concealed a thousand dangers, any one of which could make this their last good-bye. There was one quick tightening of the hands before Rogers bent toward the writing desk. And Johnathan Evans stepped out into the darkness.

2

THE MESSENGERS

As usual, Johnathan Evans and Toe-lee-ma rose with the sun. They prepared for the trail quickly and silently, and stepped outside the tent.

"The medicine was good," said the Indian. "No evil spirit from the lake disturbs the boy's sleep."

"Well, that's a stroke o' luck anyway," replied Evans. "We're long on distance to cover an' short on time."

"I will look for Rogers at the sawmill," said Toe-lee-ma. "The rangers do their work well, but there are trails which only Native eyes can see."

"Yes, you'll hev to go to Rogers," Evans said. "He's the only man here who understands the value of yer knowledge."

"And you must run a careful path," said Toe-lee-ma. "If Satanis led the Abenaki on Rattlesnake Hill, there may be danger. The French cannot control him. If he deserts them, the hatred that burns in his spirit may turn him to the long trail home along the border. It is a trail he has taken many times, and always he has covered it with the blood of your people."

"I've thought o' that," answered Evans. "But you, old friend, you will hev to be even more careful how you set yer feet. Rogers will want an eye out in the woods watching over every move the French make. Give me a week then start leavin' sign in our old places along the Richelieu. If Amherst drags his feet, I'll be back before the real push on Montreal starts."

"The forest is filled with evil omens," Toe-lee-ma replied. "They say we will not meet again soon, but still, I will leave the sign."

A simple raising of hands signaled the moment of parting. Between companions such as these, words were an unnecessary burden.

Uncle John returned to the tent to wake his nephew. "Put your things together, Tom," he had said. "We're goin' to tell the folks along the border they kin breathe a mite easier and, while we're at it, we might as well put up these recruitin' posters. The general's goin' to need more men if he's goin' to Montreal; know a man or two who might have the time to go rangerin' agin if it means the end of those French. Devils and their crazy priests turning the Abenakis and Cauhnawaugha's loose to kill and burn along the frontier."

It did not take the boy long to get ready. He reached for his belt and tied it securely at the back of the linsey-woolsey hunting shirt that hung down over the fringed buckskin trousers. Then he stuffed some pone and jerky into the overlap of the shirt and reached for knife and tomahawk. Tom always enjoyed getting ready for the trail and had made a kind of ritual out of his preparations. Carefully but quickly, he crossed his hands, placing first the knife under the belt on the left side and then the tomahawk on the right. Next came the leather pouch, with its chunk of lead, his brass mould for casting bullets, flint and steel, and a few cast lead bullets. Then he slung his powder horn and stooped to tie the rawhide thongs that fastened the long cuffs of his moccasins to the ankle, fastening first the left and then, after shifting feet, the right. Finally, Tom straightened himself to his full height, simultaneously picking up his rifle with the right hand and placing it by his side. The rifle, fully five feet long, barely reached the top of his shoulder.

When he reached the lake, Uncle John was already in the canoe. Tom stepped in without a word, and they headed across Lake Champlain and turned south down the drowned lands, moving roughly parallel to the southward course of Lake George some miles to the west. The noontime sun found them in East Bay at the mouth of the stream that joins Wood Creek, and Uncle John turned the canoe into the shore. They could not have landed far from the spot where, thirteen years earlier, Regaud, with five hundred French regulars and Canadians and two hundred Abenakis seeking revenge for the slaying of Chief Cadenaret, had left the younger DeMuy, with thirty men, to guard the canoes that were to take them back to Crown Point after the attack of Fort Massachusetts.

"We'll hide the canoe before we take a bite," said Uncle John, and Tom knew that they were not expected to take the news down Wood Creek to Fort Ann and Fort Edward. He wanted to ask why, but he knew that his uncle would not waste time on words while there was work that demanded his complete attention.

They were a full thirty minutes hiding the canoe. Uncle John was a most careful man. When he had the time, he always acted with a care for the future. After he was satisfied that nothing short of an act of God would betray the canoe to an enemy, he leaned against a tree and reached into his hunting shirt for a piece of jerky.

"No need for us to go to Fort Ann or Fort Edward," he said. "They'll git the news soon enough. We'll slide along Skene Mountain to the Batten Kill, go over to the Hoosic River, and down into Fort Massachusetts. It's not likely we'll see anything, but we'd better look pretty close just the same. That murderin' devil Satanis was with the French at Fort Ti. He knows that the war paths to the border won't be open much longer. He's in the woods right now tryin' to figger out some way to git one last good lick in before the French go back to Canada."

They sat in total silence, the young man and the man no longer young, held from the future and forced into a painful past by the magic in the name Satanis. To the boy, the Abenaki Satanis was truly a magician, a magician who had come from St. Francis to Fort Massachusetts on a war party led by his uncle, Chief Cadeneret, and had gone home vengeful and defeated, mourning his uncle's death, but he had returned again and again to murder and destroy along the border. In fifteen years of almost unceasing activity, he had killed at least two hundred settlers and had been himself untouched. Some folks said he was not just a tool of the French priests but an agent of the devil, operating under the devil's guidance and protection. There was no other explanation, they said, for his success or his power.

Satanis had early become an obsession in the life of young Tom Evans. In the fourteen years since Uncle John's return from Louisbourg, Satanis had been more than a legend and a superstition. Half of the people Tom knew along the border had had relatives scalped, tomahawked, or taken captive by Satanis and his warriors. Three times, Tom himself had seen the Abenaki's bloody work and joined those who trailed him in vain along the warpaths that led to Canada and safety. But at the heart of the myth that Satanis became for the boy was an experience of absolute terror that disturbed and commanded the boy's idle waking hours and haunted his sleep with an image of flames so real that he cried out in pain. In his dreams, he saw again and again the Williams's cabin at Number Four, where he had stayed with his mother while Father and Uncle John were at Louisbourg fighting to strike a crippling blow against the French power that unleashed such dogs as Satanis. He saw the burning putlog, followed by some of the clapboards it supported, fall through the opening to the loft and crash on the floor. Over and over he heard the earsplitting howls of the Indians and the heavy thud of their battering ram against the batten door. He heard wood groan and split as axes smashed in the heavy wooden shutters over the window holes, and he saw the most evil face in this world looking down a rifle barrel. Then the rifle seemed to explode as fire lunged out from the muzzle. Across the room he saw Mrs. Williams fall against the wall and a spring of blood gush from her throat and fall down her breast. He felt himself being jerked straight up from the chimney. He heard the grating of the iron smoke oven door, and then he was shoved in. The door banged shut and he was alone in the oven, halfway up, and on the left side of the chimney. The blackness of the oven and the smell of burned corncobs and hickory chips terrified him, and he lay shaking and sobbing silently, listening to the struggle below.

The boy twitched and trembled in the black hole. Screams of bitter agony and exultant, soul-shattering shouts of savage joy seemed to split through layers of heavy, dull thuds and groans. Suddenly, the half-formed and half-heard thunderings of Reverend Cushway's Sunday meeting services mingled with the confused welter of sounds below, and the boy, only four, understood hell. His own scream started in his throat, but a blackness crushed his mind and shoved the scream back. The oven was silent.

The next sound the boy heard was the familiar grating of the oven door. He could not see the hands that reached in and gently curled under his arms, pulling with careful strength, but he recognized the voice of Jed Hawkins, quiet but excited.

"It's little Tom Evans. Thank God they didn't have time to find him." The boy resented the cloak that was thrown over him before Jed handed him out of the chimney. He wanted to look for his mother, but he was too confused and frightened to move.

"Take him back to the fort. Mrs. Johnson will take care of him." And take care of him she did, for nearly a year, until the Indians forced the settlers out and the fort was abandoned, and Uncle John, broken in spirit by his brother's death at Louisbourg, took the boy down the Connecticut to Northfield to live with the family of Dick Webster. But the orphaned boy never forgot the day of terror in the cabin at Number Four, nor the hideous face at the window, which he now believed had been the face of Satanis.

Tom felt a slight breeze drying the beads of sweat that had formed on his forehead. He looked up to see his uncle staring down at him. Tom could not tell if Uncle John had guessed his thoughts, but he saw understanding in his uncle's eyes.

"We'd better git on the trail, Tom, if we're goin' to camp on the Batten Kill tonight. Can't do so much trailin' at dusk." He waited for Tom to stand up before he stepped out upon the narrow path that led through the forest.

Hour after hour, Tom followed the slender, bent figure that trotted effortlessly ahead with short, easy strides. Uncle John could easily move fifty or sixty miles in a day on one of these Indian trails, and that was as much distance as the best Narragansett pacers could cover over the roads. Tom's longer strides ate up more ground, but it was he who tired first and, as always, he was thankful for those infrequent, brief stops occasioned by his uncle's experienced eye. Throughout the long afternoon, Johnathan Evans paused to solve the mystery of each suspicious disturbance of the forest floor, but the boy sensed that his uncle was not quite satisfied. Finally, they approached the Batten Kill, and Uncle John stopped and pointed at a thick stand of pines.

"It's getting too dark to track," he said. "We'll find one of them pines where the wind don't blow in. I don't expect it's goin' to be too hot to sleep."

Tom shivered. Even here, at the foot of the mountains, the nights could get awfully cold at the end of July. He knew there would be no fire as he trailed after his uncle into the thick, jumbled pines.

"Pick yourself a tree," his uncle said, "and chew on some jerky. Maybe in the mornin' we'll see some sign of Satanis. I half-thought he might be somewheres between Wood Creek and Batten Kill, but we surely didn't see his sign."

Tom knew that conversation was ended until the morning. He wormed his way through the thick lower branches of an old tree and sank down in the sweet needles, leaning his back against its trunk. He placed his rifle carefully in the fork of a branch and reached into his hunting shirt for supper. As he ate, he wondered about his uncle's concern over Satanis. Could that bloody demon really be heading toward the border, and if so, how many of his murderous comrades had he brought with him? *Well, no matter,* he thought. *I'll find out soon enough.* And with that thought, he stretched out and went to sleep with that marvelous self-discipline that characterizes the true son of the border.

———————————

Dawn found Tom squatting at the edge of the pine stand, hands gripping the barrel of the rifle in front of him. He stood up and moved toward the trail as Uncle John, returning from his habitual, precautionary morning scout, came into view.

"Couldn't find a thing," said Uncle John as he turned to follow the trail southeast to the Hoosic River.

Tom swung in behind and once more matched his longer stride against the pace of that slender, stooped body. Again the hours sped by, and the two halted only briefly while Uncle John, with some satisfaction, examined the evidence of the trail. The sun was overhead when they stepped from the forest onto the broad road that ran along the Hoosic River. If they stayed on the road, they would soon be out of York State and approaching the valley where, cut off by the high mountain wall of the Hoosacs and reachable only by the old Mohawk warpath through the Taconic Hills, lay the township settled in 1749 and fortified with a blockhouse just three years ago.

"Well, Tom," said Uncle John, "it doesn't make sense now to do anythin' but head straight into Fort Hoosac. It's certain no war party has come this way from Fort Ti. Mebbe we can learn more from the folks at the River Bend than they can from us. Besides, it's been way too long since I had a 'yard of flannel.'"

Tom never said a word as he followed his uncle along the river road. He hardly noticed the old farm houses of the puddin'-headed Dutchmen until the last one disappeared in the distance behind him, and they headed into Massachusetts. The sun had moved on ahead of them and drooped down in the west before Tom saw the huge sign that announced to all weary and hungry travelers that rest and food waited.

The River Bend Tavern, built by Colonel Simonds in 1750, was for more than a dispensary of delectable food and heart-warming drink. It was a second meetinghouse, where the men of West Hoosac ironed out their political and religious differences, and the banquet room was the scene of the biggest parties given in the area. The tavern served as a recruiting office for militia, rangers, and provincial troops, and, in times of peril, provided safety for the settlers who could reach it. It offered travelers a desk to write letters, a bed for the night, and a sustaining breakfast in the morning. These, and a hundred other services, made the River Bend more of an institution than a tavern. Tom followed his uncle through the door leading into the taproom and felt the heat from the gigantic fireplace, which was a full ten feet wide and six feet deep and as high as Tom himself. The three militia men and the ranger seated at the first table wore familiar faces, but Tom could not think of any of their names. They exchanged casual nods with his uncle and went back to their ale and small talk. On the right side of the taproom, seated along a round table, engaged in an animated discussion, were four men who began calling to his uncle as soon as they saw him. One of the group, a short, stocky man who looked like a tree trunk with arms and a head, pushed his chair back from the table and stood up grinning hugely and waving his stumpy arms furiously.

Uncle John grinned back at the tree trunk and waved his hand in a greeting that included all the men at the table, but he kept walking straight up to the bar where the host awaited him.

"Well," said the tavern host, "it's been quite a while. I heard you were called back to Fort Edward to help lobsterbacks go agin Fort Ti." The host glanced briefly Tom. "It's good to see you, lad," he said and turned to Uncle John. "Get the road dust out of your throat start talkin' before I lose my manners. Tell me everything that happened just as fast as you can tell it, before those A-rabs over there git hold of you." He waved good-naturedly at the men seated at the round table.

"Nothin' better than hard cider fortified with rum for trail dust," said Uncle John. "And while yer at it, git one of them good pewter mugs and make a space on the shelf for Tom. I'd say he's earned one."

Uncle John turned and headed for the large board mounted on the wall over the writing desk. "Don't you ever take anything down off this board, Bill?" he asked. "I've got to put up a recruitin' poster that will give these men somethin' to think about."

Tom followed his uncle across the taproom, glowing with pride and pleasure and feeling better than he had ever felt before in his whole life. He knew that, in his own way, Uncle John had just announced publicly that Tom was a graduate of the Johnathan Evans School of New Hampshire Rangers. It had been a full four-year course too, culminating in the official service at Fort Ti and, what was even more important, that mug was a diploma every man Jack would respect because it was a gift of Johnathan Evans, man of legendary adventures and guardian of the border by appointment of Governor Shirley himself.

They stood looking at the board while Uncle John searched for a place to tack up his poster. "Here's the spot," he said, taking down a poster of similar size and handing it to Tom. "I hear Goreham's boys have been at Quebec since June anyway. Besides, the best way to help Wolfe is to help Amherst put pressure on Montreal."

Tom held the poster at arms length, remembering with satisfaction that Uncle John had served with most of the great rangers—Goreham, Scott, Rogers—and read slowly:

> All able-bodied, fit men that have an inclination to serve his Majesty King George the Second, in the First Independent Company of Rangers, now in the Province of Nova Scotia, commanded by Joseph Goreham, Esq., shall, on enlisting, receive good pay and clothing, a large outfit, with a crown to drink the King's health. And by repairing to the Sign of the Bear in King Street, Boston, and to Mr. Cornelious Crocker, inn holder in Barnstable, may heed the particular encouragement, and many advantages accruing to a soldier, in the course of the duty of that company, too long to insert here; and further may depend on being discharged at the expiration of the time inter-tained for, and to have every other encouragement, punctually compli'd with.

As John was tacking up his poster, the men in the tavern crowded around the board to read it. The man who was like a tree trunk urged Uncle John to join his table.

"C'mon, John," he said. "We know you got the news we been waitin' for, or you wouldn't be here, and we ought to know. First." His eyes fairly danced, and again he began to wave his arms furiously. "Tell us how far them Frenchies has run so we can spread the good news. By golly, I can't wait to tell Jessie." The man was so excited and his body jiggled up and down so much as he hopped around that Tom thought he would fly right up to the rafters. Tom smiled to himself at the thought of a flying tree trunk.

Uncle John spoke over his shoulder as he headed back to the bar where the tavern host waited between the two pewter mugs.

"Later, Dick," he said. "Me and Tom got some mighty serious refreshin' to do first."

Me and Tom, not "me and the boy," or "the lad and me," but "me and Tom." Tom nearly floated up to the rafters himself his head was so light. From now on he was going to be Tom—and that meant his uncle really had graduated him. From now on he knew that the most difficult tasks would be his, and he would be held strictly accountable for his every action. Uncle John believed in him and respected him as a man. Was there ever, he thought, a more glorious day than this July 28, 1759?

At the bar, Uncle John took a deep draught from the pewter mug and reached a decision. "Bring us a trencher full of oysters and a noggin of beer," he said to the host. "We'll work on that while you get us a couple of boiled pigeons and three or four conners ready. I never tasted blue perch any better than the ones that come out of your bake oven."

Uncle John and Tom sat down at a table where they could feel the warmth of the fire. Tom admired the elaborately designed firedogs, on which the basket spit with its joint of meat was turned slowly by the clock jacks. Others could have their beef or pork out of the bake oven, but as for Tom, he would take his off the spit anytime. He eyed the gridiron used for broiling and the huge copper kettle. He calculated that the kettle could hold up to fifteen gallons. "I'll bet that kettle cost four hundred dollars, if it cost a farthing." He shook his head in awe and tried to calculate the total cost of the fireplace equipment with its skillets, frying pans, pots, kettles, griddles, and trivets, but the task was too much for his limited knowledge, and he turned his attention to the oysters.

The tavern host came over and set down one trencher with the conners and boiled pigeon and another with peas, carrots, and potatoes. He looked like he wanted to sit down and join the two busy eaters, but he turned away without speaking a word.

"Poor old Bill," said his uncle. "His curiosity almost got the better of his manners there."

Tom secretly surveyed the taproom, turning his head slowly and looking out of the corners of his eyes. Suddenly he felt the tension and the excitement in the tavern, and he realized that Uncle John was the force that held it in.

Tom pondered the idea as he ate. More than respect kept these men at their tables talking intensely but quietly. It could not be possible that they in any way doubted or mistrusted the veteran border warrior, and certainly they could not fear him, for most of them had the kind of courage that is born from conquering fear, and yet Tom felt something in the atmosphere that he neither liked nor understood.

Uncle John finished the last sliver of beef and ate the last spoonful of baked beans. A wave of his hand brought the host with apple pie and strawberries floating in rich, thick cream. The conversation at tree trunk's table got louder, and Tom heard anger in the men's voices, but the strawberries and cream were much more interesting, and Tom devoted his full attention to them.

"Well," said Uncle John, pushing an empty trencher away. "We're goin' to have to give an account of ourselves pretty soon." He patted his belly and smiled appreciatively. "I guess we're about ready for it, at that." He stood up and walked toward the bar. The tavern host waited for them, a pitcher in each hand. One pitcher contained a mixture of eggs beaten up with sugar, nutmeg, and rum, and the other was half-full of ale, just heated to the boiling point. The host poured the contents from one pitcher into the other, over and over again, until the mixture was smooth. Then he brought a loggerhead, red hot from the fireplace, and plunged it into the pitcher—now the drink had that burnt, bitter taste so dearly loved along the border.

"One yard of flannel," said the host as he poured the flip into the pewter mugs, "and stand the cost."

By this time everyone in the tavern had come to the bar. They pushed and jostled each other as they tried to get as close as they could to Tom and Uncle John—that is, everyone but one man and his handsome companion, who remained seated at the round table on the right of the room, silently watching the noisy crowd.

Uncle John held up his hands for quiet. "Just like you all guessed," he said. "Fort Ti has fallen." Uncle John's words acted like a spark applied to gunpowder. The room exploded in cheers and shouts. Toasts were offered to the provincial troops, to the rangers, and to the militia. Men locked arms and turned in circles, stamping boisterously on the tavern floor.

Uncle John waited until the noise subsided. "What's more," he said, "the Frenchies didn't even stay to fight. They blew up the fort and hightailed it down the lake to Crown Point, and if the Gen'ral was to ask me, I don't think they'll stop runnin' 'til they get on the Richelieu River."

"How long, at the outside, do you figger it'll take to drive 'em out of Crown Point?" asked a tall, thin man standing near Tom. He spoke for all in the taproom. Once the French were gone from Crown Point, the major point of departure for the Indian war parties would be closed, and the activities of the autumn—the reaping and the harvesting—would at last be safe.

"The way I see it," said Uncle John, "a ranger'll be comin' through any day tellin' you the French ran away from Crown Point jest like they ran from Fort Ti. There's no way they can stop an army like Amherst's there. No, they'll head north to the Richelieu and try to stop him at Isle-Aux-Noix. They've got both arms of the river closed with chevaux-de-frise, and Bourlemaque's got a force on the island equal to Montcalm's at Fort Ti in '58. Besides that, they've had plenty of time to set up artillery and fortifications. They been workin' on it since spring."

"Now if we could get rid of them devils at St. Francis, all our troubles would be over," said the same tall, thin man, who was, judging from his homespun clothing and gnarled appearance, one of that remarkable breed of men that is constantly moving farther into the forest darkness, clearing a space for cabin and fields, and moving on when the light created draws other and more permanent settlers.

"Your troubles won't be over until the French are driven out of Canada," said Uncle John. "And that hasn't happened yet. Wolfe's been more'n a month at Quebec, and we got to give him some help. I saw you all readin' the recruiting poster. You give that poster a lot of careful thought. If we can help old Amherst git past Bourlemaque and up onto the St. Lawrence, Montcalm'll have to take forces out of Quebec and head 'em toward Montreal. Mebbe we can give Wolfe the ladder he needs to scale the walls of Quebec."

Tom noticed the agreement on the faces around him as the men began to form back into their own little groups to pursue one of their favorite occupations, the discussion of ideas which left room for opinion, and Tom had heard enough of these discussions to know that anyone who entered them had better understand his facts and organize them logically if he didn't want to get laughed out of the room. These men were town meeting trained, inheritors of a tradition of rationality and common sense which had been sharpened and made practicable by the frontier life, and a man had better know what he was about, whether he argued the meaning of a passage of Scripture, the need for a new tax, or the direction of the wind in the morning.

Tom also knew that there wasn't going to be any great rush to join Amherst's army. There was still danger along the border, and there were strong arguments for staying home and protecting what had been won at so bitter a cost, but the idea of driving the French out of Canada was always certain of approval.

By this time the tree stump, whose name was Dick Wells, had worked his way to Uncle John's side. They exchanged words in such a low tone that Tom could not make them out, and, joined by a third man, they headed for the table where the parson and the dark-haired man sat.

"C'mon, Tom," said Uncle John. "You an' me's goin' to git educated. Over at that table they got a real hoot-n-holler preacher; a converted Frenchy; two selectmen, including Dick here, who was once a deputy to the General Court of Massachusetts; an' a school teacher. I don't think you could find the like of 'em in Boston—at least not all sittin' at one table."

Tom didn't know what to think as he followed the three men toward the table. He walked a few paces behind and was apparently unnoticed by a fourth man who left the table where he had been sitting alone and joined the crowd. They reached the table and sat down without introductions; Uncle John and Dick Wells sitting opposite the Frenchman and the preacher, and the other two arranging themselves around the end of the table. Tom sat next to his uncle, pushing his chair away from the table so he could get the warmth of the fireplace on the middle of his back.

The Frenchman set his brandy on the table and looked right at Uncle John. "I know," he said, "as you do, that we will never be safe until the French are driven out of Canada, and I have as much reason as anybody for wanting to see them gone. I have no love for the people who destroyed my father's trading company and drove us out because we were Huguenots, but I am not so foolish that I will be deluded by hopes and dreams. Whatever their defects might be, the French regulars are great soldiers, and they have in Montcalm a general who understands the situation and his troops and uses both to the utmost advantage. As long as he leads, Canada will not be conquered and the borders will not really be safe. I think we had better not run off to join Amherst and leave our women and children to the Indians."

"I never said it would be an easy task, Mr. Bouchet, nor even a certain one," said Uncle John, "but it has to be tried, and right now is the best time. If Amherst and Wolfe can unite in Canada, the French are done, and even if Amherst gets no farther than the St. Lawrence, he'll force the French to split their forces. As a matter of fact, it surprises me that you aren't servin' one or the other already. A man that's lived in Quebec and Montreal, that's trapped and traded with the Indians, and has friends from Detroit to Louisbourg ought to be pretty valuable to somebody's army." Uncle John never took his eyes from those of Emile Bouchet, but Bouchet did not shift under the relentless gaze.

"It appears to me we could spare you Amherst," broke in Dick Wells. "You got no family here and no fields to harvest either. I think you can trust us to care for our women and children."

"Now, now, Dick," said the Reverend Roger Cant, a benign smile enveloping his craggy, emaciated features, "you wouldn't talk like that at town meeting."

Dick Wells, recognizing the justice of the reprimand but not liking it any better than he liked the Baptist preacher, scowled and reached for his mug of flip.

"You don't have to say anything, Roger," said Emile Bouchet in a quiet voice that belied the anger in his Gallic heart. "I know I will always be an outsider here, but I had hoped the mere fact that I am French would not obscure the fact that I know more about French Canada than any man here, nor the fact that I have been of more than a little service to this township."

There was silent agreement at the table. Emile Bouchet had moved along the border for ten years, staying mostly with the Reverend Roger Cant when not pursuing his trapping and trading interests. It was true; he had been of service to West Hoosac. He had helped them fight the Abenaki, he had contributed his time and effort to the establishment of new settlers, and he had used his connections with the Indians to help arrange for the return of captives to their homes.

The men at the table might not have liked him, but they had to admit the truth of what he said. "If you think for a minute," continued Bouchet, "you will realize that I only say what you know from bitter experience. For years you have been fighting the Indians and habitants led by the *coureurs-de-bois*. You know full well how devastating they can be. You have seen the changes in the French since Montcalm arrived. Captain Evans was at Ticonderoga in '58, and I'm sure he would admit that the Marques de Montcalm-Gozon is not an ordinary general. And whom do the British send to oppose him? First, old Nambycrabby, and now Amherst the turtle, who never moves until victory is certain. Personally, I do not think he will move now in time to be of any use to Wolfe. First, he will build forts, and then ships for the lake, and finally he will decide that it is too late after all to move against Isle-Aux-Noix. The French have leaders like Levis and Bougainville to send to Bourlemaque's aid. Whom do the British have? When Howe was killed at Wood Creek, they lost the only officer they had who knew how to fight in the forest. How can you hope to defeat the French with such leaders as Britain sends you, and, for that matter, who ever heard of Wolfe? The British themselves said he was mad."

"Yes," broke in Winthrop Smith, "and King George said if Wolfe was mad, he wished he'd bite some of his other generals. Besides, the French aren't as strong as you say. In the first place, it's no secret that Governor Vaudreuil hates Montcalm and throws every obstacle he can find in his way. In the second place, the Canadians hate the French regulars worse than old Abe Simons hates the British, and, in the third place, the Indians aren't of much use in siege actions and regular battles—and neither are the habitants."

"That's right," Dick Wells exclaimed. "The French deserters from Fort Ti for the last year all claim there aren't enough troops in Canada to keep the habitants in order. New France is an apple that's rotten right to its core!"

"It's true that New France has its problems," said Bouchet. "But what you don't understand is that, beneath the dissension, there is a unity provided by the church and a natural love for Canada that will bring the habitants flocking to Montcalm, once they see it's a matter of survival. Do you think they don't love Canada as much as you love Massachusetts? Do you suppose Vaudreuil would let his dislike for Montcalm interfere with the defense of Quebec? I think, personally, that Montcalm could defend Quebec with half the troops he now has. Quebec is impregnable. It is more a fortress than a city."

The brief pause occasioned by Bouchet's reply was interrupted by a nervous cough. Robert Stevens, the schoolmaster, ran his hand over his hair and down along a lean jawbone, ending the motion by turning his wrist to rub his nose with the knuckle of his index finger. He was used to being the extra man at the table, living as he did with different families throughout the school year, and he had the mannerisms of the man who is never at home and never among friends.

"I hope you will pardon my observations, gentlemen, but I must say that New France will fall." He let his hand pull at his chin. "It is not a matter of generals or of strategy or tactics. It is not a matter of ability to fight, or of courage and will either. Nor is it a matter of numbers. It is a matter of ideas."

The men waited for the schoolmaster to explain. Robert Stevens might be peculiar, but he was in no way foolish. He had been to both Harvard and Yale, and he knew Latin, Greek, and Hebrew; and what was truly remarkable to the settlers, neither the colleges nor the learning had addled his brain. He was an odd duck, no question, and no one felt comfortable in his presence, but on those rare occasions when he offered an opinion, everyone listened.

Stevens leaned an elbow on the table and pulled at his ear. "Massachusetts," he said, "represents political and spiritual freedom in a church and state unified because each man is free and individually responsible for keeping the covenant with God. He who builds upon that covenant can look forward to success in this world and salvation in the next. In New France, either a man looks up to see how he can purchase the favor of the powerful, or he looks down to see what he can take from the weak."

Tom looked at the men seated around the table. He could not follow the argument at all. He wasn't sure what political and spiritual freedom meant anyway, and when the schoolmaster talked about unifying them in church and state, Tom's mind went blank. He was surprised to see that Uncle John was leaning forward, looking slightly puzzled but evidently much taken with Stevens's idea. Dick Wells's shaggy brows were puckered, and his eyes had the squint of concentration, but he looked completely bewildered. Win Smith stared straight down at his mug, while Reverend Cant, head tilted up and mouth open, looked like a hound dog getting ready to let loose his beller, if only he could just get the scent of the fox. Emile Bouchet sat as if he were at attention, and Tom could not guess what he was thinking.

"I guess we all know the difference between the colonies and Canada," said Win Smith. "We been fightin' 'em for fifty years here on the border, an' we understand 'em better than anyone else does—an' them hellions they set loose on us too!"

"Yes," said Uncle John. "And I know right now we got 'em on the run. If Amherst and Wolfe can unite their armies in Canada, the war will be over, and I can't see as how liberty has anythin' to do with gittin' that done." The words were straight from the shoulder, the tone was questioning.

"What I'm saying, Captain Evans," replied Stevens, "doesn't alter the facts of the matter, but it does help to explain them. You were at Louisbourg in '45. French Canada could never have thought of or carried out such an expedition. They had no William Vaughan to come up with such an idea. They had no Governor Shirley to see its possibilities and shepherd the plan past the Assembly. They had no man with the common sense and goodwill of Welsh Billy Pepperell, and they didn't have the men of Massachusetts, Connecticut, and New Hampshire. You are well aware, Captain Evans, that the English themselves thought it a mad scheme. The success of the expedition can't be argued now, but it certainly was then."

Dick Wells, who also had been at Louisbourg, nodded his head in agreement. Here was something he could understand. "The teacher sure has got his history straight there," he said.

"They all said a bunch of farmers and mechanics couldn't do such a thing, but we took it all right—and then them stupid British went and gave it back." He shook with indignation and anger at the thought.

"The point is," said the schoolmaster, "that the idea came from Massachusetts. If the expedition had failed, Massachusetts would have had another idea, because Massachusetts is free in a way that even England is not free."

The Reverend Roger Cant was angry and puzzled. He did not like either the conversation or the man who dominated it, but he could not seem to find an opening to change its course. He was further irritated by the interest the men now seemed to be taking in the schoolmaster's ideas, and he had just decided to plunge blindly into the middle of things when Emile Bouchet spoke.

"I've always had an interest in history, Mr. Stevens," he said. "But is this the time for a history lesson? We'll have plenty of time to explain the fall of New France after it has fallen. I think now we should be discussing what we are going to do here on the border until New France does surrender. Our danger is by no means over."

"You are the one, sir," said Stevens, "who not long ago offered the opinion that Quebec would never fall. I don't see how you can plan your actions of the border intelligently until you are convinced that Quebec will fall. I am trying to explain why Quebec must fall as the only way to make you believe that it will fall."

Uncle John looked at the teacher with new respect. "I, for one, want to hear the teacher out," he said. "I reckon I should have spent more time at book learnin' than I did." He turned to Tom. "I guess maybe I shouldn't have taken you out on the trail as soon as I did either. A year or two more in Northfield wouldn't have hurt none."

Win Smith and Dick Wells nodded their approval. The way Stevens had handled Bouchet had pleased them both immensely, and they wanted to see just how much longer Reverend Cant could control his tongue. They leaned back in their chairs and called for drinks all around.

Now Mr. Stevens really warmed to his task. The nervous motions of his hands ceased, the tone of his voice became intimate, and he leaned far out over the table.

"Since you have an interest in history, Mr. Bouchet," he said, "I'm sure you know the story of ancient Rome. You will remember that the Romans made a great discovery. They discovered that they could gain the loyalty of the people they conquered by allowing them to keep their own gods, their own languages, and their own customs. The Romans also knew that a man must have a full share in a system if he is to make a full return, so they gave the rights and privileges of citizenship to everybody throughout the entire Roman world."

"What you say about the Roman Empire is common knowledge, Mr. Stevens," Bouchet said, "almost as common as the knowledge of its fall, but since you seem determined to finish your little lecture, I hope you will be able to come more directly to your point."

"Pacts are common, Mr. Bouchet," replied Stevens. "Knowledge is not. The point is that the Roman system lacked the choice of representation. The larger the empire got, the stronger the central government got, until life in the parts simply died away. The popular assemblies of the Roman world were like town meetings; they confined themselves to the business of the town. It just never occurred to them that they could choose representatives from among themselves and delegate to them the political power of the town, to use that power away from home and out of sight of the citizens themselves."

"Mebbe they learned you can't trust some people when they git out of sight," interjected Win Smith, for the first time really absorbed in the schoolmaster's argument. "I can name you some deputies in the Massachusetts Assembly that couldn't be trusted at high noon if they were sittin' right in the stocks."

"Yes," replied Stevens. "And if we had no system of representation at all, I'm sure you could convince me that one would never work. Not only that, Mr. Smith, but if you didn't already know about representation, you wouldn't think of it. You just don't invent institutions of government for the people of Rome or New England or any other people anymore than you can sit down and invent a setter's nose for a partridge."

The common sense of the New England mind could find no fault here, and the inborn sense for logic in Bouchet's Gallic heart agreed too, with so obvious a truth.

"Your observation, Mr. Smith," Stevens continued, "shows the perils the idea of representation faced. On the continent, representation could not stand against king and church, and our struggle against New France is rooted in the defeat of representation by the Roman idea of authority. How very fortunate we are that the English spirit of representation was finally joined by the Puritan revolt against spiritual despotism; otherwise, the Stuart kings would have made England 'Roman.'" Stevens sensed the approval of the Massachusetts men.

They might need a philosopher's stone to clothe his abstractions with the facts of border life, but they understood their own heritage.

"A very wise man once said," Stevens continued, "that God never meant that in this fair but treacherous world in which he has placed us we should earn our salvation without steadfast labor. This has certainly been true of our experience. While our forebearers in England defended their liberty against the Stuarts, our forefathers in Massachusetts, unfettered by the old despotic institutions and free from British interference, secured for the world a new era."

The table had come under the spell of the schoolmaster's learning and intensity; it had become a classroom and the men pupils, but the spell was broken new by the Reverend Roger Cant, who had never been at ease in a classroom and who had, in truth, never spent enough time in school to get used to it.

"Now back up there just a minute, Mr. School Teacher," he said. "I don't know all what happened in them times yer talkin' 'bout, and the rest of us don't neither, but I listened—thought I might learn somethin'. Well I did, but it wasn't what you figgered. You should've left them unregenerate Puritans outta yer fancy talk, fer I know 'em first hand. They've drove me out of three towns and robbed me of three congregations becuz they can't stand in the light of the truth that comes to me when I read the Bible. They ain't no such thing as freedom anywhere you find a con-gregationalist, and that's the same thing as a Puritan."

Dick Wells jumped up with such force that his chair toppled over and hit the floor with a thud. Tom had the odd thought that Wells didn't look anything like a tree trunk now as, his face fiery red with burning anger, he struggled against the iron grip Uncle John had placed on his arm.

"I'll give you freedom, you weasel," he exploded. "I'll throw you right out the door, and mebbe the free air will clear up your teched head!"

"Now, Dick," said Uncle John quietly, "we been through before. It don't do no good to raise a fuss here. The reverend just plain forgot where he was for a minute let that slip out. Looky there, Dick. You knocked over mug and spilled all that good flip. I'll stand fer drinks around the table, if the reverend will buy the next round. Is that agreeable, Reverend?"

The Reverend Roger Cant nodded his head. He knew from bitter experience that there were places where his kind of light shone, but dimly, and he cursed himself for his forgetfulness. He knew too that Emile would be angry. Bouchet had told him time and again that he must curb his tongue if he wished to exert any influence in West Hoosac—but that teacher with his bookish nonsense would drive any man to distraction!

Uncle John released his grip on Dick Wells and reached down to grab the fallen chair by the bottom of a back leg. In a seemingly effortless motion he restored it to its place at the table and turned to Mr. Stevens.

"If you don't mind," he said, "I think we'd like to hear more about them forefathers of ours."

Mr. Stevens was obviously upset by the flare up. He leaned back in his chair, and his previous intensity had left him, but he continued, probably more from some inner necessity to finish his point than anything else.

"People have suffered indignities when they placed themselves in conflict with Puritanism," he said, "but that's another issue. I was speaking of the part played by Protestants in establishing the victory of representation over absolutism, Reverend Cant, but I can also assure you of this: New France will be able to trace its fall to a Puritan doorstep."

"Well," said the Reverend Roger Cant, his mottled face belying his conciliatory tone, "I reckon we could all follow that if you'd said New England or Massachusetts, instead of Puritan."

"Reverent Cant," said Stevens, "it seems that there are some people with very faulty memories whose bandaged fingers kept wobbling back to the fire. The Puritans who came here first were almost exclusively English—country squires, yeomen, and ministers all in perfect agreement—thrifty, prosperous, moral people. They were not fanatics. They didn't aim to remodel human nature or the basic institutions of family and property. They simply wanted to live their lives according to the covenant they had all made with God. They formed their government by voluntary compact, and they made covenant between themselves and their officials. In short, the people had the right to choose their own form of government, and the right not only to choose their own officials but to turn them out if they didn't enforce God's laws. Here was the perfect union of sovereignty and liberty; a state wherein the citizens and church members were one and the same, all under covenant to obey God's laws. Here for the first time was a society bound together by common hopes, interests, and duties, based upon the only true foundation of stable freedom: conscience, reflection, faith, patience, and public spirit, and this society elected their governors from among themselves, supported their clergy, defended and educated themselves without help, and determined for us the certainty of the fall of New France with its spiritual and political despotism."

The Reverent Roger Cant placed on his face an ingratiating smile meant to impress everyone. "Well now," he said, "I don't rightly know if I'm allowed an opinion at this talk or not, but it still appears to me somethin's not right here. Mebbe you people don't think what happens to poor, old Roger Cant counts for very much, and mebbe drivin' me out of my livin' and keepin' me from preachin' the Word of God accordin' to my own light comes under the headin' of 'another issue,' but I wonder if Mr. Stevens would call what happened to Roger Williams another issue? He was back there around the start o' things, and they drove him out, just for speakin' his own mind."

The schoolmaster grabbed his forehead with his fingers and hooked his thumb under his cheekbone, closing his eyes and letting his head bend down for a moment. Then his hand dropped slowly to the table and he looked up at Roger Cant.

"Well, well, Reverend," Stevens muttered, "error and truth are always in contention in this world, and the difference between the two is not always easy to see. Even the Puritan, tho' he feared ignorance as the devil's own tool and cultivated his mind as a weapon against it, sometimes fell short of perfect vision."

"Well," said Roger Cant triumphantly, "I can't see the virtue of a system that sends the truth packin' into the wilderness in mid-winter."

The teaching habit could not let such an opinion pass unchallenged.

"Some goodness in the heart of Roger Williams was sent packin,' Reverend, but not the truth," said Stevens. "A few men in history, John Winthrop was one of them, have had the wisdom to see that a lesser good must sometimes be sacrificed to prevent a greater evil. Williams had tunnel vision, the congenital disease of fanatics. The only eyes he could see the world through were his own."

"As far as I can see," said the Reverend Cant, "all yer doing is callin' names, and that ain't good enough fer us." Once again he directed an ingratiating smile around the table, noting with satisfaction the lack of opposition to his words.

"What a chaotic world this would be if we didn't have names," observed Stevens. "The mischief doesn't occur until the name doesn't fit the fact. Did you know, Reverend, that Roger Williams taught that the churches of England were un-Christian, and the king's patent invalid? He said it was a sin to accept land from a public liar, by which he meant the king, and the only way to expiate such a sin was to return all the settlers to England. He thought a regenerate man couldn't pray in the company of any unregenerate person, including his wife and children, and finally he got to the point where he thought only his own wife was worthy enough to have Communion with him. Well, when he realized how alone this made him, he got a little common sense back, so he turned his error inside out and decided he'd better preach and pray with everybody! That's the way it is with the fanatic. He has to be on one side of the coin or the other, and, what's worse, he can't ever abide the other side.

"Mind you, now," continued Stevens," the Puritans produced Williams, and they wouldn't have driven him out if he'd only listened to reason. In a society where every man is educated and holds his own opinions, there's bound to be some pretty wild errors, but logic and reason are supposed to overcome them. The only people the Puritans drove out were the fanatics who wouldn't wait for time and reason to work on the system, but tried to destroy it one way or another. Now, no one at this table could afford to let a lunatic destroy him on the grounds that the lunatic thought he was the only one with the truth, any more than the Puritans could let Roger Williams or Mrs. Hutchinson or the Quakers destroy them before the foundation on which all New England rests was fairly set."

"Hold on just a minute," interrupted Roger Cant, whose anger was again about to get the better of his discretion. "I smell somethin' here, and it smells like a dry, dusty old book somebody threw up in the loft. Now mebbe you got some o' them things right, I don't know, but a half-truth is wors'n a whole lie, as far as that goes. I guess we all know what happened to Roger Williams, and we've all heard what kinda' man he was. I calculate you'd tell the same kind o' lie about Reverend Whitefield, but I wouldn't listen to it any more than I'm goin' to listen to what you just got done sayin'. Years ago, I was put by the Lord in the way of salvation, and I was washed in the blood of the Lamb—born again—thanks to the preachin' of Reverend Whitefield. A light come over me, just like come over so many others; I been a-preachin' ever since, and I'm goin' to bring that light to all God's children that want it, even if I have to use a tree stump for a pulpit."

The Reverend Cant's eyes glowed with his zeal and sincerity, and he managed to look almost like a saint. Tom felt a sudden sympathy for this man, whose sufferings had only strengthened him in his convictions. He might be wrong sometimes, and maybe he had caused the others some trouble, but Tom admired a man who stuck to his beliefs.

Tom's thoughts were interrupted by Win Smith. "And all those that don't want it too," he said. "You 'New Lights' always do the same thing. You start by sayin' you have some special truth that nobody else has, and then you start saying that everybody who doesn't see yer special truth is unregenerate and unconverted. You howl and squall, an' you won't pay yer taxes and you won't obey the laws, an' if you don't git yer own way, you pull out, takin' those you've corrupted with you. You don't use no reason and no common sense, an' when you don't git yer own way, you smash and destroy. You won't accept bein' the same as the rest of us, an' you don't believe that the right thing to do comes out of the meetinghouse, being as you think yer the only one who knows what's right, an' you finally wind up screamin' 'bout persecution."Uncle John pushed his chair back from the table and stood up, dropping his hand on Tom's shoulder. The chair scraped and grated on the floor, and everyone's eyes turned toward him. His face was absolutely without expression, matching the tone of his words.

"I reckon Tom an' me don't have time to git into one o' yer religious arguments," he said. "The sun'll be up before we're fairly rested as it is, an' we've got a long haul tomorrow."

Emile's hand on Cant's elbow had the same effect as if he had placed it over his mouth—Cant's open mouth at the touch, and whatever he had been about to say a secret. Bouchet looked straight at Uncle John and spoke earnestly.

"I wish you would stay just a minute, Captain Evans," he said. "I have to leave on a business trip myself; I've neglected my trading too long, and I'm afraid I might have some serious losses if I don't go to Boston and Albany and check on my interests there. You've just come from the action at Fort Ticonderoga. Did you see any sign at all of a war party down along the Mohawk Trail? If you did, go to Boston first."

"No sign at all," said Uncle John. "If there's a party between here and Fort Ti, it's got ghosts for warriors. Now, we left the drowned lands at East Bay, so I can't guarantee nobody went down Wood Creek toward Fort Ann, but with the French withdrawin', and prob'ly gone from Crown Point by now, I can't see no danger in the trip to Albany."

"That's good news," said Bouchet. "Then I'll start for Albany in the morning. Say, there wouldn't be any chance we could leave together, would there? I'd be happy to have you and Tom with me even part of the way."

Uncle John looked at Bouchet closely. "Now, what reason would we have to go back the way we came?" he asked. Then he laughed a little self-consciously. "No, Bouchet," he continued, "we're goin' west to the other border forts and up the Connecticut to Number Four."

"Of course," said Bouchet. "I should have thought before I spoke. Naturally, you have business at Fort Massachusetts—recruiting posters and other things—and you can check just about every place any war party might be hiding, waiting for a chance to do some deviltry, right up to Number Four. Have you decided which path you're going to take out of Number Four back to Ticonderoga, or are you planning to head for Crown Point?"

"The only plans I have," said Uncle John, "are to go to a cabin raisin' up northwest of Number Four. They's a fine young couple settlin' in up there, and some of us old-timers want to make sure they git settled right. I'm lookin' forward to it mightily."

"If I didn't have to go to Albany," said Bouchet, smiling pleasantly, "I'd join you. There isn't anything that pleases me more than seeing young people making a beginning and meeting friends I haven't seen for a while. A cabin raising is truly a double pleasure, and if you have the chance, Captain, I would appreciate it if you would give the young couple my name and tell them that Emile Bouchet is always ready to help. I can appreciate how much you are looking forward to the event. Perhaps your old friend Toe-lee-ma is there now? I haven't heard that anyone has seen him for some time. You know, I was surprised that he didn't come with you from Ticonderoga." Bouchet's tone turned this last statement into a question, although he did not look as if he expected an answer.

"Toe-lee-ma comes and goes as he pleases," said Uncle John. "I've never tried to cut his trail for him, and I'm sure not startin' now. As long as you got the information you needed, Bouchet, Tom an' me wish everybody a good night and turn in."

Several "good nights" followed Tom and his uncle out the door and into the cool evening.

A cold wind swept through the valley, but to Tom, it offered a welcome relief from the smoke and turmoil of the tavern. He threw back his head and took a deep, grateful breath, letting the air cleanse him, inside and out.

"Didn't care much for that business in there, did you, Tom?" said Uncle John. "Well, there's always things a man has to put up with—but that Bouchet; I never trusted the man, and I don't like the int'rest he showed in our doin's. It ain't natural for him to want my company. I don't see as how I told him anythin' he can use—still, he's a clever devil, an' he gives me an uneasy feelin' I jest can't get rid of. I reckon we better not spend any more time at the forts than it takes to spread the word about Fort Ti and tack up the posters. It won't hurt none to git to Number Four a day early."

Tom followed his uncle over the tavern's home lot toward the barn. He climbed the ladder to the hayloft and sank down, suddenly too tired in mind and body to worry about tomorrow. He was asleep instantly, even before his body had fairly settled itself in the hay.

3

THE SEARCH FOR SATANIS

The eye of the St. Francis Abenaki, accustomed to forest details, did not linger upon the misshapen trunk of the giant oak at the edge of the small clearing. In the forest along the New Hampshire-Massachusetts border, where not one infant tree in a thousand lives to maturity, abnormality is as normal as gloom and silence, and the grotesque postures of the dead and the dying testify to the ferocity of the struggle to exist.

The Abenaki's eye was more attentive to the clearing itself, and his mind more appreciative of the testaments to struggle found there. He noted with satisfaction the pine saplings struggling up where lately corn, beans, and pumpkins had shared the black soil. The charred, decayed wood that had once been a tree and then a foundation log and now looked almost like any other debris of the forest floor nourished his flickering hope that the forest, with the aid of tomahawk and rifle, would one day completely reclaim its own. And so, satisfied that no unwanted presence here threatened him or his hunting grounds, eyes and feet turned northeast, toward the Connecticut and Fort Dummer.

Had the Abenaki turned his relentless eyes once more to the clearing, they would have been attracted instantly by a slight, mysterious movement of the hump that deformed the giant oak, and, although the disturbance was brief and unrepeated, the mystery would have been solved by instinct and experience. The motion would have become an involuntary shudder, then the fringe of a deerskin jacket, and, finally, the figure of a young man, and the Abenaki would have had a decision to make: could he safely kill now without betraying his presence on the border and jeopardizing his plans for the future?

The young man who had so fortunately benefited from the Indian's carelessness listened intently for sounds that would signal his uncle's return from his early morning scout.

What could possibly be takin' him so long, thought Tom as he watched the sun steadily rise up the trunk of the ancient pine at the eastern edge of the blearing. *If he did find any sign, he wouldn't follow it very far without comin' back for me.*

The boy listened to the chucking of the squirrels and the screams of the blue jays above him and the scuttling of deer mice near his feet as the sun continued to climb until it topped the pine and moved over the blearing. The life of the forest momentarily subsided. The mid-morning silence brought ominous thoughts that enflamed Tom's imagination. "What could have gone wrong?" he asked himself. "The Indian who could outsmart my uncle hasn't been born yet."

Mebbe that man Bouchet has something to do with this, he thought, remembering how Bouchet's questions had upset Uncle John at the tavern. *He certainly wanted to know our plans. Even wanted to know where Toe-lee-ma was.*

A picture of Bouchet formed in the boy's mind. He realized he had disliked the man from the moment he set eyes upon him.

That Frenchman's a bad one, he thought. *Uncle John said so too.*

Tom's brow furrowed in wrinkles of concentration as he tried to recall Bouchet's every word during the scene at the tavern, but, other than the man's surprising interest in their activities, he could think of nothing that connected him with his uncle's failure to appear.

Just the same, thought Tom, *it was Bouchet who caused Uncle John to change his plans.* He remembered the haste with which they had traveled from West Hoosac to Fort Massachusetts and how quickly Uncle John had given the news of the victory at Fort Ti and departed. There had been some hasty conversation with a young lieutenant of the militia, evidently all Uncle John needed to arrange for the posting of the recruiting notices along the border and south down the Connecticut, a quick mid-morning meal, and then they had taken to the forest. The actions of the journey from Fort Ti were repeated, only with more care, Uncle John frequently departing from the path to make a short but thorough circle through the forest, returning wordless and expressionless to take up the trail again. They had made huge semicircles around Forts Pelham and Shirley, covering every possible access from the north, but they had not gone near the settlements. Finally, dusk had overtaken them, and they had stopped at this deserted settlement between Fort Shirley and the Connecticut. Tom ground his teeth in despair and frustration and groaned inwardly. Why didn't Uncle John confide in him more?

Why did he always have to be so secretive about everything? Sometimes he acted like a magician, letting his purpose unfold detail by detail, without explanation, until suddenly the trick was accomplished, leaving poor Tom with only a general idea of how the details had been fitted together.

Tom was momentarily distracted by a woodpecker industriously pursuing the interests of his stomach. Tom couldn't help thinking of a wood chopper as the busy bird cocked his head up and to the left and delivered a rhythmic series of blows against the tree and then turned his head to the right and repeated his attack. Bits of bark came crashing down through the silence, unaccountably angering Tom, who reached for a large piece of bark that had landed near him, intending to throw it back at the bird, when the light touch of a hand on his shoulder chilled his backbone and froze him motionless.

"A man in the forest oughtta listen to the warnings of the blue jays and the crows and fergit about them woodpeckers," said Uncle John, "leastways, if he wants to keep his scalp."

Burning hot shame flowed through Tom's veins and drove out the ice. His hand dropped to the ground, and he shook just a little as he shoved himself upward and turned to face his uncle.

"Jest follow me," said Uncle John, "and I'll show you what I mean." They stepped out of the trees, followed an old furrow down the clearing's edge, turned east for a few rods, and reentered the forest, stopping by an oak stump that had put out a number of long shoots.

"Satanis," he said and pointed at the ground.

Tom's eyes sighted down the finger and picked up the faint impression left in the tangled leaves.

"Satanis," said Uncle John again, squatting down so his index finger could trace the print of the moccasin. "See how the left foot points straight ahead and the print is deeper than you'd expect on the outside edge?"

Tom bent forward, trying to refine the gradations of the print and memorize them. It didn't bother him that he could not really see the subtle differences in the depths of the impression in the leaves, because he knew that if he studied the track intensely enough, he would absorb the feeling of its uniqueness as surely as if Satanis had stepped in the middle of his memory.

"He stood there several minutes," said Uncle John. "It's a mighty fortunate thing you weren't thinkin' about woodpeckers then, Tom, or he'd a-spotted you for certain. I'd give a wagon-load of beaver skins to know what he was doin' down here all by his lonesome."

"Think he came down here lookin' for somebody?" asked Tom.

"Mebbe so, but if he did, he didn't find him," replied Uncle John. "They ain't another print to be found anywhere near here. I made sure of that before I came back.

"It don't do no good to stand here," he said. "Wherever Satanis is goin' to strike, it ain't goin' to be this clearin,' and it's not likely he come from Crown Point by himself. No, he's lookin' to give us somethin' to remember him by fer a long, long time. Now, we know he didn't come down the Mohawk Trail because that's the way we come, so that leaves three ways he might have come in with a fairly large war party, say twenty to thirty braves. No, Tom, we can't outguess him, so we're goin' to have to find him. The question is, where do we start lookin'?"

"Well," said Tom, "it's certain he went across Lake Champlain and through the woods to Otter Creek. Then he could follow the Otter up to the highlands and portage over the Green Mountains to the West River, and go down to Fort Dummer; or he could curve up the Otter to Mill River, portage over the mountains, and take the Ascutney Trail down the Black River. If he went that way, he could hit any settlement between Number One and Number Four."

This last probability was so strong that Tom made it instantly into a fact. "He must have done just that," he exclaimed. "There's no other way he would have come."

"Mebbe," said Uncle John, "but then what's he doin' down here, forty miles to the south? I'll grant you it ain't likely he's goin' to do his murderin' around here, what with all the militia and rangers along the border between West Hoosac and the Connecticut and north up to Number Four. It's just too risky for anything big, and he wouldn't chance having his escape route cut off. The closer he is to the trails leading to Champlain, the better off he is. As far as that goes, if he hits as far north as Number Four, he can run right up the Connecticut to Lake Memphremagog."

"Yes," said Tom, "and he wouldn't attack a strong point like Fort Dummer, even if the Wantasiquet Path was still open to him. He must aim to hit somewheres between Number One and Number Four."

Uncle John shifted his weight from one foot to the other and looked north. "There's so little time, Tom," he said. "I might be willin' to make a guess and stand on it if only I knew the size of his party—but even then it'd be mighty poor odds." He turned to face Tom, the giant of decision again in his eyes. "We've got to find him, Tom. He'll wait for the best chance he can get, and mebbe that'll give us the time we need. You know the valley northwest of Dummer where the West River runs between the Hills of Dummerston and Putney. If he's goin' after the fort or any settlement near it, we'll find his sign there."

Tom his uncle entered—not into the forest as they headed north toward the West River. He knew how little time they had because Uncle John had not bothered to follow the trail Satanis left from the clearing. *If it'd been me,* thought Tom, *I'd of at least found out what direction he was takin'.*

The miles went swiftly as they trotted along the broad, well-used trail without stopping. By the time they passed west of Fort Dummer, Tom had done a lot of thinking about Uncle John's haste, and he believed that he understood the unspoken cause of his uncle's great concern. Uncle John just had to be thinking of the cabin raising north of Number Four, of the young couple he was so fond of, and the neighbors who might come from as far away as thirty miles to join in the work and the fun. Satanis might well think that such an event was ideally suited to his purposes, isolated as it was from protection and yet gathering enough people to satisfy both his lust for blood and his greed for plunder and captives. How Uncle John must have been tempted to guess that the force of Satanis would be small and that the cabin raising would be his target! But his sense of obligation to the entire border, and the habits of years of rangering devoted to its protection, would not permit him to overlook the consequences of an attack on Dummer or the fort at Number Four.

The hills on the east and west closed in on them as they entered the valley and continued to run northwest, following the course of the river. The Hills of Dummerston remained close on the west, but when the land began to open up on the east, Uncle John crossed the river and halted.

"If there's a war party here waitin' for Satanis, they're somewhere up in them hills that'll get 'em to Dummer in two or three hours, dependin' on how careful they are. It's certain Satanis wouldn't have chanced leadin' 'em through the valley before he left 'em. If it's Dummer or any smaller fort around it they're headin' for, they left the river somewheres near here. To hide in the hills."

Uncle John looked at Tom very intently. "Tom," he said, "Satanis is the craftiest devil alive, but he can't walk on air, and if he left the river here, we'll find sign of it. You go back into the valley to where the cliffs come closest to the river. If he's tryin' to trick us, he'll come out there. Don't expect to see a lot of sign on the ground. Thirty of them devils can cross like they was one man, but a sign they will leave, an' you'll find it. If you don't find nothin' between the river and the cliff, come on back along the base of the hills, and Tom, make sure there's a couple of hours of daylight left when you git back."

Uncle John turned and headed north along the river. Tom watched him move away, standing there feeling the full loneliness of the forest, fighting the images that raced through his thoughts: the evil face at the cabin window; the black smoke oven that held the screams of all the fiends of hell; his father lying in the woods outside of Louisbourg with his head split open by a hatchet; the charred, smoldering ruins of a cabin; a figure fallen across the doorway, the head bloodied and scalpless, and the body's strange, black mixture of burned flesh and clothing.

Suddenly the boy began to truly understand the responsibility that had marked and lined his uncle's face and bent his figure, and he turned to his task with his five senses so sharpened that they amounted almost to a sixth. For the first time, he carried to his task some of the magic powers ascribed to his uncle by the border people and the Indians.

As Tom followed the river south toward the cliff, his new-born intuition, simply because it was too new to sustain itself in the welter of physical facts and the theories arising from them, gradually deserted him. The life of the river bank unfolded before him, mirroring the struggle for survival that character-izes all life, from the sapling struggling toward the sun in the dense, tangled forest, to the settler fighting the more varied and potent forces that seek to take from him life, liberty, and prop-erty. His eyes caught the print of the raccoon and followed it to the water's edge, where the animal had fished for his break-fast. He passed tufts of fur fluttering on the ground, where the crafty fox had overtaken a rabbit, and he looked at the torn and bloody ground, where mink and muskrat had fought with all the vicious hatred of natural enemies. *The marten waits in ambush to surprise the squirrel,* thought Tom, *and all the time his relative, the fisher, sits on a tree branch and awaits his chance to eat the marten. Sometimes it's awful hard to understand God's plan.*

Tom had reached the place where the weathered cliff came within several rods of the river. With utmost care, he examined every inch of the area, including the ferns and flowers, looking for any sign of disturbance, but he found nothing. Not a blade of grass was in any way out of place. Everything was completely normal to the river and its life. Tom turned north to work his way along the base of the hills and back out of the valley.

The course of the sun and a fierce gnawing in his belly told Tom he had returned on time. He reached into his hunt-ing shirt for a piece of jerky to chew on while he waited. The intensity of his search had drained his energy and his emotions, and he waited, passively free for the moment from worry and speculation.

When Johnathan Evans arrived, he nodded his head in what might have been a silent comment to himself on Tom's appearance, although the nod was allowed to pass for a greeting.

"Not a thing, Tom," he said. "Still not a sign. I'd bet my scalp they haven't been here." Worry wrinkled his forehead, and fear unbalanced the scales that had carefully weighed out the facts of his scout. "But I can't afford to bet somebody else's scalp, dammit! It's always possible we missed somethin'. We couldn't make the Black River now before dark anyway. I don't like it, Tom. I don't like it, but we're goin' to have to pray to God that Satanis hasn't picked his target yet!"

Uncle John paused to look at Tom, inviting comment, but when no comment came, he looked up to the sky and then out over the hills.

"We just can't stand here and waste daylight, Tom," he said. "Won't be no use, but we got just time to check them trails that lead over the hills and down into Dummer. Mebbe it'll help us some day to know we done every last thing we could."

The habitual action of following the bent form ahead of him through the forest began to work the numbness from Tom's mind. Although his uncle had given little outward sign of the fears that boiled inside him, Tom felt his apprehension. Each step drove a new doubt into the boy's conscience. Since he could not doubt the thoroughness of his uncle's scout or the truth of his conclusions, he began to doubt himself.

They could have crossed over and I never saw the tracks, he thought. *I know I was tired before I reached the cliff. There's no doubt I might have overlooked something, or maybe I looked too hard at a sign that didn't mean anything. Could anybody study that mess in the mud where the rat and the mink fought so furiously and still see the hidden sign their hatred had obscured?*

When the first trail yielded no evidence of Satanis, Tom began to hope fervently that the second would reveal the presence of the enemy. *There will be plenty of time to warn the fort,* he thought. *It won't matter that I let Uncle John down. Mebbe we can even ambush Satanis, and—*

"Tom!" Uncle John's voice, low but exasperated, brought Tom back to reality. "I don't know just what you're thinkin', Tom, but whatever it is, stop it. We need to keep our wits about us now more'n ever. There's nothin' on this trail either, and I'm certain sure now they've come out of the mountains somewheres up on the Black River. If they don't hit some place tomorrow morning, we still got a chance to stop 'em."

Tom was heartened by his uncle's words and manner. After all, as long as Satanis was still in the forest, the chances were that his magician uncle would find him, and when he did find him, perhaps he would arrange a reception that would stop his deviltry permanently!

"It's almost too dark to see," said Uncle John. "We'd better git off the path here and find ourselves a spot to sleep. It's better'n twenty miles up to the most likely portage onto the Black. The goin' ain't too rough, and I reckon we'll skip the mornin' scout and get movin' before sunup. In fact, if we get real lucky, we might find Satanis first and let him lead us to the pack of murderin' wolves he brought with him.

Tom, his doubts laid to rest as much by fatigue as by his uncle's words, settled down on the forest floor and enjoyed the sparse meal of the ranger on the trail. Then he closed his eyes and fell instantly asleep.

Tom felt the weight of his uncle's hand on his shoulder and wondered how a touch so light could be so commanding.

The same touch had awakened him hours earlier in the pre-dawn blackness of the forest, drawing him almost instantly from the depths of sleep and magically preparing him for the day ahead. Tom had marveled at the skill with which his uncle had penetrated the invisible tangle of trees and brush as they came down out of the hills and headed north toward the Black River. The sense of wonder was with him still as they stood before the tiny brook that tumbled down the Green Mountains, leaping and bubbling in frothy laughter as it widened and deepened the channel; it was so industriously cutting into the valley of the Black. Tom wished the tiny stream luck and hoped it had powerful magic that would protect it from landslides, droughts, and all the ancient enemies of embryonic rivers.

Uncle John seemed to sense Tom's thoughts. "That's a fine little brook there," he said, "workin' hard to amount to somethin'. I've watched it grow for years, an' I'd be the last one to wish it bad luck, but sometimes God's wonders are used by wicked men. See how the stream cuts into the valley and almost reaches the river before it peters out? Now, supposin' you were Satanis, and you wanted to come down out of the mountains and get to the Black River without leaving any sign. Got any idea of how you'd do it?"

Tom blushed inwardly. Again, his mind had not been on the task at hand—and the price of his failure could be the lives of his neighbors.

"Of course," said Tom, "I would come down this brook, stepping on the stones and making sure I didn't leave any print in the mud; that is, would if I was thinkin' at all."

"Not to worry about it," said Uncle John. "There's no harm done. The important question, Tom, is where do we start lookin'."

"Well, if he used the brook to get to the Black, he had to leave it where it peters out around those flat rocks, so there don't seem no point in climbin' up the cliff and goin' back to see where he went in."

"You're right, but there's more to it than that. For one thing, we ain't got the time to go up into the hills, and for another, there's too many other spots off the portage from Mill River over the mountains that's just as good as this. I've been trackin' Indians down the Ascutney Trail for near fifteen years, and the one thing I'm certain of is you can't never be certain where they're goin' to hit the Black. Satanis might not lead his party across here just because he'd figger it for the first place we'd look; on the other hand, he might figger we'd be a mite careless checkin' such an obvious spot, and that would give him his best chance to sneak through, so we'll start from the foot of the cliff. You take the north side, and don't miss a pebble or a leaf. If he's leadin' a big party, one of them might git careless too."

Tom went to the edge of the cliff and bent to his work. Mindful of his uncle's warning, he scrutinized every inch of the stream's course. No detail escaped him, but when he finally arrived at the flat, black rocks, he found nothing. A sudden heaviness hung about his heart and, for a moment, he was close to despair. How could they hope to find Satanis in time when he had so many miles of nearly impenetrable forest to hide in?

Tom straightened up and looked wearily at Uncle John, who leaned on his rifle, his face absolutely without expression.

"Looks like we got to move on north," he said, the tone of his voice so absolutely without feeling that he sounded inhuman. He threw his hand at the river a few feet away. "It would take a midget to walk in that trickle that spills over the rocks toward the river," he said, "and a giant to leap off the rocks into the river. No, Tom, we got to go on north to find our crossin'."

Tom looked at the tiny fingers of water that lapped over the flat, black rocks, each ending in a tangle of mud, pebbles, and torn, soaked leaves. As he watched, a tiny current ran over the rocks into the largest finger, floating two more recent arrivals, not as wet as their companions, aside. Tom wondered how long it would take before they too would sink down and intermingle with the sodden leaves below. Then he turned to follow Uncle John, who was already moving north up the valley.

As he ran behind his uncle, Tom had the feeling that their hope of stopping Satanis dwindled with every step, and yet there was nothing they could do but keep on looking. Somewhere in this valley was the fact they were looking for. Sooner or later they would find it. The question was whether or not they would find it in time.

Tom's thoughts were interrupted by his uncle.

"It's purely unreasonable to go any farther up the valley," he said. "We've jest got to turn around and go back. If I hadn't seen his track outside of Fort Shirley, I'd almost say he didn't come this way at all. I'll take the other side of the river, and if you don't find where he went in, mebbe I'll see where he came out."

Tom nodded and headed down river. He knew that the area along the river bank was his primary concern, and he promised himself that he would do better than he had down on the West River. He didn't want any of those second thoughts about his concentration that had bothered him the night before. If they didn't find Satanis, Tom wanted to be absolutely sure that the cause was not due to a defect in his character.

Tom worked the riverbank slowly, fighting off the desire to hurry that pushed his every movement. Constantly he would be struck by the extraordinary sameness of the struggles along the two river banks, and each time he would force the intruding thought away and re-study the sign. The intensity of his efforts absorbed him so completely that he did not hear his uncle's approach, and the sound of Uncle John's voice startled him so much that he straightened up frantically, almost losing his footing in the sand and mud.

"I just can't seem to find a thing," said Tom self-consciously, feeling the heat of his embarrassment creeping into his face.

"I haven't done any better, Tom," said Uncle John. The lines around his mouth were cut deeper by fatigue, and he could no longer keep the mounting concern and frustration out of his eyes and his voice.

"We missed somethin', Tom," he said. "I don't know how we could have, but we had to miss somethin'. Either that, or he really didn't come down the Black—but I would've bet two months of good beaver trappin' he did." Uncle John shook his head in slow, painful bewilderment. "I swear, Tom, I jest don't know what to do. If we left right now we could make the Ottaqueechee before it gets too dark. Now it don't make no sense in the world at all that he took the French Trail, and I know it don't, but God knows what we been doin' don't make no sense either. I jest got the feelin' in my bones that we ain't goin' to see nothin' here we didn't see before." Again he shook his head, as if he were tryin' to shake away some deep, abiding pain.

Tom, upset as much by his uncle's attitude as by their failure to find Satanis, leaned silently on his rifle, thinking his own thoughts, waiting and hoping for Uncle John to pull himself together and set a course of action. They stood for several moments facing each other, hands wrapped around rifle barrels, a pair of discarded bookends enclosing nothing but empty space.

At last, Uncle John broke the silence. "I went over everything I saw that looked unnatural," he said. "Every broken twig and rolled-over pebble, and I couldn't make any of it come out of Satanis. I tried to think of every sign I almost looked at twice, and then didn't. Finally, I just went over anything I saw that int'rested me for any reason at all; the whole sum come to zero, Tom. If he went by the Black, he's whipped us, that's all. Mebbe we ought to get up to that cabin raisin'. If we can't do nothin' else, at least we can protect our own."

For the first time in his young life, Tom felt sorry for his uncle. The feeling made him strangely restless and uncomfortable, and he shut it out instantly, turning his thoughts against himself. *It has to be me*, he thought. *Whatever happens is goin' to be my fault. If only I could think...*

"Now, Tom," said Uncle John, "if you're settin' there punishin' yerself, that won't do no more good than we're doin' settin' here an' all, the time has come to make a guess and hope to God we're right, and I'm guessin' he's goin' to hit somewheres around Number Four."

"I can't help it, Uncle John," replied Tom. I get this feelin' that it's my fault. If he's here, I missed somethin'. There's jest no other explanation!"

Uncle John nodded his head. "All right, Tom," he said softly. "A few more minutes here won't make no difference now. Let's go back to the brook, where we started this mornin'. Was there anythin' there that stands out—that keeps comin' back to you?"

"But that's the trouble, Uncle John," said Tom. "I can remember everythin' I did, but no one thing seems to mean more than another. As far as that goes, that little stretch of brook between the cliff and the river had less sign than most any place we looked. It wasn't nothin' but a pretty little brook tarrying leaves down to wash over them flat rocks and float around soakin' up water."

Uncle John looked at Tom with mild interest. "I don't recollect any leaves floatin' in any of that spillover," he said, his voice betraying just the slightest trace of disapproval. "There was a lot of leaves in them fingers, all of 'em stuck together and sodden, like they should be. Been gatherin' all summer, like always, one er two at a time."

Tom hesitated, trying to get the morning's picture clear in his mind. If he had let himself see what he imagined instead of what was really there, no doubt he had done the same thing in several other situations—and it really *was* his fault that Satanis and his warriors had crossed the Black undiscovered!

Suddenly Tom found himself talking. "I was standing right next to the rocks," he said, "almost on top of 'em, when the water kinda surged over the hollow in the middle rock and ran into the largest finger in the spillover and hit right between two leaves that were caught together. I remember now, they didn't float, but they split apart at the bottom and stayed hooked at the top, and then they moved back together, but I could see that they were hooked on top to each other and to the leaves beneath 'em."

Excitement animated Uncle John's features. "That could be it," he nearly shouted. "If it is, we've still got a chance. C'mon, Tom, we're goin' to do some real runnin.'" And without further explanation, Uncle John spun around and headed south.

Tom followed, trying to figure out the mystery of the floating leaves. The pace set by his uncle was cruel; after the first hour a fire burned in his lungs and he began to breathe solely through his mouth. By the time they halted at the flat rocks, Tom's chest was racked with pain and black spots danced before his eyes. Uncle John knelt down and carefully parted the two leaves that seemed to Tom to have sunk down farther in the water, since he had left them behind in the morning.

Uncle John handed Tom the two leaves. "Still not quite as wet as the others. That's why they haven't sunk down and mixed with the others even now. Look at the leaves underneath. They're a good half inch too deep for the level of the bed. We'd have seen that right away if it hadn't been for those two leaves on top."

Tom squatted on his heels and watched closely as Uncle John carefully removed the remaining leaves. "Look there, Tom," exclaimed his uncle, "he's the devil himself. He crossed the whole bank from the rocks to the river over that spot."

Tom looked at the moccasin print in the mud and knew from its depth that it had to be the last of many moccasins that had carried their owners to the river.

"From the very beginning, I had a hunch he would do somethin' like this," said Uncle John excitedly. "From here, he could go on down the river and hit any of the three townships below Bellows Falls, or he could go almost due west and hit Number Four. At any rate, the settlements are safe, at least for today. No matter how early he got up this morning to cross over, he couldn't hardly get position to attack much before noon, and noontime attacks don't suit his darkened soul."

As he listened to his uncle and the thrill of the discovery of the moccasin tracks began to diminish, Tom felt his apprehension returning. After all, it was already late in the day, and the vital question of Satanis's target was still unanswered. *Supposing Satanis took the Black right down to the Connecticut just above Number Two*, he thought. *Of course, he wouldn't actually go into the Connecticut—the risk would be too big—but it'd be dark before we could get far enough down the Black to start lookin' for his exit.*

He turned toward Uncle John. "What are we goin' to do?" he asked. "There's not much more than three hours of good daylight left."

"I know what yer thinkin', lad," his uncle replied. "And the way yer lookin' at things, we ain't got much reason for but look at it this way. I don't know what happened when he left Fort Ti, but judgin' by the depth and size of that print, it don't appear that he could git more'n thirty warriors to go with 'em. Now that's goin' to limit his plans considerably."

Tom nodded his agreement, taking heart from his uncle's attitude. Uncle John was once again the masterful forest magician, seeming to understand the situation so thoroughly that he could control any event that might issue from it.

"He's certainly not going to attack Number Four," said Tom confidently. "There's always militia there, and like as not a party of rangers too. He'd need at least a hundred men and all the help the devil could give him to take the fort." Uncle John seemed satisfied with his nephew's reasoning.

"That's right, Tom," he said. "As far as that goes, he's not goin' to attack any fort—not with only thirty men. Indians don't attack forts anyway without some robed demon or French half-breed leadin' 'em. It's not their style of fightin'. Besides that, Satanis knows he's goin' to have to settle for a few scalps and a little booty this time out. He come in travelin' light an' he's going out travelin' light.'"

Tom's face fell. "Well," he said, "if he's goin' to hit some settler's cabin outside the forts, it don't seem likely we got much chance of guessin' which one."

"If we had to guess," said Uncle John calmly, "now that we know where he is an' how many men he's got, I reckon we could cut the odds down some. In the first place, the French probably planned to desert Crown Point same as they did Ticonderoga, and Satanis would surely know that, so he'd plan to avoid Lake George and most of Lake Champlain. That means his natural escape route is up the Connecticut north of Number Four, and then up the Winoski to the northern end of Champlain; that is, if he intends to join Bourlemaque at Isle-Aux-Noix; or, if he's gittin' home, he might go way up the Connecticut and on into Canada by way of Lake Memphramagog. Either way, he's not goin' to hit very far south of Number Four and git cut off by forces from the fort. In the second place, he's not goin' to settle fer one isolated family, tho' he jest might plot out a route where he could safely hit four or five."

Tom was still confused, but he continued to take hope from his uncle's calmness. "I still don't see how that helps us pinpoint where he's gonna hit," he said.

"Of course, we don't know exactly where or when that devil has decided to do his murderin'," said Uncle John, "and two of us wouldn't do much good anyway, even if we did, but we can git plenty of help at Number Four. We can send out enough parties to collect most of the settlers in the fortified cabins until we can find Satanis and drive him out, and I can find rangers fast enough to get to the remotest cabins and smart enough to get their people back to the nearest fort. But first, we got one chore left—and jest enough time to do it. Seein' as how Satanis has such a small party, an' seein' as how he come into the Black right where I thought he would, the chances are pretty good he's goin' west to hold up somewheres outside of Number Four, figgerin' he's safe enough for the time bein,' and if he did, I'm bettin' he took the Mooserack Path."

Tom tried to prepare himself mentally for the task ahead. He knew the pace would be torturous, and indeed it was. Uncle John set out across the valley at full speed, and as they entered the forest that clutched at their clothing and slapped at their faces, coals burned in Tom's lungs.

"There's a deer trail that runs along the ridges up into the hardwoods," said Uncle John. "It never gits too far from the main path, the cover is perfect, and in daylight, it's not that hard to travel. Right here it ain't more'n thirty yards away. If

Satanis came this way, no doubt it was this mornin', but we better watch ourselves jest the same."

Tom watched his uncle step from the Mooserack Path into the brush, admiring the skill with which he avoided the snares of the tangled forest floor. Although Uncle John made no attempt to conceal himself from Tom, within seconds he could neither be seen nor heard. For several minutes Tom stood still, waiting, then he heard a squirrel chuck twice, and he went to join his uncle on the deer trail.

Tom saw several signs of the war party before he reached his uncle, who had moved on up the trail. "They sure must have felt safe in here," he mused, "'cause they didn't take any pains to hide their tracks."

Uncle John ignored Tom's observation and pointed to the ground. "What do you make of that?" he asked. Tom looked down at the moccasin print. "They've got a white man with 'em," he said. "Must be one of the runners-of-the-woods, the *coureurs-de-bois*." Suddenly a chill of apprehension set Tom's spine a-tingle. "Lord, Uncle John," he exclaimed, "all the while we been figgerin' on Satanis making the decision. If this Frenchman is important enough, he'll be runnin' things, and that changes everythin'."

"Mebbe so an' mebbe not, but I know that print—made it my business to know it a long time ago. Tom, that print belongs to Emile Bouchet, an' I got the feelin' you had better learn it too. It's an easy one, bein' way out like that and pressin' so deep on the inside of the heel." Uncle John shook his head. "I never liked that Frenchy," he growled. "Never liked him an' never trusted him, for more reasons than one. They's no tellin' what he's doin' here or how much influence he's got on Satanis, but I can tell you I don't like it. Tom, we'd better get back on Mooserack Path and git into Number Four just as fast as we can."

Tom looked up at the sky as he headed for the path. It was almost dark, and the trip into Number Four would be hard. It was difficult to trail through the woods in the daytime. To move along a narrow path up and down hills and over marshes and streams in the absolute, total darkness of the forest required incredible skill. Involuntarily, Tom closed his eyes, for soon he would be running blindly. The moon and the stars would not penetrate the forest canopy, and he would move solely by the sound of the footsteps ahead of him, and Uncle John, moved by the new urgency caused by the discovery of Bouchet's print, would run heedless of the perils of rocks, roots, holes, vines, and branches—heedless of the twistings and turnings of the path and the protruding tree trunks—of the thousand and one obstacles thrust out in the blackness.

Tom would never forget the pain and the labor of that run. He stopped counting the times the path tripped him and the trailside trees knocked him down. He ceased to worry about rips and the holes in his hunting shirt and trousers. He no longer felt the branches scratching his face, and he became too tired to notice the pain in his bruised and bleeding knees. A blackness rose up into his mind to match the blackness of the forest, and he knew no reality but the sounds that moved on ahead. Finally, he stumbled against a dark object and fell again to the ground; this time he could not rise. The sound he followed was gone. There was no sound, and he could not move.

"Tom … lad … we're here, boy. On yer feet, Tom, we're here. There are the walls of Number Four right ahead." Tom felt himself being lifted to his feet. He felt a tenderness and gentleness in the touch that confused him. He opened his eyes and put out his hand to touch the kindness that held him.

"Good lad, Tom," the voice spoke again. "Yer a man to run the trail with, I'll tell the world. Look straight ahead there, Tom. There's the gate to Number Four, an' we ain't got time to rest now."

Tom was still confused, but the warm praise was enough to start him toward the gate of the fort, and by the time his uncle exchanged greetings with the guard, Tom was himself again—in pain and near exhaustion, but ready to face whatever might come.

Tom felt a great sense of security as he stood within the stockade of Number Four, listening to Uncle John and the guard swapping information. The fort itself was a square enclosing about three quarters of an acre; each side measured a hundred and eighty feet and was bounded by squared logs laid one upon the other and interlocked at the corners, which were manned by flanker-boxes raised above the ground on posts. Backed against the outer wall of the fort were the small houses of its inhabitants, built so that their low roofs served as firing stations. So strong was the fort at Number Four that Captain Stevens and thirty men had successfully defended it against a force of over three hundred French and Indians, and yet, Number Four was nothing more than an isolated outpost of civilization, buried in forests that spread unbroken to the banks of the St. Lawrence, resting unprotected on the banks of the wild and lonely river that served as the highway for marauding bands of Algonquins, Caughnawaga Iroquois, and St. Francis Abenaki.

Tom felt traces of pain as he bent to pat two of the fort's dogs, who were not only children's pets, but also valued allies in detecting the presence of Indians and tracking them to their hiding places. "Good dog," he whispered. "Good dog. Down, boy, down. I don't have time to play right now."

Uncle John, his brief conversation with the guard over, turned to Tom, deep concern again showing in the tone of his voice.

"Bad luck, Tom," he said. "Most of the men have gone south to the other townships, and some have gone down as far as Dummer. There's somethin' awful wrong 'bout this, but I can't guess what it is. We got to get right over to the Ely cabin and find out what's happenin'. There's a cider and melon party goin' on, and I suspect most of the people left in the fort will be there."

A cider and melon party! Some of Tom's weariness dropped away at the thought. There was one such party a year ago at the Williams cabin down at Fort Dummer that he never would forget. He still wasn't sure how that had happened, but somehow, after all the guests had left, he had found himself sitting on the choice, but he had never known why. After all, he had not had the same chance as the others, ranging the woods as he did with his uncle, to impress this golden girl of the frontier with such talents as he possessed. Yet he had been the one she had chosen! He was still shaking his head in wonder as he followed his uncle through the batten door of the Ely cabin.

Uncle John stood just inside the door of the cabin, squinting and adjusting his eyes to the light and, at the same time, searching the cabin. The appearance of the two rangers, unexpected as it was, drew the partygoers to the door with a mixture of questions and greetings.

"Why, Captain Evans, a pleasure to see you, sir!" and "John, what brings you here at this time of the night?" Tom listened as his uncle responded to the greetings, making light of the rather unusual circumstances of their presence, quieting the people who crowded around them and somehow or other making it known to Joseph Ely that there was a need for private conversation.

"Eph, git that fiddle of yours a goin'," said Joseph Ely, "while I get these men somethin' to take the chill out of their bones. Why, a stranger'd think we'd forgotten our manners." He made a path toward the corner nearest the fireplace, and the people willingly fell back as Tom and Uncle John followed Mr. Ely across the room.

"All right, John," said Joseph Ely, pouring flip into two quart mugs sitting on the puncheon table and turning to the fireplace to heat a flip dog. "What is it?" He pulled the red-hot dog from the fire and plunged it into the flip.

In the fireplace light, the worry on his face turned to fear.

"Well, that's the trouble," replied Uncle John. "I just don't know, an' I'm hopin' you can help me put the pieces together. Out at the gate, Sam told me the men have gone south down the Connecticut, and that don't make sense, under the circumstances."

The two men sat down at the table to match facts, each hoping that, between them, they had the information necessary to explain the situation. To Joseph Ely there had been, of course, nothing to explain until the moment he saw Captain Evans step through the door of the cabin. He understood that the key to whatever mystery Captain Evans had brought with him lay in the events at Number Four that had led to the decision to march south. For some time there was silence as Ely went over yesterday's details, discarding some, selecting others, and trying to arrange them into a meaningful pattern. Tom watched the working on the man's face as Ely struggled with his own desire to know what had brought the rangers to his cabin, and the temptation to blurt out immediately the one major fact that had sent the men of Number Four hurrying for their trail clothes and rifles. The self-imposed discipline necessary to frontier survival and the inner rationality of his Puritan heritage triumphed over the weaknesses of the moment and the raw emotions, and finally Joseph Ely was ready to begin.

"Yesterday was a big day at Number Four," he said thoughtfully. "'Bout as big a day as we've had this year. It ain't easy to know where to start. The Browns and the Dormans was up early gettin' ready to go up an' help Josh Foster raise his cabin. The boat came up to Bellows Falls with rum, salt, and other necessaries. Billy Williams and his family came up from Dummer on their way to help young Foster, though I was surprised to see his missus, even if she is kin to Josh's wife, seein' as she's expectin' again so soon. Then there was the runner who brought the good news about the victory at Fort Ti, and we all went over to Joe Woods' cabin for a little celebration." Ely paused as he ordered his remembrances of the impromptu affair at the Woods's cabin. "Well," he continued, "we'd been over to the cabin 'bout an hour and a half—it must have been around one o'clock—drinkin' a toast to the runner, an' the spirit of Lord Howe, even to that old bloody back, Amherst—everybody talkin' about how wonderful it was goin' to be to go to bed without worryin' about gettin' burned out an' havin' yer scalp lifted, or goin' out to hoe corn an' not needin' any weapon but a jug of cider—when the Frenchman came in."

Johnathan Evans's eyes seemed to throw sparks back at the fireplace, and Joseph Ely, again in full control of his faculties, noticed it at once.

"You know him, John," he said. "Bouchet, the French trader who stops with that 'new light' preacher down at West Hoosac. Emile Bouchet."

"Bouchet!" Uncle John's mouth barely had time to silently form the name before some ancient reflex slammed his body back against his chair, exactly like a man taking a musket ball full in the chest. A terrible energy consumed his features, transforming his face into a ring of burning fire, and the source of that energy was unmistakably the essence of hatred. Tom had never before and would never again look upon pure passion. For the first and only time in his life, he turned away from his uncle, turning instinctively toward Joseph Ely. But the turning was useless, for Joseph Ely sat paralyzed by a cold agony that had struck the pit of his stomach and fingered its way outward and upward, immobilizing him in his chair.

"Bouchet," intoned Uncle John again, but this time the name was audible. "The same Bouchet whose footprint we found this afternoon on the Mooserack Path along with the footprints of Satanis and thirty Abenaki hellhounds."

The spell placed upon Joseph Ely by the ranger's terrifying display of hatred was broken. He bolted upright like a man who has been slapped in the face. "Good God!" he cried. "What does it mean?"

That was as far as he got. With incredible quickness, Johnathan had risen to his feet, with one hand grabbing a mug of flip and pressing it into Ely's hand and with the other raising his own mug in a toast.

"Be quiet, man," he said. The intensity of his voice was all out of proportion to its softness. "Do you want to have everybody in the room over here shouting questions and arguing before you can tell me what Bouchet was up to?"

"I'll drink to that kind of future," he said. His performance was perfect. His tone was the happy toaster's tone, and the volume was not one decibel too soft nor too loud for the occasion. The startled eyes that had turned toward Ely's explosive cry turned casually away.

Joseph Ely had recovered himself. After raising his mug to drink the toast, he sat down and went back to work. His mind teemed with images of Bouchet, Satanis, burning cabins, and murdered settlers, and when he began to speak, his thoughts were far from organized, but he was determined not to let Captain Evans down again. The life of a friend might well depend upon the completeness and accuracy of his recollections.

"As I way sayin', John," he began, "everybody was celebratin' when Bouchet showed up, an' somebody shoved a glass in his hand an' somebody else proposed a new toast an' we all drank to it. I remember Bouchet laughin' and jokin', tellin' us how he first celebrated the victory with you and Tom down at West Hoosac. In fact, he was braggin' that he was prob'ly the first man in Massachusetts to drink to the victory at Ticonderoga and makin' a big thing outta his part in spreadin' the news along the border and north up the Connecticut. Well, I soon got tired of listenin' to that, I can tell you, and I turned away an' forgot all about him—an' I'm thinkin' now that mebbe that's jest what he wanted. He looked at me an' knew a fool when he saw one."

Johnathan Evans's finger tapped on the puncheon table, but his voice and manner were very calm. "There wasn't any way you could know what he wanted," he said. "But there's one thing so far that bothers me. You keep talkin' about Bouchet like he was alone. There must have been somebody with him."

"No, John, not a soul," Ely said, "and I didn't figger that was unusual. He's been tradin' around these parts, on and off, for a good many years; it ain't strange at all to see him travelin' alone."

"Of course, ye're right," came the reply. "I was thinkin' of somethin' he said down to Hoosac. It don't matter anyhow, Joseph. What I'm wonderin' is what he did after you lost track of 'im."

"I kin make a pretty good guess," said Ely. "It wasn't only 'bout a half hour later I spotted him over at the door sayin' goodbye to Sally Williams. I remember it 'cause Miz Williams was hollerin' to Sally to git a move on." Ely permitted himself a quiet chuckle. "She was sure riled at Billy for stayin' too long and drinkin' too many toasts. Can't say as I blame her either, considerin' her condition." He permitted himself a second chuckle. "I'll bet Billy got her up to Foster's before supper. He's a movin' man when he's got that many drinks under his belt, and when the cider wore off, I'll bet her tongue made him wish every step he took was his last one."

Tom took as much delight as Joseph Ely had taken from the plight of poor Bill Williams. He could picture the man now, stumbling along a forest path, leading a horse from whose back Mrs. Williams delivered an embittered sermon full of biblical quotations concerning the fate of the drunken man, but when he looked over at his uncle to share this joke, Tom's laughter died away. The deep lines about his uncle's mouth seemed carved in stone, and the brows were knotted and pulled down so far that his eyes squinted.

Johnathan Evans had good reason for his grimness.

In truth, the last thing he had consciously heard was the name Sally Williams. His mind had flashed back over the past two years, using the light supplied by the girl's name to drag truth from the shadows of time and circumstances that had hidden it. He saw an earlier cabin raising where Sally Williams, a woman at fourteen, ran toward him through the midday meadow, her hair a yellow gold that took its color from the sun, and her eyes the color of paradise. She came to him, laughing and holding her skirt higher to run the last steps before young Tom could catch her, and the golden brown curve of her calf took his breath away. He remembered laughing at the sight of his trail-hardened nephew, changed into an oafish schoolboy, stumbling along behind her; and then he remembered the look in the eyes of another visitor to the cabin raising who stood nearby, his face unmasked so that the corruption of his soul shown through. Instinctively Johnathan Evans knew that he had found the moment that had triggered Bouchet's decision yesterday, and immediately his thoughts began to turn his intuition into a description of the truth.

That's when he decided, he thought. *Right there, when he found out the Williams were goin' up to help Josh Foster raise his cabin. He knew his usefulness along the border was over as soon as he found out the French were bein' driven back to Canada, so he went lookin' for the worst thing he could do to us and the best thing he could for himself before he left, an' he found it here. He must have figgered he could talk Satanis into hittin' the cabin raisin'. God knows he can promise that red devil plenty of blood and booty at such an affair.*

He decided to keep his own counsel, at least until Joseph Ely finished recounting the details of Bouchet's actions, and he directed at Ely a questioning look that prompted the man to continue.

"Well," Ely resumed, "it wasn't long after that when I saw Bouchet over in the corner talkin' to young Charlie Turner, who had given away enough rum and cider to git hisself elected lieutenant at the last Train Bank Day. I could see they was awful earnest from the way they had their heads together. Bouchet was waving his hands around, Charlie was gettin' excited, and some of the 'listed men were gatherin' around, noddin' their heads an' pokin' at one another. Next thing I knew, young Turner was wavin' me an' Jack Spafford over with one hand and shovin' that worthless old Zeke Potter away with the other." He stopped to spit disgustedly on the floor. "I kin understand a man's weakness as well as the next, but that Zeke Potter!"

Ely stopped momentarily to collect himself and then began again. "When we got over to the corner, young Turner couldn't git his men quieted down, and everybody was comin' over to see what the hubbub was all about, so Jack an' me pulled him over to the other side of the fireplace where we could at least hear, and left the rest of them to their squabblin'. Bouchet jest naturally seemed to follow along. Now that's the thing that sticks in my mind, John. Bouchet never started anythin'. It was mostly Charlie Turner's doin'."

"Mebbe so," said Uncle John, "but somethin' had to set Charlie off, somethin' Bouchet told him before you and Spafford were called over."

"Why, it's easy enough to see what set him off," said Joseph Ely, "but you wouldn't say Bouchet meant to start anythin' if you'd been here. He was just bein' friendly, really. After the Williams left, he didn't know anybody else, so he naturally drifted over to the corner where the militia was drinkin' an', by way of gittin' himself into the conversation, he jest happened to mention how glad he was that the Williams were goin' north from the fort, where they'd be safe, instead of south, where there might be some danger. Well, young Turner, he said he couldn't see how there could be very much danger in any direction, seein' as how the French were bein' driven out of Champlain. Now, the way I got it, Bouchet didn't say nothin' for quite a while, just stood there thinkin', an' the more he thought, the more he fretted, I reckon, till he finally decided he'd better tell Charlie what was on his mind."

"Now, Joseph," interrupted Uncle John. "If Bouchet had some reason for wantin' the able-bodied men out of the fort, you wouldn't hardly expect him to make a public announcement out of it. He wouldn't just walk up to young Turner an' say, 'Lieutenant, collect yer militia an' as many householders as you kin' git to go with you an' head down the Connecticut!' Jest the same, he wanted the men out, and he got 'em out. I swear, he's closer to the devil than Satanis is. He came to Number Four without nothin'—not even a plan. He looked around, saw that young fool Turner, an' used him to walk out of here with the whole lot of you in his pocket. You've got to tell me how he did it."

Johnathan Evans calmly accepted the sudden surge of profound respect he felt for Bouchet, because it sharpened his awareness of the depths of the man's guile without in any way diminishing his hatred of him. Joseph Ely came to his own defense.

"I tell you, John, everythin' happened jest as natural as water runnin' downhill. There wasn't a body here that thought we done the wrong thing. Why, it was you yerself that warned Bouchet agin' goin' into Albany on account of the Indian sign you saw near the Mohawk Trail on yer way down from Ticonderoga. There ain't a man on the border who'd doubt yer word on such matters."

"Except that I never told Bouchet I saw any sign of Indians, 'cause I didn't," said Uncle John quietly.

"But there wasn't any way we could know that, John," Ely quickly replied, sensing that he had made his point, "any more than we had any reason to doubt Bouchet's word when he told us 'bout the sign he saw outside of Fort Shirley. Now, he didn't make any big thing out of that either. Said he only saw three or four tracks, an' he couldn't make much of 'em, 'cept they was Abenaki and up to no good. Well, you kin imagine how we took that! Abenaki print outside of Fort Shirley? That couldn't mean anythin' but a last bit of deviltry somewheres along the border. Then Bouchet told us that Cap'n White had already sent out what militia he had along with some rangers to protect the border east to the Connecticut and the frontier north to rummer, seein' as how there was so few troops an' so many miles between Dummer and West Hoosac."

"All right, Joseph," said Uncle John. "He made it sound reasonable enough, I'll bet my flintlock agin' an' old British musket it wasn't long after he got you all stirred up that somehow he got that fool Lieutenant to thinkin' how easy it would be to git himself elected Captain if he got movin' south quick enough."

"I can't say as how that's true, John," Ely said. "I never heard nothin' like that goin' on. Anyhow, it don't matter. We all decided we had a duty to protect the frontier as best we could, and we all figgered we had to help the settlers down the Connecticut, so there wasn't nothin' left to do but pick out the men who could best be left here to defend the fort."

"Well, that's it then," said Uncle John. "There ain't no doubt in my mind now about what Bouchet plans to do." All the breath seemed to go out of him at once; his head fell forward, and his shoulders hunched down after it.

Tom and Joseph Ely sat and waited. Their minds were tortured with doubts and apprehensions, but, because they had been unable to form any clear picture of what was about to happen, they had been spared the utter devastation of the soul that had suddenly struck their companion.

Johnathan Evans raised his head. Now that he was certain, he would put the situation squarely before the others. Not only was it his duty to lay the truth out before them, but also it would be necessary for each of them to act, and his deep Puritan heritage told him that they would each individually be held fully responsible for whatever judgments they made and whatever actions followed from them. His inherent concern for the true value of life both in this world and the next would not allow him to succumb to the temptation to protect them from their own fears.

"It ain't hard to figger what's happened," he said, "once you make the connection between Bouchet and Satanis. That's what had me fooled. I don't believe Satanis ever went to Crown Point. He took off from Fort Ti when the French blew it up, takin' whatever hellions he could git to go with 'im on the spot. He went across Lake Champlain up the Otter to Mill River and over the mountains, stoppin' somewheres west of the Black—jest far enough away to be safe and jest near enough to be within' a day's march of any target he had in mind—an' hid the war party. Then he headed south to meet Bouchet. That's why we found his print near the clearin' outside of Fort Shirley." He turned toward Tom. "Mebbe he did see you there under that tree, careless as you were. If he did it must've been mightly painful for him, weighin' the value of the scalps he was plannin' to take agin yers, considerin' how long he's waited to git at me for the trouble I've caused him."

Tom whined inwardly, remembering especially how he had foolishly lost his temper over the actions of a woodpecker, but he was in no way tempted to interrupt his uncle.

"Satanis must've been disappointed when he met Bouchet," continued Uncle John. "If I know that murderin' devil, he expected to git right at his bloody work. At any rate, Bouchet couldn't make up his mind, so he talked Satanis into goin' back to the mountains an' waitin' while Bouchet did some investigatin'. No doubt Bouchet did stop at several forts to spread the news of Ticonderoga, like he said, but he was lookin' for information about militia placements an' whatever else he could pick up. Like all good liars, he used jest enough of the truth to make his lies believable."

Watching his uncle's face intently, as if he expected its features to convey a meaning deeper than words, Tom suddenly had the feeling that his uncle was going to retreat into some inner world of thought and say no more, and, in fact, what he must say next had made Johnathan Evans pause momentarily.

The pause was marked, yet briefer than a heartbeat. "When he got to Number Four," Captain Evans continued, "Bouchet made up his mind. No doubt he'd had the Foster cabin in the back of his mind all the time, it bein' as exposed as it is. At the very least, he could promise Satanis plenty of scalps and a quick escape route up the Connecticut, an' when he saw a chance to get Sally Williams for himself, he jest couldn't resist the temptation. He decided right there to hit the cabin raisin' an' steal Sally."

For some reason the looks of shock and disbelief on the faces of his nephew and Joseph Ely angered him. "What's the matter with you?" he said fiercely. "Have I suddenly become a filthy, disgustin' old man? You, Joseph Ely! You know Bouchet's reputation along the border. What have I said that's so hard to believe?" His anger passed as quickly as it had come, and he spoke again calmly, not wasting time on an apology that was neither expected nor needed. "He made his decision knowing full well there would be no comin' back for him, so he had nothin' to lose by tryin' to send the militia south where they couldn't follow his retreat into Canada. If it worked, he'd be clear outta the country before his lies were unravelled; if it didn't, the escape might be a little touchier, but he had already decided to take the risk. As it is, his luck held out, an' he's left us here with no hope of stoppin' him unless he has trouble with Satanis."

Tom sat stunned. The numbness began to spread upward from the pit of his stomach again. He saw the painted face at the cabin window just before the darkness rising from below shut him back in the smoke oven. Shrieks of agony and cries of anguish mixed with the smell of burning timber and corncobs, and then he felt the hands, incredibly soft and gentle now, pulling him out of the darkness into the light.

"Tom, Tom," He looked up and saw his uncle standing beside him, felt his hand on his shoulder, heard his voice. He wondered why he had never realized how much Jed Hawkins looked like his Uncle John.

"C'mon, Tom, C'mon, lad. There's still hope. There's yet a chance, if we act quick enough."

A chance? A chance for what? thought Tom. *What is he talking about?* He accepted the words now as his uncle's, and he tried to understand their meaning.

"He's exhausted," said another voice. "Just plumb tuckered out. He's got to git some rest, or he'll be too sick for any doctor to cure."

Joseph Ely, thought Tom, *that's Joseph Ely.* As he turned toward the voice, the sights, the sounds, and the odors of the Ely cabin pressed in on him and brought him back to the present.

"I'm all right," he said. "Jest tired is all. I reckon I give you quite a start, driftin' off like I did, but I'm all right now."

"Why, sure you are," said Joseph Ely. "I'm plumb wore out myself, fer a fact, an' I ain't done nothin' all day. It must be way after midnight, an' time I got these folks on their way. Tell you what! There's a place up in the loft where you'll sleep sweet as a newborn babe. You go on up, son. Yer uncle an' me'll take care of things down here."

Tom was overwhelmed by a new understanding of the goodness in Joseph Ely's heart, but he did not move from his chair. He sensed that now, for the very first time, he was the one man his uncle needed and depended upon.

"Wait jest a minute," said Uncle John, talking to Tom but looking at Joseph Ely, "an' I'll go on up with you. I don't rightly know if you really understand this situation or not, Joseph, but young Foster's cabin is eight miles northwest straight through the thickest part of the forest. Most of the way the path ain't no wider than yer shoulders, an' there are stretches where a man workin' in the dark would take as many steps away from the cabin as towards it. Even if we left right now we couldn't git there in time to warn 'em. The only sensible thing to do is to git our sleep now while we can't do nothin' else. Tom and me'll leave at four an' take the main trail out. We kin follow that fast enough in the dark to git to the cutoff pretty close to half past five. By then the sun'll be comin' up, an' with a little luck, it'll come up fast enough to light the swamps and them stands of hardwood where they ain't no path at all. I figger about four hours, altogether, if everythin' goes jest right, an' we git the light we need."

"I understand the situation clear enough now," said Joseph Ely, unable to hold back his anger. "Yer plannin' on stoppin' Satanis with no more help than you can git from this boy. Now, John," he said, his anger disappearing as he spoke, "I know how you feel, but be reasonable. If you go up there alone, you can't do anythin' but git yerself and the boy killed. We've got to git the others over here an' talk this thing out. If there is an answer, we got a lot better chance of findin' it together."

Johnathan Evans did not return Ely's anger. "I'm afraid this isn't the kind of decision that you kin put up to a town meeting," he said. "The only thing we have to do is face up to the facts. I don't plan on stoppin' Satanis. I couldn't do that if I took every man in this room with me and risked leavin' the fort defenseless. But I do know what I can do. Traveling jest with Tom, I kin get to the cabin around eight o'clock, and, if Bouchet and Satanis couldn't git together or if for some reason you'n me could never guess, they delayed the attack, we could lead everybody back to Number Four. On the other hand, if it's all over … " He stopped, but regained his self-control immediately and forced himself to go on, using the same words. "If it's all over, they'll likely split into two parties to confuse us. If they do, I'll follow one, an' Tom'll follow the other. That way mebbe we can still do somethin' to help."

"I don't know," said Ely. "It's like ye're countin' 'em dead already. There's got to be somethin' else we can do."

"You know in yer heart there ain't, Joseph," he replied, "an' we ain't got time to justify our helplessness by talkin' about it. Why, man, you've got plenty to do. Tom an' me'll need a good breakfast and rations for the trail. You'll have to find a reliable man who can go south and bring back the militia. Somebody's got to see if there's any rangers free to follow us if we have to go after Satanis."

As Uncle John headed for the ladder that led to the loft, motioning Tom to follow, he turned for a last word with Joseph Ely.

"I've got a terrible feelin' inside me," he said, "that savin' anybody up there depends on how quick you kin come after us, not on how quick Tom and me git there."

4

MASSACRE AT DAWN

n the pre-dawn blackness of the first day of August, 1759, Emile Bouchet and Satanis led their Abenakis down the mountain slope and across the meadow that bordered on Josh Foster's corn field. Bouchet, who had spent half his life with Indians and had found both their ways and their maidens to his liking, moved expertly and confidently through the darkness. He had no fears; no doubts about the future. The years of spying were over, and today he would burn into the frontier a monument to his mastery of both parties who contested for it. Few men ever walked in the wilderness with lighter step or happier heart than Emile Bouchet at this moment.

Bouchet could not stop appreciating himself as the Indians moved into the cornfield. He let Satanis position them for the attack while he settled down to wait for the sunrise. He wanted to devote all of this final hour to yesterday.

It is only the leaders who count, he thought. *Abercrombie with fifteen thousand men could not take Carillon with thirty-five hundred, but when you add Abercrombie's stupidity to one side and Montcalm's genius to the other, the equation balances. How easy it was for me to work upon the fears and ambitions of that young idiot of the militia. And the others, the elders ...*

His inner laughter fed upon itself and grew too joyous to be contained. Satanis, waiting nearby, looked at him in questioning disapproval, but Bouchet deliberately turned his head away. He did not want his thoughts interrupted.

It is too bad I could not have turned as I left and said to them, "This, then, is your town meeting mentality. Look what one clever man can do to you. The defect, gentlemen, is in the system, but you can look to New France to cure it for you shortly."

Bouchet knitted his brows briefly. He had wanted to spend more time enjoying his triumph at Number Four, but Satanis's glance had distracted him.

Ah, you, my friend, he thought. *You are quite another matter. No fears, no misguided philosophy to weaken your judgment. Your incorruptible hatred places you above the mere reordering of facts. You have only one way to look into a man's soul, but when you do look, nothing that is primitive can be hidden.*

Bouchet's admiration of Satanis was genuine. He knew that Satanis allowed himself to be used by the French only where his goals and theirs coincided. In truth, there had been times when Bouchet had wondered, in spite of his historical sense, whether he used Satanis or Satanis used him.

But this time, Bouchet thought, *the impetus is clearly mine.*

The satisfaction he felt stemmed from his respect for the Abenaki. His mind went back to the pine stand where he had convinced Satanis that the Foster cabin was the best place to strike. At Satanis's request, they had squeezed under the sheltering boughs of a giant pine and sat in a deep carpet of fragrant needles. He had waited, conscious of the awesome size and power of the Indian, for Satanis to speak.

"Has my old friend found a way to plant the Lillies of France in the fields of New Hampshire?" Satanis spoke in French, something he rarely did, although he knew the language well enough. For a moment, Bouchet allowed himself to consider the reasons behind this unusual behavior, but only for a moment.

"The French are not planters, as my brother knows," replied Bouchet carefully. "They are traders, who give rifles and blankets for beaver and mink. The French do not cut down your forests and build cabins. They live in your houses with you, as brothers should. The French do not cover your valleys with corn and pumpkin so they can breed children who, in turn, will breed more children to destroy your hunting grounds. The French marry your women and become hunters and trappers because, like the Abenaki, their spirits must be free. You know that this is true, or I would not speak it."

"There are Frenchmen who like Indian ways," said Satanis. "They come and live with us for a time and take our women as squaws. There are traders who bring rifles and blankets with them, yet first, they try to get our furs with rum. But we should not argue over the alliance of the French and the Abenaki against the English. That was decided for both of us a long time ago. I am satisfied that your people do not want my hunting grounds, Bouchet."

Emile Bouchet was not disturbed. He knew that Satanis had chosen the pine as a conference site because the close quarters and natural setting enhanced the psychological advantage of his great size and savage ferocity. He knew also that Satanis's opening remark carried a calculated insult designed to test his will. Bouchet's intuition told him that his reply had been successful and cautioned him that he was expected to wait for the Abenaki's next move. He did not have to wait long.

"My warriors have risked much to wait for the words of Bouchet," Satanis continued. "Every hour increases the chance of discovery, and already it is too late to return to Crown Point. It is time for Bouchet to say what he has found."

The Frenchman began to feel the pressure of the arrangement. He did not like tilting his head so far back to look up into the Indian's face. He began to feel the element of danger always present in such a situation. He was like a mouse caught between the open paws of a giant cat, but he did not lose his nerve. He would stick to his plan as long as he could. When the decision to strike the cabin raising came, he wanted it to come from Satanis.

"Where the risk is great, the reward is often greater," replied Bouchet. "It is a truth I have learned from Satanis himself. But I have no warriors. It is not for me to say what is true here. Satanis must weigh the value of my information against the waiting time."

The Abenaki simply nodded his head; the preliminaries were over. It was time to get at the facts.

"I have been at the forts east along the border and as far north as Number Four," said Bouchet. "Nothing has changed—the English celebrate the victory at Carillon as if it marked the end of the war. They talk of larger crops and more children, and already a few of the younger ones are busy cutting deeper into the forest. Satanis knows the situation as well as if he had walked in my steps."

The presence of Satanis seemed to magnify itself until the Frenchmen felt that he was being physically pushed backward against the pine boughs. Lightning flashed in the Indian's eyes and Bouchet expected thunder in the voice, but there was only derision.

"An evil spirit has entered Bouchet's eyes so he has looked without seeing," said Satanis. "He has looked at strength and he has looked at weakness, but he has not seen the difference. The Abenaki will pay again in blood for his trust in the French."

Bouchet fought down the impulse to place his plan at once before Satanis. The effort calmed him, and he found time to marvel at the Indian's ability to instill terror in a heart as resolute as his own.

"I am protected from all evil spirits by the great charm that hangs from my throat," said Bouchet, pointing to his silver crucifix. "I have counted strengths and weaknesses from West

Hoosac to Number Four, but I did not think Satanis wanted them recounted here. The forts and the outlying fortified cabins are still the houses of safety. Militia guards the forts and sentries are posted."

As he spoke, Bouchet tried to read the Abenaki's face, searching for the slightest change of expression that might guide the direction of his words, but Satanis had turned to stone. Almost in desperation, as he felt his own will weakening, he threw the burden back on the Indian.

"I only wished to assure Satanis that nothing has happened on the border to interfere with his plans," Bouchet spoke, using just the right amount of injured pride and self, but inwardly he began to feel that Satanis was looking into the depths of his guilty soul.

"Bouchet knows that thirty warriors cannot attack a fort. We do not have time now to besiege a fortified cabin. Whatever we do must be done quickly, with one eye on the enemy and the other on the escape path. Bouchet says his eyes have been clear. Then let him say now what they have seen that will give the Abenaki revenge for the warriors they have lost, and payment for the land that has been stolen."

The Indian's words heartened Bouchet immensely. They meant that Satanis had not been able to make any satisfactory plans of his own. Perhaps he now regretted the haste that had sent him hurrying from Carillon with only thirty warriors. Satanis was as proud as he was bloodthirsty, and his anger could well be directed more at himself than at Bouchet.

"I am sorry that Satanis has brought so few warriors with him," said Bouchet boldly, "for through the power of my silver cross, I have made it possible for the Abenaki to walk first among the children of Onontio at Quebec. Had Satanis but one hundred warriors, this day would the fort at Number Four fall. Even so, we can still do much damage to the English. Their hay still is in the field, their wheat and oats are unreaped, the corn is not yet gathered, and they keep their cattle in the meadows.

The great triumph must be forgotten, but we can burn them back to Number Four and put hunger in their bellies in the winter."

The Indian's face remained stone, but he looked straight at Bouchet and, for the first time, spoke personally.

"When we met on the border, you understood that my force was small and you knew what to look for. Now you talk of great honor and great victory, knowing that I had left such hopes at Carillon. I will not listen to your words, because they tell me you are afraid of what is in your heart. Do you think you can shame me into throwing away the lives of my warriors on some foolish French scheme? We will do what little we can and go home to St. Francis."

Bouchet struggled to conceal the tremendous pride and confidence that surged inside him. Satanis's psychological tricks had not worked. He had been able to look behind Bouchet's screen of words, but he had imagined the wrong thing. Bouchet felt that he had the Abenaki right where he wanted him.

"Satanis is truly a wise chief," said Bouchet. "His wisdom has made me see that I have spoken as foolishly as the young brave back from his first warpath. The truth is," he smile engagingly, "I have had such complete success in fooling the English that I wanted to build up to telling you about it. I confess I wanted to prove that my trade requires, in its way, as much skill as yours. Ah! But I should have told you right away!"

Bouchet managed to look sheepish. "Forgive a Frenchman his little weakness," he said. "I realize that the how of it doesn't matter now." He interrupted himself with another smile. "There'll be time for that later—but I have managed to send the militia and most of the able-bodied men out of Number Four south from the Connecticut. The area around Number Four is ours. We can pick any spot we choose."

Satanis did not congratulate Bouchet. "There is still much to consider," he said. "St. Sacrement and Champlain are British lakes now. There will be troops and rangers from Fort Edward to Missisquoi Bay. We cannot return to Crown Point, and the northern end of Champlain is dangerous. There is no time now to bring back canoes, and we will have to find new ones if we go north up the Connecticut. The journey home will be difficult even without prisoners; the English are swift and diligent in their vengeance, and we must make sure we have enough time for our purpose."

When Bouchet offered no advice, Satanis continued. "I must know how many men are left at Number Four," he said. "If we burn the cabins and the fields close to the fort, the smoke will draw our enemies to the one point from which they can follow our retreat in force."

"There are not ten men at the fort who can follow us as far as the White River Junction," said Bouchet, "and twenty more could not be gathered in less than hours. There are not more than three rangers homesteading in the area, and no part of the militia will return in the morning. We could go in three groups and burn enough corn and wheat to make their babies cry in February and, if the spirits are friendly, we will take back a few scalps to hang on the poles of St. Francis. The Onontio in Quebec will be pleased to hear that his children have not left Carillon and Scalp Point empty handed."

"Onontio would be happy," replied the Indian, "because he does not wish the border English to help Amherst move on Montreal, but the Abenaki will not take needless risks to burn grain and cabins. We have not come from Carillon to practice what the French call tactics. We have come to take revenge and scalps now, in the old way of the war party, by striking unseen in the gray dawn and disappearing into the forest before the alarm is raised. I will not triple the chances of discovery to do French work, nor will I risk separation to move in the French manner. The Abenaki will make their own plans, and leave Onontio to his."

"Satanis listens to the words of his old friend as he listens to the words of an enemy, balancing every word against truth and deceit, but my words carry no liar's burden. I did not ask Satanis to attack the fort, and I have freely admitted that good fortune alone made the fort open to attack. If there were anger beneath my words, it was anger at the fate which offered an opportunity that an earlier fate had already taken away." Bouchet raised his eyes until they gazed directly into the eyes of the Indian. "But this fact remains," he said, "the area around Number Four is ours, and the fate that would have given us the fort has provided an alternative, less glorious but more fitting to our situation."

"When the honey stump is filled with angry bees, the wise bear visits the berry patch," said Satanis. No observing eye could have detected in the Indian's features the confusion in his mind, but Bouchet was quick to grasp the hollowness of the reply and press the advantage.

"Tomorrow morning," said Bouchet, "the young friend of Wobi Madaondo, the White Devil, will raise his cabin in the heart of the forest eight miles northwest of Number Four. Settlers will come as far as thirty miles to bring gifts and to help in the work. Even the family of the golden-haired girl, the beloved of the White Devil's nephew, has come up from Fort Dummer. *Mon Dieu!* I would like to stay behind long enough to see the look on the White Devil's face when he comes to view the place of sorrow!"

Still nothing changed in the Indian's appearance, but his heart pounded against his chest. The anguish he would cause Johnathan Evans would be almost as good as killing him, and the scalps would bring a fine price from Onontio's men.

Greed possessed him momentarily, and he calculated the possibility of turning fifty scalps into sixty. The French were not always careful in the counting of scalps, and Satanis had fooled them before. Then, uttering a deep, bass grunt, Satanis regained his self-control and returned to the game he played with Bouchet.

"We will take our revenge at the cabin raising," he said. "We will strike quickly and take scalps, not prisoners. We will carry away only small items of value, like the silver objects the white man uses to put salt in, but to please Bouchet, we will stop to burn the cabin site and the fields around it before we go home to St. Francis. Does Bouchet agree?"

Again, the Frenchman forced himself to look straight into the Abenaki's eyes. "Bouchet agrees that Satanis should do these things," he said. "Bouchet is happy to give his good friend the opportunity for revenge and scalps. For my own part, I ask nothing but the chance to prolong the agony of the White Devil and his nephew."

"If Satanis is willing to give Bouchet two braves, Bouchet will take the golden-haired girl captive and go west by the Winooski to Lake Champlain. We will leave sign along the river to say that we are many, and when the ranger captain comes, he will follow the sign of the captive. He will know he is too late, but he will follow anyway, to Quebec itself, if necessary, and somewhere he will make the mistake that will deliver him to us. What words does Satanis have for the plan of Emile Bouchet?"

Huddled now immobile in the Foster cornfield, the answer of Satanis seemed to Bouchet to float toward him from the edge of the world as his eyes caught the faint red glow just appearing in the east. "Satanis is satisfied," the Indian had replied. "Bouchet's plan is good," and then Bouchet was brought back completely to the business at hand, as Satanis glided silently to his side and pointed at the approaching dawn.

"I have sent Abissanehraw, who needs no light to see, and Tatabekamateosis, whose magic makes him brother to the dog and wolf, to scout the camp," he said. "They will see how the settlers sleep and find the golden-haired girl. When they return, they will be your warriors until you reach Isle-Aux-Noix."

Bouchet nodded his head, and the red man and the white waited, each absorbed in his own devilish thoughts, until the two warriors materialized out of the early morning mist.

Abissanehraw gave the report, bending close to the damp earth to trace in the dim light the outlines of the positions of the settlers.

"Here," he said, moving the point of his knife from east to north across the dirt, "is the cornfield." The knife moved west. "Here are horses and an ox, near the meadow," Now the knife moved west again, and then made a semicircle to the southeast. The knife rose and fell, repeating the semicircle. "These are felled trees from which they will cut logs for the cabin." The knife rose again and made a horizontal cut in the soft earth. Then it made a series of vertical slashes above the cut. "These are trees already cut into logs and men with rifles sleeping among them." The knife continued to move, gouging two holes in the dirt and marking off a square between them. "Here is the spring," said Abissanehraw. "Here the half-faced camp, which the white man and his wife have lived in during the summer, and here is the place where the cabin raisers have placed their packs." The knife continued to move southeast, and again made several vertical slashes above the horizontal cut. "Here more men with rifles sleep along logs, and here," the knife cut a series of X's into the dirt and joined them with straight lines, "are the shelters set up for the women and children and the cooking place."

The warrior looked up from his work as the point of the knife fell on one of the X's. "Here," he said, "the Frenchman's yellow-haired girl sleeps with her mother."

Satanis spoke before Bouchet could question the scout. "How many men with rifles?"

Abissanehraw moved the knife. "Six here, four here, eight here. Not many."

"More will come later," said Bouchet. "It is only the first day of the raising, the day of log cutting and foundation laying. Some will not come until the third day."

Satanis quieted Bouchet with an impatient glance. "How many women and children?"

Abissanehraw paused briefly before answering. "I looked only for the Frenchman's girl," he said. "I could not count the women and children, but they are not more than twenty."

Satanis held up his hand. He could not conceal the gleam of satisfaction in his eyes. This was the situation he had longed for so many times as he sat before his fire at St. Francis, letting his imagination play with his hatred for the English. To steal upon the enemy at dawn, to see terror on their faces before the kill, and to disappear without the loss of a warrior, rich with scalps and prizes, was, for Satanis, the ultimate success in warfare.

The Abenaki leader turned to Bouchet. "Abissanehraw and Tatabekamateosis will take you to the shelter of the girl. When you hear the first sound of our work among the logs, take the girl and go to the White River Junction. Mark the trail so the ranger captain will think we came to the junction as one party."

The trace of a smile shaped Satanis's lips as he turned away. "I hope Bouchet does not take so much pleasure in the object stolen that he forgets the reason for the theft," he said, at the same time signaling Abissanehraw and Tatabekamateosis to move out with Bouchet. Then he turned to his war, first sending six warriors after Bouchet to make certain that no women or child escaped, and then grouping the rest for the attack upon the unsuspecting guardians of the camp.

Satanis wasted no time in moving his men from the cornfield. The sun itself was above the horizon and the habit of the pioneer would soon stir the settlers from their sleep. The Abenaki hearts beat tumultuously in their red breasts, but the disciplined Abenaki feet moved slowly and noiselessly. No careless moccasin snapped a twig. No imperfection rustled a leaf. A British general would have thought the movement the creation of a madman. The irregular, zigzag advance of what the general would have equated with ranks and files would have been a military monstrosity on the plains of Europe, but it was perfectly suited to the purpose of Satanis.

The Abenaki lines reached the second series of felled trees, and Satanis looked down upon the unsuspecting enemy. A wave of his hand spread out the warriors on the flanks. He raised his tomahawk and screamed out the incredible intensity of his hatred. Centuries rolled backward as the Indians raced savagely toward the satisfaction of their primitive obsessions.

Hatchets rose and fell, biting into the skulls with a soft thunk and splatting dully against the bones of desperately turned faces. The last organized moans of pain and terror, smothered by the wild screeching of the warriors, expired, but the sounds of massacre continued as knives cut around hairlines and fantastic dancing figures shook tangled, dirt-ground knots of skin, blood, and hair.

The first war cry of Satanis unleashed yet another primitive force, this one in the unregenerate heart of Emile Bouchet, who moved with his Indians toward the temporary shelter where Sally Williams and her mother lay sleeping.

While Tatabekamateosis placed one hand on the mother's mouth and slit her throat with the other, Bouchet and Abiss-anehraw bound and gagged the daughter and carried her out of the shelter and across the clearing. Bouchet entered the forest to head north to the White River Junction, threw the girl over his shoulder, and fled at top speed from the horror in the clearing.

The physical exertion demanded by the quick pace and the weight of the girl on his shoulder soon restored Bouchet's perspective and brought him to a halt. Quickly he put the girl down and knelt beside her, talking softly as he cut the bindings.

"Don't be afraid," he said. "There is no danger now if you keep up the pace and show no fear. I have made a bargain with the Indians, and they will keep it as long as nothing happens to upset them. Soon we will be safe with the French, and I will make arrangements for your future."

The girl gave Bouchet a look of helpless confusion and fright that might have been the salvation of a man less habituated to evil. Though she had been spared any sight of the massacre, the bloodcurdling shrieks of the Indians and the screaming of the children had made the journey on Bouchet's shoulder seem like the continuation of a nightmare. She struggled to find reality in sounds of her own making.

As the words tumbled out incoherently, a part of the terror that had paralyzed her broke. Tears flooded her eyes and spilled down her cheeks. Emile Bouchet leaned closer to wrest what advantage he could from the situation. His hand went up, fingers spread wide, and his lips made a firm, silencing sound as he let his head swing slightly toward the watching warriors.

"There is no time for explanations," he said. "You must get up now and stay close to me. I can tell you only this. There was an attack on the Foster cabin, and everyone is probably dead. I did all I could, but you were the only one the Indians would let me save."

He rose as he spoke and took Sally's hand, pulling her to her feet. "Remember," he said, "you are safe only as long as you stay close to me."

As Sally rose to her feet, she caught a glimpse of the Abenakis. Abissanehraw stood silent and menacing while the traces of a wicked grin molded the lips of Tatabekamateosis. The two represented a study in the unpredictability of the Indian temperament, and sudden fear moved Sally closer to the Frenchman. Bouchet represented both civilization and her only chance of survival and eventual reunion with her own people.

The simplicity of the situation penetrated her fears, and she resolved to follow Bouchet's advice as closely as possible. As terror turned her thoughts inward, she saw herself stumbling and falling to the path as Tatabekamateosis, angered by her clumsiness, stepped toward her and started the downstroke of his cruel hatchet.

They did not stop again until they reached the White River Junction. There, Sally, once again bound hand and foot, watched Bouchet and the Abenakis hurrying back and forth over the trail, seemingly aimless in their movements and performing actions unfathomable to the girl, and yet, as incoherent as the movements and actions seemed, they were performed with great speed and intensity, and stopped as suddenly and mysteriously as they had begun.

Bouchet came over to the girl and reached down to cut her bindings. "Don't be so frightened," he whispered. "Things are going very well. I don't think the pursuit will come close enough to excite the Abenakis into harming you. From here we go to the Winooski, where I have a canoe to take us to Champlain and up the Richelieu. We won't stop until we are safe at Isle-Aux-Noix, unless the danger of discovery makes the cover of night necessary. The Abenakis will make me bind and gag you when we approach Champlain, now that the lake is British, but you'll be safe as long as you are quick to do exactly what I ask you to do."

As Bouchet straightened up from his task, something disturbing in the touch of the man's hands prompted Sally to ask one question. "What are you going to do with me when we reach Isle-Aux-Noix?" She had heard firsthand about the unhappy fate of border women who had been turned over to the French.

Bouchet took the time to answer, enjoying the situation and wondering fleetingly if he might pull the girl closer and wrap her in his arms as a protective gesture.

"I have spent many years in Canada," he said, "and I still have important connections there. We will go to Quebec, and you can live in the house of one of my friends until you can be exchanged. You will find the people very civilized and their style of living both gracious and grand. Quebec will be a new world for you, and I hope you will learn to appreciate the city and its people."

As Sally followed Emile Bouchet down the path, she deliberately shut out the fears and doubts about the fate of her parents and the settlers at Foster's cabin. Under the circumstances, it might be months before she would find out what happened, while the behavior of Emile Bouchet was vital to her own survival. She sifted through everything she had heard over the years about Bouchet, but nothing could explain his presence at the massacre in the company of the Abenaki warriors.

Perhaps, she thought, *he was on one of his trapping or trading expeditions and just stumbled onto the Indians as they were preparing their attack, or maybe he was on his way to the cabin raising himself when the Indians captured him.*

Sally's forehead wore the wrinkles of confusion. Neither theory accounted for Bouchet's evident freedom, so she began to analyze his actions in the forest. The one fact that kept coming to her mind was Bouchet's seemingly genuine concern for her welfare.

I don't see how anyone could be kinder, she thought, recalling the gentleness of his touch, *and he must have taken great risks to save me. But somehow, I don't like what he said about living in Quebec. If all I am is a prisoner to be exchanged, what difference does it make how I feel about Quebec? And as far as appreciating the people goes, I think I know all I need to know about the French!*

5

THE CHASE

The truth that one mind chooses to ignore often becomes the obsession that another feeds upon, and Captain Johnathan Evans stood immobilized on the trail, extracting the evil from the black wood smoke that suddenly appeared in an opening in the forest canopy. He stood on the trail with his mouth open and the skin stretched tightly over his cheeks and jawbone, trying with some animal reflex to catch the odor of the burning wood. He stood there until the darkest oaths capable of man's unregenerate nature found explosive voice and parted him from the evil the sight of the smoke had forced him to share. Then he began to run. He ran blindly and stupidly, and the tension in his body kept the tremendous energy that drove him from its natural transformation into swiftness and robbed him of his endurance. He ran on through the forest obstructions, weaving now and then, sometimes stumbling, until he broke from the woods and stared directly at the desolate scene. It occurred to him that it was a little after eight in the morning.

Now Tom stood at his uncle's side. Across his mind flashed the picture of another Mrs. Williams, blood gushing from her throat and falling down her breast. The smell of the burning cornfield in front of him became the smell of burned corncobs and hickory chips, the blackness of the smoke above him became the blackness of the bake oven where he had trembled terrified years ago; he heard the thunder of Reverend Cushway's Sunday sermon, and, for the first time since he was four, he understood hell again. He thought of his mother, massacred below that terrible oven, and of his father, lying dead somewhere outside of Louisbourg with a hatchet sticking in his head. The boy burned with an immortal hate that matched the devil's own hatred of God and mankind.

At last, Uncle John began to move, and Tom followed. They stood between the burning foundation logs of the cabin site and the half-faced camp, where the Foster's had spent the summer, and looked at the temporary shelters where the women and children had slept, awaiting the dawn of the new day when the cabin raising would begin and a new life would start. They saw, not far from a pine tree, a flattened, elongated ball of pulp, hair, and dirt, and, against the base of the tree, they saw the grotesque, shapeless broken trunk of the body discarded as soon as one final smash had severed it from its head. Not far away was a child's leg, carelessly draped over a smoldering log, completely burned through at the knee joint. Tom turned away, nausea contending with rising hysteria, unable to control either. As if from another world, he heard his uncle's voice, unreal in its calmness, and ungodly in its tone, though it quoted the Bible.

"Vengeance is mine, saith the Lord," it said, "but we are surely meant to be the instruments of God's wrath. The Lord has given us a task, and we have no time for grief until God's work is done. There is Bouchet's track. Follow it until you're certain of its direction. Then meet me here and we'll decide what to do."

Uncle John turned and moved toward the line of logs that partly concealed the first activities of the massacre. He had his own work to do, his own decision to make.

Tom, grateful for the chance to find release from his emotions in action, went about the business of following the track of Emile Bouchet. The chore was surprisingly easy. Bouchet had made no attempt to hide his escape. In moments, Tom had traced him to the edge of the clearing, stopping where Bouchet had stopped for his last glance at the deviltry of the Abenakis, nothing that some unknown fear had suddenly set Bouchet into a panic. Soon he came to the spot where Bouchet had recovered himself and put his prisoner down to cut the bindings. He studied the prints of the two Abenakis as they waited for Bouchet to unbind his captive and then followed four sets of tracks directly to the White River Junction. There he viewed with amazement the sudden proliferation of the tracks of his enemies, understanding immediately their purpose, wondering what had forced Bouchet into such a waste of time and energy. Within moments he had picked up the tracks heading west toward the Winooski, following them just far enough to be sure the trail was not another piece of trickery before hurrying back to the site of the massacre.

As he stepped from the forest, he found his uncle completing a message to Joseph Ely. Without looking up from his task, and evidently once again in full control of his passions, Captain Evans outlined the situation to his nephew.

"Satanis has taken his warriors and gone straight home to St. Francis," he said. "He's going right up the Connecticut to the two big curves they call the Cohose Intervales and hit the Ammonoosuc, where Major Rogers built a fort for Benning Wentworth four years ago. Then he'll strike across the upper waters of the Ammonoosuc on his way to Lake Memphramagogg. It's about sixty miles from Number Four to that fort, and about one hundred from there to the lake. He'll have to go a little to the west to get around them bays at the north end of Memphramagogg, but then he kin head for the St. Francis and home. There's no point in following him. He didn't take prisoners and he'll move fast. If he needs anything—canoes, food, or whatever—he kin git it from the Indians on the upper Connecticut."

Uncle John paused and shook his head. "I've made that trip before," he said, "an' if there's any tougher travelin,' I don't know it. There's no game between the Ammonoosuc and Memphramagogg eceptin' owls, and when you git to the Lake you can't find nothin' but moose, if you git lucky, and the wood is so hard it won't never burn. That Memphramagogg is hills and mountains, swamps and logs, and wind an' rainstorms. Then you got to go up and down them high hills and across them terrible, rushin' brooks chuck full of huge boulders, and fight that thick, tangled undergrowth … "

He stopped, as if suspended in some painful part of his past, but only for a moment. "No," he continued, "there's no point in chasin' him an' givin' that agent of the devil, Bouchet, a chance to hide Sally where we won't never find her. His trail's the one we got to follow—and follow just as close as we can." He looked at Tom expectantly.

Tom stared at his uncle, unable to reply until he could accept the fact Sally was the prisoner Bouchet had carried with him. The state of near hysteria in which he had followed Bouchet had kept him from the realization that the captive had to be Sally Williams. Now his mind returned to the cabin of Joseph Ely at Number Four. He remembered the look on his uncle's face when he had told them that Bouchet would get Satanis to attack the Foster cabin so Bouchet could steal Sally. He remembered the shock and disbelief he and Joseph Ely had shared, but now prophecy had become fact. All the uncertainty was gone, and Tom was ready for the ordeal ahead.

Tom began to get the feeling that fate had already decided upon the final outcome of these tragic events for every person involved in them; he felt that his uncle was the medium through which flowed all the experience of his life. He saw him as an agent whose movements would bring retribution upon friend and enemy alike, and he hastened to provide the information that would set things in motion.

"I followed Bouchet straight to the White River Junction. He and the two Abenakis he has with him left a lot of useless signs, and then took Sally and headed for the Winooski. It looks like he's going over the French Trail right to Champlain."

"Yes," replied his uncle, "that's what he figgers to do. Then he'll go down Champlain to the Richelieu and report to Bourlemaque at Isle-Aux-Noix. Where he'll go from there is anybody's guess. He may try to leave Sally at Fort St. John's, or he may take her on to Montreal, or he could go down to Quebec. But he's got connections all over Canada, and he might hide her at some settlement along the St. Lawrence; still, I don't think he'll git very far away from her, and I don't think he'll leave her at St. Francis or any Indian village. That'd be too risky for him. The only thing we can do is head for the Winooski and pick up his trail. I don't think we can catch him before he hits Champlain, because he's got at least three, nearer to four, hours start on us, but you never know what might happen. At any rate, we got nothin' to lose by followin' him, an' if we kin stick close enough to him, we may git some idea of where he plans to hide Sally."

Tom nodded his agreement and picked up his rifle, moving quickly to keep within a pace or two of his uncle. The swiftness with which Johnathan Evans moved at the beginning of the trail told Tom that this chase would be desperately cruel and hard, and Tom made a silent vow that he would run himself to death, if need be, rather than hold back his uncle one second.

Now hidden in a swampy area along the banks of the Richelieu River, surrounded by cattails, marsh grass, and lily pads, Tom renewed his silent vow. The water that nearly covered him had chilled him to the marrow of his bones, and his body shook so violently that he imagined unnatural, betraying, ripples reaching out into the current of the Richelieu. The chase after Bouchet had been even crueler and harder than he had anticipated. Before it was over, Tom had more than once thought of that desperate journey from the Mooserack Path to Number Four, right after they had discovered that Bouchet had joined Satanis. Incredibly, it had been only the day before yesterday, but Tom knew that without that experience and the overwhelming need to rescue Sally, he would not have survived the last twenty hours.

In fact, in his present condition, Tom's grasp of time was uncertain and penetrated by fantasy. He remembered his uncle's expression of disgust when they had found the place where Bouchet has secreted the canoe that carried him down the Winooski.

"I expected as much," his uncle had said, "but we'll never catch him now—not with them Abenakis on the paddles."

Then everything had gotten progressively dimmer as they sped toward Lake Champlain. Tom repeated over and over and over his vow not to hold back his uncle. He couldn't remember arriving at Colchester Point, but he remembered waiting for what had seemed an interminably long time in a broken, squatting sleep, until he heard Uncle John talking in low tones to some rangers who had been reconnoitering the lake and hoping incidentally to pick up a scalp or two. Then he had felt himself lifted into a canoe. He remembered the waves of Champlain slapping against the bow, and then nothing until the canoe touched the east side of the Richelieu with a gentle bump. A kind hand had put him ashore, handed him a knapsack, and whispered apologetically, "There's most of a whole bologna, a bag of meal, and a cake of chocolate left, but I'm afraid there ain't much rum left in that canteen. May God curse me fer my weakness and put blessin' on yer brow, fer yer a disarvin' lad if ever I've seen one." The hand and the voice disappeared, and Uncle John guided him through the blackness to his hiding place. It must have been hours ago, even if the sun did still hide behind the gray early morning mist.

"You've got to hold on, Tom," his uncle had said. "We've got to git a prisoner from Isle-Aux-Noix. It won't be long before the scouting parties and the wood cutters will be on the lake, an' mebbe some fishermen will be out early trying their luck. The mornin'll be perfect for bass feedin' in the shallows, with this mist hangin' on the river, an' if them Frenchies know any-thin', they'll be castin' their lines right at us. If any boat comes near, you listen for a blackbird callin' in the rushes. When you hear the call, swim out and tip the boat over toward this shore, because that's the side where I'll be. Then shove the boat into the reeds, so it's hidden, and I'll take care of everythin' else."

The anxiety in his uncle's parting words still haunted Tom. "Can you do it? Hev you got enuff left to do it, boy?"

"I kin do it," he had replied, and as his uncle moved away, he began to shiver and to repeat to himself with each tremor of his body. "I kin do it. I kin. You won't lose a step or a second because of me."

Now the call of the red-winged blackbird, sounding as if he were perched on a cattail behind him, focused what was left of Tom's energy on the fishing boat that drifted toward him, slowly bumping its way through the mist that seemed to enclose it. The boat's occupants, partly obscured by the vapors that rose from the river, were young Canadian militiamen, probably no older than Tom himself. The one in the bow was having some kind of difficulty with his pole. Tom, as he came upon the other side of the boat, could hear him cursing softly in French. The militiaman in the stern leaned over the side of the boat, prob-ably to check his line by hand. Tom sank under the cold waters, placed his hands on the boat, and thrust upward with all the power in his legs and arms, his momentum carrying him waist high above the water. He saw a hand rise out of the Richelieu and grasp the arms of the militiaman who fell from the stern. He heard the soft thunk of Uncle John's hatchet, and he knew the Frenchman was dead before he hit the water. He heard the other militiaman thrashing about in the current, then the sound of flesh striking against flesh, and in the silence that followed, he pushed the boat out of the river and deep into the concealing reeds and cattails. He pushed himself halfway up on the bottom of the overturned boat and let his overtaxed system collapse. Unconsciousness lapped over him in waves, and he felt that he was sinking after the Frenchman to the rocky bottom of the Richelieu. But there could be no rest now. The business at hand had to be completed. His stomach tried to throw back the rum that Uncle John poured into him, but somehow he held it down, and somehow he managed to slide off the boat and follow his uncle to the edge of the forest, where Uncle John picked up the Frenchman, bound and gagged and still unconscious, and headed east toward the hills.

Again the journey was cruel, as they went through the nearly impenetrable heart of the woods to avoid any chance of discovery, nor did it improve when they reached the foothills and began to climb the cliffs of jagged rock, fighting desperately for handholds on the exposed roots of the hardy pines that had so far survived their battle with the elements. But up they went, until Uncle John found what he was looking for: a cave, or, rather, a narrow cleavage that twisted back several feet into the solid rock of the hill. There, Uncle John laid his burden down and Tom, delirious with fever, fell unconscious on the cold, hard, rock floor.

When Tom regained consciousness, the first thing he felt was the hot herb tea in his mouth, and then he felt Uncle John's arm holding his head up so the Indian medicine could flow gently down to fight the poison in his blood. In the darkness of the cave and the matching darkness of his mind, Tom thought that this shadowy figure had always squatted beside him, performing over and over again this same, strange rite. His body stiffened, expecting the moans and cries that he did not yet know had been his own, and he wondered what had happened to the tremendous fires that caused him to burn inside.

"Well now, you've had quite a sleep fer yerself. More'n three days. Fact is, lad, you had me pretty worried for a while, tho I never lost faith in yer spirit or Toe-lee-ma's herb tea and ointment. I've dealt with ague afore, an' it's never licked me yet, leastways not if I got in the fight soon enough. Why, I—great Lord, lad, I don't know what's wrong with me. I'm goin' to squat here an' talk you to death if somethin' doesn't stop me. You jest close yer eyes an' git some good healin' natural sleep. When you wake up, I'll have somethin' ready that'll stick to yer stomach an' put yer strength right back into you."

As his uncle rambled on, Tom came back nearer and nearer to reality. The one thing he didn't want to do was sleep, at least, not yet. He just had to settle the uncertainties that made chaos out of his efforts to concentrate. Questions tumbled out.

"What happened, Uncle John? How did we git here? It don't seem possible I could've been unconscious three whole days." The sound of his own voice began to give direction and coherence to the half-formed thoughts that disturbed him. "What happened to Sally and Bouchet? Where is the Frenchman we took captive?" Now that his thoughts had found words, he would have rushed on beyond the point of exhaustion, but his uncle would not let him.

"There'll be time for that when yer ready, Tom," Uncle John interrupted. "We can't do nothin' till yer strength comes back, an' that won't happen 'less you do what I tell you to. I've trained you hard enough so you know that first things hev got to come first. A man can't do his job unless he's ready, an' he can't do it then if the time ain't right, tho' plenty of good men have tried and failed 'cause they couldn't put reins on their desires. You jest close yer eyes an' git some sleep, 'cause right now that's what you need most. When you wake up I'll have some hot stew ready, an' then we'll talk. There'll be plenty of time fer talkin' and plannin' before yer ready to take up the trail again."

Uncle John rose quietly and walked away, leaving Tom no choice but to follow his instructions. In fact, as soon as his uncle turned away, Tom realized the man's wisdom, and the knowledge of his utter weariness descended and closed his eyes.

Uncle John was as good as his word, as always. Tom awoke to the aroma of boiling hot stew, and although his cup was mostly broth, he found it deeply satisfying. While Tom ate, Uncle John explained their situation.

"I learned from that militiaman that a man accompanied by two Abenakis and a young woman was brought in by a Captain and taken to Bourlemaque's headquarters. He said the guards couldn't do anythin' but talk about the beauty of the girl, but he did hear one of 'em say he'd seen the man somewhere before an' knew he was important. Course, he'd have to be, to git Bourlemaque up in the early hours of the mornin.' It appears that Bouchet is even more important to the French than I suspected."

"But what about Sally?" Tom asked. "What is he goin' to do with Sally?"

"Well, the Frenchman said he didn't know about that, an' I'm certain he told the truth. He was jest a boy about yer age, burnin' with the fever, like you, and wishin' he was back on his farm along the Beauport shore. He didn't hold nothin' back, an' I did the best I could fer him, but his heart jest give out on him." Uncle John shook his head. "He was a simple one all right, so I folded his hands over the cross layin' on his chest and buried him deep."

"But what are we goin' to do now?" asked Tom. "We don"t know any more than we did before."

"Now, Tom, jest hold on till I'm finished. Fact is, we know all we need to know for the present. That young Frenchman almost didn't git to go fishin' 'cause Bourlemaque put out an order that all men who had any experience with boats were to report immediately to the dock. It appears he had planned to send a boat in a couple of days to Quebec carryin' dispatches to Montcalm, and suddenly he decided he couldn't wait—all of a sudden he wanted the boat loaded and ready to sail right away. Our poor young militiaman out there was goin' to report for duty, but his friend talked him out of it." Uncle John shook his head. "It's sure funny the way things work out sometimes," he said.

Tom was not as satisfied with the information as Uncle John was. "We're still not much better off than we were before," he said. "All we know is that Bouchet convinced Bourlemaque that he had to git to Quebec in a hurry, an' that's not much to go on."

Uncle John managed to keep the irritation he felt out of his voice. "Tom, if gittin' to Quebec in a hurry was the only thing on Bouchet's mind, why didn't he jest hop in a canoe with them two Abenakis and keep goin'? Oh, he wants to git to Quebec in a hurry all right, but he wants to take Sally with him all the way, and he wants to take her in some kind of style. Won't lose that much time, waitin' for Bourlemaque's boat, an' he kin impress Sally with his importance and his kindness. You see, Tom, the first thing he has to do is git Sally to trust him and depend on him—an' with events shapin' up the way they are, he knows he has all too little time to do that. Bourlemaque's boat was jest too good an opportunity to pass up."

Tom still felt a deep frustration and disappointment, but since he had nothing to add to the facts of the matter, he decided wisely to remain silent.

Uncle John looked at his nephew closely. "Don't you see what it means to us?" he asked. "It means we don't have to worry about Bouchet hiding Sally some place along the way. It might have taken us weeks of hangin' out in the woods around the places he might have left her, like Fort St. John's up the Richelieu, before we found out he took her to Quebec. We could have been forced to go up to Montreal, and then back down the St. Lawrence, checking every settlement, an' who knows what could have happened to us, or Sally, in the meantime? Now, in three or four days, dependin' on when yer strong enough to travel, we kin go straight to Quebec and join Wolfe. Once we git with Wolfe's army, we'll find Bouchet and Sally."

Even now, as Uncle John talked, Tom felt his confidence returning. It grew stronger and stronger as the days of his recovery passed and the ranger captain talked of the seige of Louisbourg in '45 and of his travels and adventures during the succeeding fourteen years. Names and deeds of legendary rangers, some new to Tom and some familiar, built the boy's hopes hour by hour; hopes built upon a structure of noble deeds and unwavering sacrifice. Tom could see in his uncle's eyes the heights to which the soul is moved when mere man rises above himself to keep covenant with his people and his God, but as Uncle John talked, Tom also felt the presence of some abiding sorrow, some mystery too profound, too agonizing to be shared, but the feeling escaped beneath the pictures of the heroic rangers engaged in conflicts more important than their own lives.

And Uncle John knows them all, the boy thought over and over. *There are six companies of rangers with Wolfe, and I'll bet Uncle John knows half the men personally. If there is any trace of Bouchet about Quebec, and there's bound to be, Uncle John will find him. Maybe the information won't come from a ranger at all. Maybe it'll come from a prisoner—or a deserter. But we'll find Bouchet, and we'll find Sally, too!*

Tom's impatience to be on the trail grew out of proportion to his returning health, but Uncle John, who knew full well the dangers and difficulty of the journey to Quebec, would not be unduly pressed. Tom just had to wait.

At last, the awaited day came. Tom's recovery was complete. They left the cave at dusk and headed for the path that wound north along the banks of the Richelieu. The path was really no more than an Indian trail and the going was hard and slow, but Tom welcomed the opportunity to test his endurance. Well before daybreak, they passed Fort St. John on the opposite side of the river, continuing on far enough to be out of range of any stray traffic going to or from the fort before pulling off the trail to hide in the woods.

The day and the following night of travel also passed without incident. They left the trail at Sorel to steal a canoe and headed down the mighty St. Lawrence, crossing over to the north shore and hugging it tightly to keep as much distance as possible between their canoe and St. Francis Village. They proceeded with extreme caution, because Satanis and his warriors traveled this area incessantly at all hours of the day and night, sometimes acting as pawns of the French and, at other times, carrying out some particular bit of deviltry of their own.

They paddled on carefully past the Indian Village until Uncle John discovered a place suitable for concealing the canoe. They spent the next day hidden in the woods, aware of their peril, resting without relaxing their constant vigil. At night, they moved silently out of the woods and went soundlessly down the St. Lawrence, exercising an incredible care as they approached and passed Three Rivers, just eighty miles from Quebec City. Uncle John could barely control his satisfaction as, many miles downriver, he stepped from the canoe to the shore. When they had left the canoe above the Richelieu, he had been certain there would be some kind of contact with either the French or the Indians long before they passed Three Rivers.

If this kind of luck holds out, he thought, *we'll be with Wolfe by midnight, but it don't seem possible the kind of luck we're havin' can keep running.*

This last day of hiding along the St. Lawrence shores was the most wearing of all on the patience of the two men. Uncle John, almost habitually aware of the incalculable chances and errors that impatience gives birth to, increased all of the normal precautions, hoping by overcompensation to eliminate mistakes in judgment. Thus, they waited until the darkness was overwhelming before digging out the canoe and entering the river.

The total blackness of the moonless night held time and nature in suspension. Nameless fears beset Tom and covered him with cold sweat. The hours passed in nightmarish shapes, until suddenly, Tom became aware of a light that did not disappear but came closer. Soon there was another light and yet another. Then they drifted back into the blackness. They had passed Deschambauit.

The canoe moved swiftly on the current, and in much less than an hour, more lights became visible. Uncle John moved out toward the middle of the river before risking a whisper. "This must be Jacques Cartier," he said. "We're only about ten leagues from Quebec City. By the looks of them lights, the French must have quite a force stationed here. Looks like they been up to somethin' too! There's no tellin' what we might run into from here on in, but it's too early to get off the river. I don't know where the British are, but they're a lot farther downstream than this."

Tom did not reply. *It might be a good idea to head for the south shore and hide out until we kin find out where we are,* he thought, but he knew that this was no time for discussion. Whatever action Uncle John took, Tom would follow, knowing it was based on experience and knowledge far exceeding his own.

This time, the signs of life did not cease when they passed the French post. Lights that reminded Tom of fireflies blinked on and off at irregular intervals along the shore and, high above, on the top of the cliff that rose sharply from the water's edge, other lights occasionally appeared.

"There's been action around here," Uncle John whispered. "The French have sentries along the shore and guards posted along the heights. We got to look for trouble any minute now."

But they traveled the nine miles between Jacques Cartier and Pointe-aux-Trembles without incident, and the lights remained the only signs of life. Then, passing the French encampment at Pointe-aux-Trembles, they saw clusters of lights on the shore, and Tom heard the sound of a deep bass voice breaking out over the water. There was a reply by a thin, irritated tenor, and a general squabble followed. Then the sounds were lost in the sounds of the river, and the rain that began to fall with increasing intensity.

Soon, Tom was soaked to the skin, but the wind and the rain had set the waters of the St. Lawrence into turbulent motion, and the difficulty of handling the canoe allowed no time to feel discomfort. Tom was bent over his paddle, concentrating on controlling the canoe in the swift current and keeping the bow pointed into the waves, when the sharp crackle of rifle fire caused him to stop in mid-stroke. Errant rifle balls whirred through the air about him, and he felt the paddle turn and shatter in his hands. Curses and screams rose out of the water ahead, and French muskets answered the rifles. He heard the harsh thud and scraping noise of boats smashing together and the babel-like sounds of French and English orders and oaths mingling in the frenetic language of war. Abenaki war whoops and death cries chilled Tom's spine, keeping him frozen to his broken paddle, and the fear that the fiends of hell had joined the battle flashed through his mind.

Then Tom became aware of Uncle John's shouting. "Drop that paddle and git yer rifle. We'll run right into the rear of them French, and when we do, you be ready. We're going to drive right through 'em, so have yer hatchet handy when we git to close quarters."

Anxiously, Tom grabbed his rifle and peered into the darkness ahead. Shapes began to form as they headed into a tangle of canoes, *bateaux*, and flat-bottomed boats. Tom saw the outline of a French officer crouched down in a *bateaux*, firing a brace of pistols. Uncle John drove the canoe toward the *bateaux*, and the officer turned in their direction, his pistols moving with him. Tom threw his piece to his shoulder and fired. The Frenchman fell back into the boat and Tom grabbed his hatchet. Uncle John changed course slightly and, as they swept by the *bateaux*, a private picked up one of the officer's pistols and discharged it hastily. The bullet sailed harmlessly over their heads, and they swept untouched past the *bateaux*, only to run straight into an overturned canoe. As Tom reached out to give the obstructing canoe a shove, a bitter, querulous voice rose out of the water.

"That's right," it said. "Drown me under my own canoe. Lord, but it must be a terrible bright man you are! But I'll tell you this, if you don't git yer hand off my canoe, you'll find out what the St. Lawrence looks like at the bottom."

Shock and disbelief froze Tom's hand to the other canoe until he heard Uncle John shouting, "Small Owen! By God, it's Small Owen. So it's a fish now yer pretendin' to be, is it? I always said drink would addle yer brain till you thought river water was whiskey. C'mon up outta there before you swallow the whole St. Lawrence."

"Johnny!" said the voice in the river. "Little Johnny Evans. Lord, but it's hard to find an old friend fallen so low, an' I kin jedge how far you've fallen by the company yer keepin' and the things yer saying. It's clear yer mind's so far gone you got me mixed up with some of yer drunken friends, but, no matter, git me up outta this river an' I'll see what kin be done to save you. No man kin say Owen Owens ever deserted a friend in need."

Uncle John steadied the canoe while Tom helped Owens crawl over the side. Tom could guess where the man got his nickname, for he couldn't have been taller that five feet four inches, and, dripping wet as he was, he couldn't have weighed more than 120 pounds. In this first meeting, Tom discovered what changeable man they dealt with, for now Owens was all business.

"Well, John," said Owens, "it's been a long time since we tried to take that battery at Louisbourg—near fifteen years. Oh, I've heard of ya from time to time, but ye're a welcome sight, and that's certain. Let's git rid of what's left of them French so we kin git back to camp and start swappin' stories—an mebbe you kin git yerself one of these." Small Owen pointed to his belt, and Tom saw the scalp that dangled there. It could have been a piece of seaweed.

"I got this on shore down river," said Small Owen, pointing to the scalp again, "before we run into these provision boats tryin' to sneak down to the city. They're worth five guineas each by order of General Wolfe himself."

"Well, look there, would you?" said Small Owen, interrupting himself. "Looks like there ain't nothin' left for us to do."

Tom looked toward shore in time to see French soldiers jumping out of the last provision boat still afloat and struggling desperately to get away from it. A large, flat-bottomed boat full of rangers that had been bearing down on the French veered away frantically, making no attempt to go after the struggling swimmers. As Tom watched in bewilderment, there came a gigantic explosion from the middle of the provision boat, and suddenly the air was filled with broken barrels, chests, and bits of clothing, and raindrops came down mixed with flour, rum, and brandy.

"Damn!" said Small Owen. "They were carrying kegs of gun powder and we won't salvage nothin' from that boat, but I'll tell you this, the boys is mad now, and they won't be totin' no prisoners back fer questionin'."

Small Owen turned away from the explosion in disgust "Well, Johnny," he said, "it's jest about over, an' they's no point in settin' out here in the rain. If you'll jest hand me that paddle, I'll git us on down to Goreham's Post, and you kin tell me how in thunder you an' that young feller happened to show up in the middle of the St. Lawrence River."

Tom knelt in the bow of the canoe, trying to protect at least some part of his body from the rain. He felt cold, wet, miserable, and confused by the night's events. Killing the French officer did not bother him. That was only a tiny scar added to much bigger ones he already carried with him.

The boat explosion had startled him, but he had quickly accepted it as part of the rationale of war. The scalp hanging from Small Owen's belt was also simply a detail of war. Nothing had happened that was beyond his experience or his comprehension—except the unusual relationship between his uncle and the small, wizened figure that had crawled out of the river into their canoe. There was an acceptance of each other, a kind of no-holds-barred acceptance, that seemed almost like affection. It suddenly occurred to Tom that he had two Uncle Johns, and he wasn't sure he liked this new one, who had let a little man, no bigger than some twelve-year-old boys, take command of the situation away from him. He sat listening to the two men whispering in low tones.

"There's nothin' mysterious at all about our bein' here, Owen," Tom heard his uncle whisper. "The Abenaki Satanis and a Frenchman named Bouchet hit a cabin raisin' outside of Number Four. They killed everybody but a young girl the Frenchman has had his eye on fer some time. My nephew Tom an' me followed this Bouchet an' found out he was takin' the girl to Quebec, so we figgered we'd join Wolfe's army an' see if we could run him down and git the girl back."

Small Owen's head nodded sympathetically. "That's dirty business, all right, John," he said. "'Course I've heard of the Abenaki. Even the French is afraid of 'em. He was here the last part of June and early in July. He raised billy hell with us too, afore he disappeared. As for the Frenchman, I never run across his sign, but if he's got any piece of the action 'round here, we got a fair chance of hearin' about it."

Owens' head nodded again. "So that's Matt's boy," he said. "There ain't no mistakin' he's an Evans. Appears to me yer takin him on a mighty hard trail fer such a young 'un."

"He's an Evans all right, Owen," replied Uncle John. "Evans all the way through; I'd match him agin' any ranger in yer company. He's seen plenty of border warfare, an' he was with me when we took Ticonderoga. 'Sides that, I b'lieve he's got a stake in this thing that's bigger than he thinks it is right now."

"So you was at Fort Ti!" Small Owen broke in. "When do you expect Amherst will be able to put pressure on Montreal?"

"The gen'ral sure would like to know the answer to that question! He's had us runnin' up and down both shores of the river, as far as thirty miles above and thirty below the city, burnin' the habitants outta their homes and supplies, jest markin' time, as far as I can see, till he gits help from Amherst. Why, lad, as soon as I tell the gen'ral ye're here, you'll be settin' right across the table from him, tellin' him jest what he needs to know. Now, the gen'ral, he don't keer much for us colonials, but he's got the touch of greatness in him, an' he knows men, I kin tell you. You let me handle this, Johnny, an' by God, I believe we'll make life on this rock tolerable." Small Owen's eyes glistened in the dark with expectation.

Uncle John looked out over the St. Lawrence. "I'm afraid what I'd hev to tell him wouldn't gain us no favors, Owen," he replied. "Amherst's busy building roads an' boats for Lake Champlain and repairin' forts. He ain't one to move on Bourlemaque at Isle-Aux-Noix till he's got ten of everythin' he needs one of—an' by that time, it'll be way too late to do Gen'ral Wolfe any good."

"Aaugh!" Owens expelled his breath in a long nasal hiss of disappointment. "Then it's a long, hard haul of misery an' dyin' we got ahead. We can't git at Montcalm by the Beauport shore. We already tried that, an' there's no way we kin git up by way of the Lower Town, and there's no place to land above the city that's close enough to attack the Citadel. Quebec's the strongest fortification I've ever seen—stronger than Louisbourg—an' it jest ain't possible to take it with what we got here, tho' Wolfe will try to land somewhere afore he leaves." Small Owen moaned audibly. "It's the bearer of bad news you are, John," he said, "an' I've a mind to keep paddlin' this canoe till I git all the way to Halifax." He lapsed into grim silence and began to drive the canoe with long, deep strokes, as if he did indeed plan to leave the valley of the St. Lawrence entirely.

They passed down the St. Lawrence in silence, hugging the south shore, each absorbed in his own thoughts. Tom noted three large ships going up river, but the distance and the darkness prevented him from identifying them. Some time later, a barge taking soundings along the shoreline nearly ran them down; Tom heard Small Owen cursing quietly to himself. The rain continued to fall, and Tom had just begun to have serious doubts about Small Owen's intentions, when what had appeared to be a bay turned into the mouth of a good-sized river. Reckoning automatically, Tom put the distance between the battle with the provision boats and the junction of the rivers at ten miles, and it occurred to the boy with great clarity that he would rather lie down in the bottom of the canoe and die than travel another ten miles in his present misery.

The voice of Small Owen broke in upon Tom's despair. "That's the Etchemin," said Owens. "Goreham's Post is just off the east bank. By God, if I had two swallers o' rum, I'd soon put my back to it."

He drove the canoe on angrily for a few minutes and then headed in to shore. "Ain't you the quiet one," he said to Uncle John. "I suppose you think all you got to do is set there an' wait for Owen to help you outta yer trouble. Well, I'll tell you right now, the only reason I'm pullin' in is that my belly's as empty as my knapsack—an' a lucky thing it is fer you too. Long as I got to stop anyway, I might jest as well git you situated. You ain't gonna find nobody else that knows half as much as me about what's goin' on around here."

"Well now, Owen," said Uncle John gravely. "I knew if I kept quiet you'd figger things out fer yerself. In spite of the gen'ral opinion agin' me, I always felt that you had enough sense to git in outta the rain, once you had the chance to think on it. I expect too, once you've had some rum in yer belly, you'll decide someone better tell Gen'ral Wolfe about Amherst."

"You always was better at talkin than you was at lyin'," replied Small Owen. "It sorrows me to see you ain't changed yer ways. Why, I recollect, but then," he paused to shake his head sadly, "there ain't no sense in puttin' you to shame in front o' the lad there. I jest hope Chicken don't bring up none of them fool things you did at Louisbourg. Chicken ain't much at recollec- tin' ordinarily, but them fool things you did at Louisbourg…" Small Owen gave himself over entirely to his silent laughter.

To Tom's utter astonishment, Uncle John laughed too. "Chicken!" he gasped. "Chicken Jones! You don't mean to tell me Chicken Jones is here. Why, I gave that old buzzard up fer lost years ago."

"Yep, Chicken's been here since the beginning, John," said Small Owen seriously. "We left Halifax in May with Captain Goreham, and Louisbourg June 5 with Saunder's Lot. Landed on Orleans the twenty-fifth and went with Scott's rear guard to Pointe de Levy on the first of July. Between then and now, there ain't been a place thirty miles on either side o' Quebec City that we ain't been at. I been out scalp huntin' by myself. I been out with one or two companies, an' since we established Goreham's Post, I been out with raidin' parties that had up to one hundred men in 'em! An' in between, there ain't been a night but what parties o' Indians and habitants hev been skulkin' round the roads an' the posts, waiting a chance to practice their deviltry. They really hurt us at first, but the gen'ral—I tell you, John, he's the smartest Englishman ever born—he knew how to stop 'em. He don't like us irregulars, but he's a man who looks a fact right in the face, he is."

Small Owen pointed at the shoreline ahead. "Look sharp, now, Johnny," he said. "They's a sentry here some'eres, if he ain't beat it in out of the rain. We ain't a quarter of a mile from the post." The canoe drifted as the three men searched for movement among the trees and bushes at the water's edge.

"There he is," said Owen disgustedly. "I do believe the buzzard's managed to fall asleep in the middle of the storm. Robbers three!" he shouted at the top of his lungs. "Robbers three, you idiot! Wake up and help us beach this canoe, afore I turn yer scalp in fer a Frenchman's."

"Who goes there?" the sentry's voice quavered out over the water.

"Robbers three, I tol' ya," replied Small Owen. "Are you so stupid they didn't trust you with the password?"

A lantern came to life and trembled toward the water. Partially illuminated figure stumbled forward.

"Put that damn thing out!" shouted Owens. "If you want to make yerself a target, go on down to the point and light a signal fire." He drove the canoe ashore and stepped out behind Tom and Uncle John. The lantern revealed the face of a boy of sixteen or seventeen before fumbling fingers extinguished its light. Sickness and pain had wasted the flesh to the bone and dug deep channels in the face. Dull and listless eyes hid deep in hollow sockets. A toneless voice whispered again, "Who goes there?"

"Owen Owens, first back from the expedition," came the answer. "Leave the canoe where it is and git back to yer post, lad. Everythin' will be in shortly, an' you kin go git yerself some dry, honest sleep."

Owens turned briefly before leading the way to Goreham's Post. "Ague and dysentery," he said. "Must be close to a thousand men in hospital on Orleans. They sent that one back too soon. He won't live a week." He shook his head in bewilderment. "Who let a boy like that come to this place, anyway?"

Tom thought about the face of the boy on the beach, but his own exhaustion was too complete to permit any real feeling. He leaned numbly on his rifle as Owens undid the lashings on a tent flap, wondering at the slowness of the little man who had seemed so quick in all his previous actions. Inside the tent, Tom was dully conscious of the wooden boards beneath his feet and the modern bunks. He knew he was being pampered as Small Owen and Uncle John provided him with dry clothing and urged him toward a bunk covered with thick blankets, but he didn't care; the need for rest was so overwhelming that it blotted out all other needs. Tom was asleep before his body had fairly settled itself on the mattress.

6

A RANGER FOR
GENERAL WOLFE

Tom awoke in a hot, humid, noise-filled tent, his clothing so soaked with sweat that it stuck to every square inch of his flesh. A mosquito hummed around his head and landed on his arm. Tom swatted at it viciously, feeling a surge of satisfaction as he saw the insect mangled against his skin. He heard the rain beating steadily down on the tent. His nose sorted out a strange mixture of odors: sweat, warm food, wood smoke, tobacco, alcohol, and bear grease. Now he was fully awake and looking expectantly toward the noisy group of men collected in a rude circle in the middle of the tent.

Uncle John waved an arm toward a pile of green buckskins resting on a locker near the bunk. "Tom," he said, "git into them skins an' git on over here. We've got sausage an' salt pork, beef, regular bread and greens, rum, an' red French wine. We've hit it lucky, Tom. We're joinin' up with the First Independent Company of New England Rangers, an' that means we'll eat better, sleep better, and live longer than anyone else in Wolfe's army."

As Tom dressed, he glanced from time to time at the rangers who continued laughing and joking and drinking toasts out of various bottles. He was pleasantly surprised to see the lean face of Jed Hawkins, who had pulled him out of the smoke oven so many years before, turned toward a man Tom recognized after a moment as Charlie Turner, the young militia lieutenant fooled by Emile Bouchet at Number Four. Tom slipped on the fringed buckskin shirt and walked over to Uncle John, who handed him a large trencher piled high with food, as he performed a brief but efficient introduction.

"This is Matt's boy, Tom," he said. "Tom, you know Owen and Charlie Turner, an' I'm sure you remember Jed. That scrawny little feller sittin' next to Owen and lookin' pretty much like his brother is Lloyd Jones, otherwise known as Chicken Jones. He's mastered the art of stayin' alive, but the only other art he knows is chicken stealin'!"

Since Uncle John's introduction required no acknowledgment, Tom sat down and surveyed his trencher, enjoying hugely his decision to begin the meal with the sausage instead of the beef.

"So it's a moralist then you've become?" asked Chicken Jones plaintively. "In '45, when yer belly was pinched with hunger an' hot was yer head with fever from the swamps of Louisbourg, ye ate yer chicken broth and chicken stew quick enough, nor kin I recollect yer asking at any time fer a bill of sale. Well, I'll better know how to act when the sickness falls on the tent, as like it will afore we're through!"

Uncle John was about to reply in kind, but his need for information brushed aside his wish to continue the game. "Owen said he thought there might be near a thousand men in hospital, Chicken, but the way yer set up here, it don't look like the army's sufferin' all thet much."

Chicken hesitated a moment before replying. "Ye got here on an unusual day, John," he said solemnly. "Pickin's have been mighty slim lately, even for us as knows how to pick. We got to live off the land mostly, an' remember, we been here near two months. When the land gives up something today, it takes its pay in lives tomorrow. Supplies is a great problem, John, for any army this big—an' remember, we been in damned rain. Seems like it's rained every day fer two weeks. Men wet all the time, sleeping on the damp ground an not eatin' right, jest naturally git sick. I suspect Owen is near right, what with ague, fever, an' dysentery, not to mention the accidents and the wounded. Still," here Chicken shook his head mournfully, "a thousand seems a mite high. Mebbe seven hundred would be closer."

"Chicken has the right of it this time, Johnny," said Owen. "If you'd come here any other time, you'd have two chances of see'n a plate of vittles like young Tom's got there: slim and none. Fact is, we just got back from a scourin' expedition with Goreham. Must have been about three hundred men, countin' the same number of highlanders and marines as rangers. We went down to St. Paul's Bay to take care of the habitants who been attackin' the boats and shippin' I figger they had about two hundred men in that parish. We hit 'em about three in the mornin' an' by five, we had 'em drove into the woods. I figger we burnt down all of fifty houses and barns—good ones too. Then we went to Mal Bay, about ten leagues east, and wiped out a whole parish. After that, Goreham took us over to the South Shore, opposite the Island of Coudres, where we destroyed part of St. Ann's and part of St. Roan. Now, John, when you scour like we do, you don't come home empty-handed. Why, they's five parishes on the south side of Orleans alone, with mebbe nine hundred farm houses. Now most of what we got, includin' the cattle, went to the hospital, an I, fer one, shore don't begrudge them poor devils a little meat, but Chicken, here—well Chicken figgered ten days in the field was worth a little somethin' fer the pot, so he took what he thought was fair. I swear, John, he kin hide a side of beef jest as quick as he kin pop a chicken into a sack!"

"An' it's little enough I take fer riskin' my neck twenty-four hours a day," Chicken said. "Why, John, a man ain't safe never. Them settlers has got together with the Injuns, and they jest don't behave at all. We can't even send a party to cut wood without riskin' the loss of a scalp. They don't ever let us be, an them priests is behind most o' it. Why ... " here Chicken's anger got the better of him and he paused to make a quick cutting motion with his hand. "Why, they even use their churches for rallyin' points and signal houses for the French regulars! Some o' them habitants been livin' with Injuns so long I swear they're half Injun themselves. They scalped so many prisoners the gen'ral hisself had a notice tacked up in ev'ry church door. He told 'em they'd better git back in their farms an' stop fightin' us if they wanted to keep their religion an' their freedom, er he'd destroy everythin' they owned, but it didn't stop 'em much, so we been burnin' 'em out. The gen'ral won't let us burn the churches tho, an that's his mistake. Them priests is the ones that head up the trouble. If I had my way, I'd burn every church and hang every priest betwixt here and Quebec City."

"Aye," said Johnathan Evans, smiling at Chicken's ferocity. "An' betwixt here an' Versailles, if you could, with Looie the fifteenth lightin' the torches an' tyin' the ropes."

"That's a mighty interestin' idee," said Owen. "But I'm afraid we ain't got the time to enjoy it. Gen'ral Wolfe's comin' over from the Montmorency side tonight to check on operations over here, leastways, that's what we been told, tho I suspect he come over to take another look at the cliffs above Quebec. He ain't done much on the Montmorency side an it appears to me he's lookin' fer a way to git at Montcalm from west of the Citadel. They say he's been makin' trips upriver with that feller Stobo—the one who escaped from Quebec last May—jest a-lookin' an' a-lookin' at them cliffs above the city."

Here, Jed Hawkins, who had been busily engaged in sharing a bottle of French wine and some private jokes with Charlie Turner, joined the conversation. "I hear Monckton's leavin' his headquarters at Point-des-Peres to have supper with Wolfe at Pointe de Levy," he said. "Now, to me, that means Wolfe wants to see if we're still bein' worked to death. I never knew a gen'ral so determined to wear his army out afore they git a chance to fight. Now the patrols is all right, mind ye, and the musketry practice too, tho I, fer one, don't need no practice in shooting my piece, but them consarned inspections and especially them drill parades—why, we come here to fight, not to polish buckles and march around like the local train bands in the village square."

"Well, Jed, if you'd been a lieutenant in the militia, as I hev," broke in Charlie Turner, "you'd know how important discipline is to an army. When the time fer fightin' does come, Wolfe's men will be ready. They'll do what they hev to when they hev to, no matter what, an' that's why the gen'ral's goin' to take Quebec. 'Sides, you know an army's got to keep busy, even if it's jest diggin' pits, er it'll come plumb apart—especially when the hospital's overflowin' with sick and troops are gittin' horse meat fer regular rations. You got to keep a man busy so he don't dwell on the rain an' the mosquitoes an' the scalpin' then add the fact that we bin here two months already, and we ain't no closer to takin' Quebec than we was when we landed. Why, if he don't keep this army busy, half of 'em will desert afore he finds us a way to git at the Citadel."

"At least nobody in this tent ever had to eat any horse meat," Chicken said with satisfaction, "tho I must own I ain't always been able to git all the little extrys we could use. What would ye all do without me, gittin' along on a reg'lar sojers pay o' five shilling ten a week, an' losin' one shillin' eight for clothin'? With hand soap at a shillin' an' roll tobacco at a shillin', ten a pound, you'd hev jest about enough left fer one bottle of Bristol beer. It's a short stay any of you would make at the suttler's tents come pay day." Chicken grinned widely. "Tho I must say, the suttlers has been very understandin', at least in my case, o' the needs of the fightin' man."

"In yer case!" shouted Owen, slapping his hand vigorously against his thigh. "In yer case, they ain't got no understandin' at all, er they'd put irons on you the second you stepped through the door. But we got to break this up an' git a move on if we want to ketch the gen'ral afore he sets down to supper. I know he'll eat better after he hears what Johnny has to say." Owen turned toward Uncle John. "It's nine miles to Point-des-Peres, an' figger another hour to run over to Levy and find the gen'ral's mess. We're outta gear fer two er three trail days, 'cause I got some plans o' my own, if the gen'ral ain't got nothin' special in mind fer us. You and Tom gotta get broke into the kind o' war we run 'round here, an' nothin'll do that quicker than a little private scourin' party."

Within the hour, the small party of rangers had completed their preparations and started out on the road that led from Goreham's Post to Point-des-Peres. They traveled in Indian file: Owen Owens leading the way, followed by Uncle John, Jed Hawkins, Charlie Turner, Tom, and Chicken. Ahead, Tom could see a cleared space in the forest and several tents. He glanced inquiringly over his shoulder at Chicken and pointed at the tents ahead.

"Light infantry tents," said Chicken. "They're coverin' the road from the Etchemin. Further on down they's a road leadin' off this one to Monckton's camp at Point-des-Peres. You'll be able to see an entrenched camp with support batteries on the north side and on the south ranger posts guardin' the roads to the camps at Pointe de Levy."

As they passed the light infantry post, Tom was surprised to see a squad of soldiers going through some sort of military exercise on the edge of a clearing. The men were spread out in a loose formation and seemed to be intent upon darting from one tree to another. Their coattails were tied up, and the coats themselves had been turned inside out. Mud had been rubbed into the linings, twigs stuck out from the buttonholes, and leaves camouflaged the hats. Even the musket barrels had been darkened with queue grease.

Chicken noted Tom's surprise. "They're usin' Lord Howe's tactics," he said. "Gen'ral's orders. They're savin' themselves some scalps in the bargain. If that squad don't take their trainin' as serious as they might, that ranger in charge kin remind 'em that three marines stepped into them same woods lookin' fer greens to go with their salt pork and lost their hair instead."

Tom ran in the footsteps of Charlie Turner for some time, thinking about the things he had seen and heard since he and Uncle John had pulled Owen Owens out of the St. Lawrence. He began to realize that in comparison to the siege of Quebec, the battle at Fort Ti had been little more than a skirmish.

Tom's thoughts were interrupted by Chicken Jones. "When we git up this little hill, Tom, you'll see the road that goes to the batteries at Point-des-Peres. If you look sharp, you kin see the camp of the forty-eighth regiment. To the south, you kin see a ranger post. Don't be surprised if you see a few Injuns. Jest look real close, an' you'll see they ain't Injuns at all. Seems like some of the boys has discovered they kin do better if they kin git closer to their work."

An involuntary shudder went down Tom's back. He tried to shut out the thought that a ranger "worked" for five guineas a scalp, yet he knew that both Chicken and Owen were not above such "work." Suddenly, Owen's reference to a "little private scourin' party" took on a new and terrible meaning.

As Tom trotted on, occupied with his thoughts, the signs of the vastness of Wolfe's operation became more and more visible. The number of roads leading to camps increased, and occasionally he caught a glimpse of a redoubt with mounted cannon. They passed a huge encampment that Chicken said belonged to the sixty-third, another line regiment, and soon afterward followed the road north as it turned toward the landing places at Pointe de Levy. Tom ran on dutifully until Owen halted at the crest of a knoll and gathered his small party together.

"Right down there," he said, "in that little log hut, is where we'll most likely find the gen'ral, if he did come over from Montmorency. He's used it before when he was jest passin' over, as he is now."

"Now I don't usually care to interrupt a man when he's spec-ulatin'" said Chicken, "but most of us here has already heard how familiar you are with the gen'rals habits, Owen, so we'd jest as soon git off this knoll, what with the wind comin' up an' the rain hangin' heavy over our heads."

"Someday, Mr. Jones, yer goin' to put too much stock in yer value as a chicken thief," replied Owen feelingly, "tho' jest now ain't the time to teach you yer proper place. But, as I was sayin', since I know the gen'ral's habits, an' since by rights I hold the rank of sarjent, I'm goin' to hev to be the one to go down an' see what 'rangments kin be made. I'll trust ye, Mr. Jones, to wait here with the others 'til I git back an' not go runnin' off to the docks." Without waiting for a reply, Owens spun on heel and toe like a man in ranks performing an about-face and began a rapid descent toward the building that supposedly housed "the gen'ral."

The night and the storm clouds closed in steadily on the little hand of rangers as they waited silently, each occupied with his own thoughts. The wind blew cold, and the fog off the St. Lawrence rolled in waves up the hill. It seemed to Tom that they were suspended in a hollow cavity that time surrounded but could not penetrate. He did not wait for the return of Owen; he endured, and he could not have said if minutes or hours had whirled past him when he heard Uncle John's voice call softly in the darkness.

"Over here, Owen. It's been a hard wait, an' that's sartain. I hope ye've brought back the right answer to the question that's been on our minds."

"Aye, I hev that," replied Owen. "I had some trouble gittin' the adjutant to give my message to the gen'ral, but once Wolfe heard the news I brought, he sent me to fetch you jest as soon as I could. Now, ye're the one he wants to see, Johnny, so the rest of us might better go down to the landin' places an' see what we kin find out. They's a suttler's tent outside the sixty-third's camp you kin find easy enough, and we'll meet you there."

"If it's all the same with you," said Uncle John, "I'd jest as soon hev you wait outside the cabin with Tom 'til Gen'ral Wolfe is through with me. It ain't likely Chicken, Jed, and Charlie'll overlook anythin' that might be of interest down at the docks, is it?"

"Not likely," returned Owen. "All right, I'll wait with Tom. Sides, the gen'ral's a curious man, an' he jest might want to ask me er Tom somethin' too."

They went as a group to the building in which the man selected by Pitt to command the expedition against Quebec was now engaged in finishing a light supper. Uncle John and Tom waited as Owen approached the guards posted before the door, and the rest of the party went on down the path toward the landing places.

Owen engaged one of the guards in a brief conversation, while the other guard knocked on the door. A tall man opened the door and held an even briefer discourse with Owen before motioning Tom and his uncle forward. Tom could not master the uneasy feeling that arose as they passed between the sentinels, who stood with muskets at the ready. The feeling became stronger as the three rangers passed through the door and stood at attention before Major General James Wolfe, son of Major General Edward Wolfe, and himself a soldier since the age of fifteen.

"Gentlemen, stand at ease!" The general's voice was sharp and clear, and Tom's eyes turned in the direction of the voice as he obeyed the command, but in the next instant, the boy's eyes dilated and his mouth hung open in amazement. The general's black three-cornered hat did not, in fact, could not, hide his receding forehead. Tom noted the slightly upturned nose and the mouth below that was most certainly not shaped to express resolution. Wolfe's red hair was tied in a queue behind, and his chin fell away so badly that it seemed to Tom to be in need of repair.

Tom's disappointment grew as his gaze comprehended the slender body, the narrow shoulders, and the long, thin, limbs cased in a scarlet frock with broad cuffs and skirts that reached below the knee. *This,* he thought, *cannot be General Wolfe. This must be some officer on the general's staff.*

But then, how could Tom know that the man who sat before him had, as a sixteen-year-old regiment adjutant in Flanders, already demonstrated a precocious faculty for commanding men? How could the border boy understand the marital nature of the man before him, who, entrusted with a full regiment at Inverness, though he was but twenty-three, had accomplished the difficult task of keeping the turbulent Scotchmen in order brilliantly enough to gain the special commendation of the king? Only the bright, piercing eyes revealed the man of genius and the man of destiny, and Tom knew too little of the world of men to judge properly what he saw.

"Well, gentlemen," said the general, "I detect some disappointment among you in my appearance. I daresay, the officers of my own general staff have registered disappointment in me that penetrates far deeper than appearance, so none of you should be unduly ashamed. As matters stand, I believe you have information that will prove most valuable to this expedition and to your king, so let us get at the business as best we can. Mr. Evans, I call upon you to give an account of your actions from Ticonderoga to the present moment. I must ask you to be concise, but I shall also caution you not to omit any details that may bear upon the success of this expedition."

"General," replied Uncle John, "I'm at some disadvantage, not knowing what yer lookin' fer, an' I hev my doubts as to what use my report'll be, since I left Ticonderoga the mornin' after the French blew it up and ran off to Crown Point."

"You must be aware, Mr. Evans," said the general calmly, "that matters of strategy require the consideration of items that seem useless until they are fitted into their proper places. Battles are more or less subject to the fates, sir, and the successful general, like the successful chess player, is the one who moves the proper pieces in the proper way at the crucial moment. Knowing the values and moves of the pieces is a matter of training and experience, but recognizing the moment of opportunity when it occurs—that is a matter of the genius that makes salient those details which shape the moment for victory."

Tom gazed intently at General Wolfe, conscious at first only of those intensely penetrating eyes, hearing the words only as sounds. The thought flashed through Tom's mind that the man was ill and fevered, and suddenly he became conscious of the lines that long suffering and the determination to rise above it etch into a man's face. A feeling that almost amounted to awe began to grow in Tom's heart.

"You would hardly believe, Mr. Evans," continued Wolfe, "the misinterpretations and confusions that arise among the staff here from the simplest of my own orders and intentions; yet, still, I must depend upon your information to help me judge the actions and intentions of a man buried in a wilderness hundreds of miles away. I have heard that General Amherst has written to Mr. Pitt his promise to make an eruption into Canada with the utmost vigor and dispatch, and God knows all logic demands that he extend every effort to alleviate this impossible situation under the rocks of Quebec, but I have also heard…" Wolfe paused briefly, coughed several times into a handkerchief placed beside him on the table, and began again speaking as before, quietly and calmly, "It is no secret, that a successful move into Canada by General Amherst would make our success here probable. Montcalm fears it as much as I desire it. If, however, we are not to have Amherst's help, our situation must be termed desperate. Montcalm thinks he can continue to hide behind his rocks until the season forces us to abandon our efforts, but I will not leave without making a serious attempt, cost what it will. Your information is vital to the future of the expedition. I want you to tell me what you know about Amherst and Ticonderoga!"

Tom noted now the change in his uncle's face. The stiffness had left it as Wolfe spoke, and Tom knew that the general had won another recruit in the army of his personal admirers.

"General," said Johnathan Evans carefully, "if you had asked me to say just one thing 'bout this whole business, I would've said that General Amherst is the most deliberate man I ever saw. He had eleven thousand men by the head of Lake George late in June, an' they didn't embark till the twenty-first of July. He built enough posts and cleared enough land to the rear of the army to start a new colony. He's the buildin'est man I ever saw. By the twenty-third, he'd got up the lake, occupied the heights, and brought up his artillery and had his siege set up. Now, as soon as Amherst started his approaches, Bourlemaque drew his army out, all 'cept about four hundred he left there to delay us a bit. Well, we exchanged shot with 'em for three days, when they took off too, blowing the fort up on their way out, er at least they blew up one *bastion* of it. The next day, me and my nephew here was sent down to the forts along the border to pass the news an' put up recruitin' posters."

Wolfe's eyes fixed themselves on Johnathan Evans's eyes. "What was the nature of the advertisement?" There was a tone of repressed excitement in his voice.

"Amherst wanted recruits of any kind, but especially he wanted rangers. I guess I'd hev to say, he planned on movin' up the Richelieu and on into Canada, but like I said, he's the most deliberate man I ever saw, and sometimes the plannin' takes so long they ain't no time left fer the doin'!"

Wolfe leaned forward to interrupt again, but, changing his mind almost immediately, he relaxed against the back of his chair and waited for Evans to continue.

Johnathan Evans continued, picking his thoughts with the kind of inner concentration that makes a man a world within himself, afraid to admit the distractions of the world about him, but he selected Wolfe's need for information as his classifying principle, so the work of his inner world could find its proper meaning in the mind of the general.

"I never got back to Ti because the Abenaki chief, Satanis, hit a cabin raisin' near Number Four and murdered every settler there but a girl he gave to a Frenchman to carry off to Quebec. Trailin' Bouchet is what brought me an' Tom outside of Isle-Aux-Noix, where we took a prisoner, hopin' to git some idea of what Bouchet was goin' to do with the girl. The prisoner was jest a homesick boy, scared and fevered in the bargain. I did what I could fer 'im, an' he did a good deal o' talkin'. He told me that Bourlemaque had quit Crown Point, jest as I figgered he would, an' had dug himself in on the island. Amherst had been busy repairin' the damaged works at Ti, an' as soon as he found out about Crown Point, he moved in there, an' if I got the boy right, was plannin' on buildin' another fort. He'd enjoy that more'n repairin' Ti, tho he wouldn't neglect that either. Unless I miss my guess, Amherst is still at Crown Point, explorin' the area an' buildin' a fort, er a boat, er somethin' on every space of ground that looks like it needs protectin' er connectin'. He's an untirin' worker, is General Amherst, an' there's nothin' he likes better than gittin' ready to do somethin', an gittin' ready to push Bourlemaque offa Isle-Aux-Noix would cause considerable delay, even to a man who was more interested in the pushin' than the preparation."

General Wolfe leaned forward, placing his elbows on the table and bending his head to clasp his hands behind the neck. He strained back against his hands momentarily before allowing them to unclasp and move forward to form a support for his chin. Still, he said nothing and Evans continued.

"The French hev armed vessels on the lake, an' Amherst'll hev to build some ships to protect the troops on their way to Isle-Aux-Noix. Now Amherst won't stop buildin' till he's certain he's got enough ships, an' you hev to consider that an army kin only do so much buildin', anyway. On top of that, Isle-Aux-Noix won't be easy to take. An arm of the Richelieu

flows around each side, an' each arm is closed with Chevaux-de-
frise. Bourlemaque's got thirty-five hundred men an' a hundred
pieces o' cannon, so attackin' in the front will be a risky business, so that jest leaves reducin' it by reg'lar siege, which'll likely
take more time than the season allows. No, I jest can't believe
that Amherst'll set foot in Canada this year."

Wolfe sat up rigidly in the chair, letting his hands, palms
down and fingers spread, fall down and push against the table.

"I can find no fault in either your logic or your judgment,
sir," he said, "and yet I must hope for miracles. There is time
yet for Quebec, and we must allow circumstance every possible
chance to work in our interests. Surely some personal commu-
nication from General Amherst will reach me soon."

Suddenly, the rigidity left Wolfe's body. Tom could almost
see the muscles relaxing as the general's head bent forward to
receive the hands that came up from the table to cradle the face.
Wolfe smiled in the way one friend smiles when he shares some
small secret with another."

Did you know," he said, "that I learned of the fall of Forts
Ticonderoga and Crown Point from the French? It's true. We
had the good fortune to intercept some letters, and I remember
well how happy we all were on that occasion." He continued to
smile. "And the next news of the matter came from a great, wild
creature who said he came directly from Amherst the morning
after Ticonderoga fell. He was an impressive figure indeed but
carried no proof of the authenticity of his letter or his mission.
In fact, I thought of asking to see the wings that carried him
from Ticonderoga to Pointe de Levy in such a short time. As
he was, however, such an extraordinary savage, I sent him to the
Montmorency camp, where I might have his actions observed,
and, I must say, he has not disappointed me. I am coming to the
opinion that, had I a thousand like him, I would take Quebec
before the end of the month!"

Johnathan Evans, too, had relaxed. "If yer savage is who I
think it is," he said, matching Wolfe's smile, "the wings are easy

to explain. When a man truly understands his bounden duty, the bonds become wings that carry him over such obstacles as stand in his way, an' I'll warrant Toe-lee-ma is as quick in doin' his duty as he is in helpin' his friends. I should jedge that a hundred like him, General, could push the Upper Town off its rock down into the middle of the St. Lawrence River, if it's truly the Mohegan ye're speakin' of."

Wolfe's eyes fairly sparkled now with the spirit and the intelligence that formed the man. His sense of duty to England and the military profession, loyalty to the king, and fidelity to his own ideal of the perfect soldier had led him at last to the Canadian wilderness, to Quebec, where he would decide, in one brief, brilliant battle, the destiny of North America.

"The name and the tribe are the same," he said, "and I assume my great savage and yours are also the same. I confess that I have not fairly taken his measure, nor yours, until this moment. The opportunity to take Quebec lies somewhere on the north shore. Time and circumstance are conspiring to reveal it to us, and a few men with your faith and courage will do to lead the others on to victory; for the world has no better soldier than the British soldier, when he is well-led and well- disciplined."

Wolfe was interrupted by a knock on the door. His adjutant opened the door and admitted a young major of light infantry, who advanced briskly to the table and saluted smartly. Wolfe looked up quizzically, but his return salute was delivered in a very military manner. The major stood at the most rigid position of attention possible. His jaws were drawn back taut and the cords of his neck bulged in their attempt to help the officer's chest expand beyond its natural limit. The extreme muscular effort expended seemed to have paralyzed the young major's vocal apparatus, and his words were even more indistinct and smothered than is usual in the British aristocrat.

"Major Neville Howard," he said, "attached to General Monckton's staff. General Monckton extends his good wishes to General Wolfe, and hopes he will not inconvenience him at supper by arriving a few minutes early."

"Where's the general now?" asked Wolfe impatiently.

"Just down the road, sir," replied the major. "He sent me on ahead when we were within the halfhour of arrival and cannot be more than fifteen minutes away."

"As you can see," said Wolfe, "I have supped and await General Monckton's arrival. Please ask him not to delay on my account."

Wolfe and the young major exchanged salutes, and Wolfe again turned to Johnathan Evans. "We have great need of men like you in this army," he said, "but I wish, of course, to use your talents to the best possible advantage. I have six companies of rangers, all shorthanded, and you can have my commission in the company of your choice."

General James Wolfe hesitated and then spoke with the manner of a man who has just made an important decision.

"Or," he said slowly and distinctly, "you can stay with me and serve directly under my orders. I need a man with the courage to expose himself to the most extreme danger, the skill to come away unharmed, and the judgment to evaluate properly what he sees. Intuition is a fine thing, and extra sense, in a way, but it must have facts, and the right facts at that, before it can operate properly. God forbid that I should miss the opportunity to take Quebec!"

Johnathan Evans could not reply. He tried to comprehend the nature of the trust that had been placed in him. Images of the years he had spend as guardian of the border weighed him down. Tomahawks flashed, and scalps danced across his mind. The smell of burning wood came out of the past and choked his senses. Then suddenly, across the years, leaped the dreadful image of the tomahawk that had cleaved his brother's skull as he watched helplessly, calling vainly upon God to return to his now useless rifle the bullet he had just discharged in defense of his own life. Johnathan Evans shuddered, as if he were an empire at the precise moment of its fall.

"I am not the man ye want, General Wolfe," he said. "I carry a terrifyin' burden on my shoulder that I hev to cast off in my own way. Ever since I stood beside the burnin' cabin of Josh Foster, I've had the feeling that my destiny would work itself out in Canada, alongside my nephew and my enemies. I come here to git the murderin' beast Satanis and the devil Bouchet who unleashed him, and to git Sally Williams back. The end of my trail lies here somewheres around Quebec, an' when I find it, I'll be free for the first time in near fifteen years. No, General, my sin was agin' my own family, an' it's there I've got to wash it clean. I've learned that all big things has got to start small and grow. There ain't no such thing as loyalty, or duty either, that don't start in the family. Once a man has that, he kin be loyal to a friend—or his country, fer that matter, but he's got to deep them roots, or he don't understand his covenant with God, an' he's not a man at all, leastways, not a civilized man, tho he might well be an agent of the devil."

Johnathan Evans let his head hang down and stopped all sounds and movements. Tom was riveted to his chair in dumb agony until Wolfe broke the silence.

"I shall never question the judgment of a man who has such terrifying honesty, Captain Evans," he said. "I would have gladly wagered my career against the man who questioned your understanding of loyalty, but I shall presume no further. Do what you will, and be assured of my good wishes."

Evans raised his head to look at Wolfe. "It ain't in the understandin' that I sinned, General. It was in the doin' I knew what I should've done but I didn't do it; my sin was agin' the family, so somehow it's got to be removed in the family. Of course, a man kin surely git outside o' his family—has to, in fact, I ain't got a better friend in this world than yer 'great savage,' Toe-lee-ma, and I'm proud to think he feels the same, but at the same time, I got to remember where my loyalty was nurtured, where it has its roots. A man who turns agin' his own kind is uncivilized, or worse, he's a man whose pride turned his heart to Satan. Sech a man kin be loyal only to hisself an' to the devil.

"Toe-lee-ma knows that too. Both races say in Proverbs unnumbered that a man can't desert his own kind without deserting all kinds. The pine that grows in caly becomes yellowed. The crow cannot fly with eagles, as Toe-lee-ma says. In the end, each kind must be true to its own nature an' its own kind. That's a law God has built into all his creatures, an' if you jedge a man by his actions instead of by the reasons he gives for 'em, it's as easy to tell the creature from the cur as it is to tell the crow from the eagle."

General Wolfe listened sympathetically, feeling the truth that the ranger's crude manner of expression was somehow made universal. His efforts to control his own thoughts failed, and he found himself wishing that the ranger would talk on, all night if necessary, until he had revealed every detail of the incident that weighed so heavily upon his soul. Then, in confused amazement, Wolfe found himself suddenly and unreasonably confronted with the image of his opponent, the scholarly and brilliant Louis Joseph, Marquis de Montcalm-Gozon. It was no secret that Montcalm, caught between the suspicious egotism and restless jealousy of Vaudreuil and the knavery of Intendant Bigot, a monster bloated by every conceivable form of corruption, longed for nothing so much as the soft winds and orchards of his estate at Candiac. Indeed, though Wolfe did not know it, Montcalm would have given up the chance to be Marshall of France to return to Candiac and the tender, loving arms of his wife and children.

Montcalm vanished abruptly as Wolfe's pensive eye fell upon his left arm, where he had placed the bank of black crepe in mourning of his father. His thoughts flew to the house at Blackheath, where he saw himself playing at piquet with his mother, dutifully pretending enthusiasm for the game, wondering silently when he might get out in the yard and exercise his dogs. Then his attention returned to Johnathan Evans, and it occurred to him that it was the service of king and country, which had carried him so many thousands of miles from home and had begun in his own house in the bosom of his own family.

The heavy silence in the room recalled Wolfe to the duties of the moment. The ranger captain would say no more, and Monckton was but minutes away. The affair must be settled quickly.

"Do what you will, then," Wolfe said. "Whatever you choose, I expect you will offer the king more than ordinary service."

"Since I've already joined the First Independent Company of New England Rangers," said Johnathan Evans, "I'd like to stay with 'em till I get the feel of the fighting an' the circumstances o' this expedition. To my way o' thinkin', my business here is pretty much the same as the king's, an' they'll come together afore too long, especially if I kin git together with Toe-lee-ma to work things out."

General Wolfe turned to his adjutant. "Draft an order giving this man a commission as my personal scout and the authority necessary to be independent."

Then he turned to face Evans again. "You will find your savage friend at the Montmorency headquarters," he said. "When your affairs and mine come together, I shall expect to hear from you."

Uncle John pushed his chair back from the table and stood at attention, motioning Tom to do the same. He saluted with the feeling that he should be shaking the general's hand and turned toward the pen that noisily scratched out his special orders. He waited uneasily until the adjutant finished writing, impatient to get about his own business.

"Over here, John," called Owen Owens, who had taken refuge from the weather under the protecting branches of a half-grown oak. "Jedgin' by the time you was in there, I'd say Wolfe found yer report mighty interestin', and no soldier ever suffered from havin' a gen'ral's goodwill. I trust, Johnny, you found occasion to remind him that it was yer friend, Small Owen, who hed the brains to bring you in?"

Uncle John did not answer Owen's question. "I don't know what your purpose was in sendin' Chicken, Jed, and young Turner down to the dock, Owen," he said, "but whatever schemes you hev in mind'll hev to do without me 'n Tom. Our business here is personal. We got to tend to our own int'rests first, an' right now, that means gittin' to the Montmorency headquarters jest as quick as we kin git."

"Why, John," replied Owen. "It's sartain I had nothin' special in mind, but I've found that a wise man always takes the time to find out what's goin' on about him, whereever he's at. You bein' with the gen'ral so long, it ain't gonna hurt to git on over to the sixty-third's camp an' see what the bays has learned. I'll stand for a bottle o' Bristol beer, even if it does cost a shilling six. Old friends like you an me," he said feelingly, "is always entitled to a partin' drink, fer the next one we git may be poured by the devil."

Johnathan Evans hesitated only briefly before nodding his agreement. He and Tom followed Owen closely, as the little man moved rapidly through the evening mist. Before long, they approached the camp of the sixty-third and, soon after, followed Owen into the suttler's tent, where their appearance was greeted by Jed Hawkins and Charlie Turner. Chicken Jones was busily engaged in a discussion with the suttler, which he did not judge their arrival important enough to interrupt.

Owen, struggling to keep his laughter silent, threw a finger in the direction of Chicken. "I see you didn't come away from the docks empty-handed," he said. "What's that thing Chicken's usin' to bargain with?"

"That's one of them silver salt holders," replied Charlie Turner. "Sure is somethin too. I don't know as I ever saw the like of it. Chicken says it musta come from some church 'cause the lid handle is a silver cross."

"Now you ain't hed time to loot no church while John was talkin' to Gen'ral Wolfe," said Owen. "How in thunder did he manage to pick up somethin' like that?"

"Well," said Charlie, "it seems as how they was some baggage settin' on the dock jest waitin' fer someone to load it onto the admiral's ship, an' seein' as how the guard was busy tellin' me 'n Jed how important he was to the army, Chicken's curiosity 'bout what was in all them bags jest naturally got the better of 'im."

Owen nodded appreciatively. He could picture the expert fingers of Chicken swiftly exploring the baggage that looked most promising. There was no denying it. The man definitely had a gift for thievery.

"You don't hev to say no more about that," he said. "I kin see the results, but did you take the time to do what you was supposed to do?"

Here Jed Hawkins spoke up. "Why, Owen," he said with some feeling, "there's no need to talk like we was some raw recruits that jest signed our 'listment papers. O' course we found out what we needed to know."

"I don't suppose we got the time to listen to everythin' sech expert fact finders as yerselves he's discovered," said Owen good-naturedly, "so we'd appreciate it if you'd git right to the point."

"I don't rightly know where to start," replied Jed. "Tonight's pretty much jest like any other night. We had six marines carried off from the camp at St. Anthony's, an' Murray, he's sent out parties to destroy all the houses in that entire district. There'll probably be detachments sent out from Orleans and Montmorency too, not that it'll do much good. Them Canadian militiamen ain't anxious to desert Montcalm when they know them French Indians'll be turned loose on their homes if they do, tho it must make 'em feel pretty bad to sit over there and watch their houses and their fields goin' up in smoke."

"Near as we could gather," Charlie Turner added, "the French are really tearin' us up on both sides of the river. They got big parties of settlers led by their local priests, along with packs o' Indians led by French regulars roamin' thirty miles up an' down the shore. There ain't a work party or a sentry that kin count on keepin' his scalp, day or night—er a camp in any village that's safe either."

"Ain't there no way we kin git at Quebec itself," said Johnathan Evans, speaking for the first time.

"How kin we git at Quebec?" Owen Owens said disgustedly. "Kin you grow wings on an army that'll fly 'em three er four hundred feet straight up in the air? No attack force kin git up the sheer front to the city, an' to the west the St. Lawrence is walled, mile after mile, by a range of steeps as hard for Wolfe to mount as it would be for the devil to come up out of hell and assault the gates of heaven. A few men at the top of them cliffs could stop an army, an' Bougainville is up there to defend 'em. De Ramesay is in the city, an' below the city, Montcaim is entrenched from the St. Charles to the Montmorency. He's got fourteen thousand men, not countin' his Indians. Them Canadians ain't much good in the open field, but dug in on top of the heights, they kin be trusted. If Quebec has a weak point, it's the landward flank on the left of the city, and Montcalm's taken keer of that. No, John, if things run accordin' to the nature o' the situation, Quebec is safe enough."

"Why," said Jed Hawkins, "it's only luck that got us here to start with. The French never thought the fleet could git through the traverse between Cape Tourmente and Orleans. They was so sure we'd be smashed to pieces on the rocks that Vaudreuil never put a cannon on the plateau, an that's all he had to do to batter every ship that passed. Then them fire ships could've destroyed our fleet before we ever got off Orleans. They floated 'em right at the fleet, loaded with everythin' you could imagine that would burn, mixed with fireworks, bombs, grenades, old cannon, swivels, an' loaded muskets. When they exploded, the sight was worse than any nightmare. Grapeshot rattled off the trees and our troops on the Point jest cut and run. It looked like the fires of hell had come up out of the St. Lawrence an' Jedgment Day was at hand. But them cowardly French sailors had set the torches too soon, and some British sailors, God bless 'em, rowed right up to them explodin' ships with grapplin' irons and towed 'em out o' the way. Them British sailors is jest impossible to beat, leastwise when they're playin' their own game."

"Yes," said Owen, "and don' ferget the French let us move over the South Channel from Orleans an' take Point de Levy. Course, we hed to knock some French an' Indians out o' a church to git possession of the houses an' the surroundin' heights, but that was child's play compared to throwin' up the entrenchments and plantin' the batteries, what with harrassment from the settlers and their Indians an' the guns of Quebec showerin' balls an' bombs on us constantly. They even sent over an assault party to drive us out after it was too late. I tell ye, that was some assault force," he continued, mouth twisted in silent derision, "made up of tradesmen, a few of them worthless Canadians from the camp, a few Indians, even some seminary pupils, an' only about a hundred regulars." Owen's disgust became so strong that it forced him to spit fiercely at the ground. "Them seminary scholars was so scared," he continued, "that they no sooner landed then they begin shootin' at their own party, thinkin' they was British. Then the whole miserable lot of 'em started runnin', knockin' into each other, and rollin' down the heights toward their canoes. They paddled back to Quebec without shootin' at anybody but themselves." Laughter choked off his words, and he slapped his thigh in delight.

"You kin see, John," said Hawkins, "it's pretty much by luck that we got a foothold at all. Occupyin' Orleans and seizin' the heights of Levy hes given Wolfe command o' the Basin of Quebec, an' here we sit. It's true, we've jest about destroyed the city with our cannon, but that ain't put us no closer to capturin' it. Montcalm jest sits up there on the heights of Beauport, or the rock of Quebec, or the summit of Cape Diamond, and looks down on every move we make. He knows all he has to do is watch until October when the winter sets in and drives us out."

"O' course," said Owen, "Wolfe knew what Montcalm was thinkin', an' he didn't waste any time tryin' to git him to fight. He sent Townshend and Murray's brigades from Orleans over to the north shore at L'Ange Gardien, a little below the Montmorency cataract. They wasn't no opposition, 'cept from a troop of Canadians an' Indians, so they got up the heights easy. The French didn't try to drive us out, so there we set on one side of the Montmorency, with the French on the other. Since then the siege o' Quebec hes mostly been us levelin' the city with artillery, keepin' the settlers under control, an tryin' to keep the Indians from liftin' our scalps. Course, they's always them artillery fights between gunboats, frigates, and shore batteries, but they don't count for much. Montcalm won't take any bait Wolfe offers him. He won't come out an' fight anywhere, even tho Wolfe has divided his force so the left wing at Pointe de Levy is six miles from the right wing at Montmorency, and Orleans is cut off from both by the St. Lawrence. It's shore beginnin' to look like we ain't goin' to see the inside of Quebec."

"Owen's right," said Jed Hawkins. "We can't get at Quebec unless Montcalm will come out an' fight, an' he's too smart fer that. Wolfe got so desperate he tried to land on the mud flats of the Beauport shore, but everythin' went wrong. We hed over four hundred men killed an' wounded, an' I hear the French didn't lose one soldier. We did find a way to git men an' ships above the city, but we couldn't find no place to land an army where we could git at Quebec. About all we did was extend the battle line thirty miles west, as far as I can see. That's why Wolfe is over again tonight, accordin' to the men we jest talked to on the docks. He's goin' upriver to look fer some place we kin land an' git an army up on the heights west of the city, but it won't do no good. He's been up there before with an officer they say was a captive at Quebec long enough, so the French sort of give him the run of the place—Stobo's his name, Major Robert Stobo—well, this Stobo was supposed to hev some way o' gittin' up on the plains of Abraham, but I notice nothin' ever come of

it. Looks like Montcalm hes all the cards in this here game, tho'
I s'pose Wolfe'll throw in all his chips an' call one more time
before he gives up an' goes home."

Johnathan Evans had listened very closely to the accounts
of both men and decided that he had heard enough. "No matter
what happens between Wolfe and Montcalm," he said, "me 'n
Tom has our own work to do, an' it's past time we was about doin'
it. I see Chicken's done with his hagglin' and comin' over, so you
men kin decide right now whether you want to help us out fer a
while er whether there's better things you might be doin'."

As Evans finished speaking, Chicken Jones joined the
group. In his hand he still held the standing salt. Exasperation
was written large on his face; irritation lent a cutting edge to his
voice, yet the others sensed that a counterpoint of good humor
ran beneath the turbulent surface.

"That suttler is gittin' more cunnin' and more connivin'
every second of the day," he said. "I swear, I believe he's got
enough gall to start cheatin' officers. There ain't nothin' lower in
the human race than a man who robs the very men that's dyin'
to keep 'im in business. Wait'll you hear how he tried to steal
my salt from me." Chicken's voice had been by no means quiet,
and now he turned to shake his treasure at the suttler.

"That kin wait, Chicken," interrupted Johnathan Evans.
"Right now, the only thing that int'rests me is whether or not
you boys're goin' to help me an' Tom git over to Wolfe's headquarters an' find Toe-lee-ma. You know what brought us to
Quebec, so you know our own work comes first. Now I ain't
never been the one to put himself between any man an' his duty,
but it appears to me yer pretty much on yer own, so if you kin
spend a few more hours, we'd appreciate yer help."

"Now, John," replied Chicken. "There ain't no need to take
that tone. You know that of Chicken hes helped you out in
circumstances a hell of a lot tighter than this. 'Course I'll help
ye find yer red friend, an' while I'm at it, mebbe I'll find a way
to trade off my salt." Chicken grinned widely and lowered his

voice. "It's a mighty distractin' item, my salt is," he said con-
fidentially, resting the heels of his hands against his ribs and
patting his hunting shirt with his fingers.

"Naturally, we'll go on over with you," said Owen Owens.
"The action's all the same fer us on either side of the river anyway. A parish is a parish an' a settler's a settler, whether he's
on the north bank er the south. I don't see how Jed er Charlie
showed no inclination to argue the point."

So Owen led the rangers toward the river. The night had
turned incredibly black. A cold, light rain drove against the
men, and the trees moaned their complaints against the wind.
A natural misery that extended from heaven to earth enveloped the figures that moved silently and swiftly toward the St.
Lawrence.

7

GUERILLA WARFARE

The full force of the rain struck the rangers as they stepped from the protection of the forest to the open landing place. The wind blew the water angrily against the rocky ledges near shore. A wretched sentry reflected upon the insanity that would drive men to launch a mere canoe against such a tempest, and his thoughts dwelt upon their fate long after the night and the turbulent water had hidden them from view.

Indeed, the passage of the canoe across the water was fraught with danger, though not one of its occupants considered the journey perilous. Still, the sentry's light blinking in the mist was a most welcome sight. The formalities of identification were quickly conducted, and soon after, Tom and Uncle John were following Owen down a trail too narrow to deserve the name. They were aware that a large encampment holding the Louisbourg Grenadiers lay on the west and that Otway's regiment was to the east, but they traveled in a solitude unrelieved by any sign of life, animal or human. The path became dangerously steep, and even these trail-hardened veterans were forced to labor to ascend it. At last, lights were seen ahead and the path leveled off. Owens answered the challenge of a sentry, and Tom could see that the lights came from a small house. They had finally reached Wolfe's headquarters.

Uncle John and Owen accompanied the sentry to the door of the house that faced the river. A few words were exchanged at the door, and Uncle John stepped inside, already reaching for the paper that contained his orders from Wolfe. Soon, he reappeared and his companions gathered around him, almost as if there were a common realization that he had now assumed the responsibilities and position of their commander.

"There's a small detachment of volunteers forming up at the redoubt just up the hill. They're a punitive expedition, stemming from the loss of the marines at St. Anthony's. Toe-lee-ma is there serving as scout for a Sergeant Hargreaves, and I intend to join the party."

Evans turned to Owen Owens. "It seems to me this will be work to yer likin', Owen; since it's a party of volunteers, I'm sure they'll be happy to hev you an' the boys go along." With that, he turned and climbed toward the redoubt and his long delayed meeting with Toe-lee-ma.

The rangers followed Evans past the gaping mouths of the cannon and across the planks that spanned the ditch between the banks of the redoubt and its inner square. Uncle John's practiced eye rested on a squat, powerfully-built figure whose very stance revealed the attitude of a man accustomed to issuing commands. Tom spotted Toe-lee-ma standing apart from the fifteen or sixteen men who had grouped themselves loosely together like a herd of cows all facing in one direction to put their rumps to the wind. Tom was certain that the Indian and his uncle had seen each other, but their disciplined natures would withhold any sign of recognition until the proper moment arrived.

"Sergeant Hargreaves," called Johnathan Evans, approaching the short, low-slung figure now before him, "Captain Johnathan Evans, First Independent Company of New England Rangers, on special orders from General Wolfe."

The men exchanged salutes, and the sergeant, who was a Johnny Bull from Bragg's twenty-eighth regiment, accepted the orders and called for light. The lantern revealed a square jaw, a generous nose colored and distended by excessive drinking, and honest blue eyes, whose expression clearly showed that the sergeant was not overjoyed by the arrival of Captain Evans.

"What brings you here, sir, to my small detachment, on a night such as this?" said the sergeant with the air of the man who does not wish his command or his plans altered by outsiders.

"As you can see from my orders," replied Evans, "the gen'ral has put me on special duty to look out fer his int'rests an' given me commission to act as I see fit. Now it jest happens that I have need o' yer Indian, but as I know the nature o' yer work tonight and the value o' the man to sech an expedition, I have no wish to deprive you of his services entirely. It's my suggestion, Sergeant, that you go on with yer job as planned, leavin' me an' my rangers to tag along an' help out as best we kin. These men are New England rangers, Sergeant, near as good as Toe-lee-ma himself when it comes to smellin' out the enemy in the woods er puttin' a torch to a house er a cornfield."

Sergeant Hargreaves thought but a moment. "'Tis true that these ugly forests hide a thousand demons," he said. "We have learned pretty much how to deal with 'em after their own fashion, but I daresay men such as yours may help us keep our scalps on. What do you think of putting the Indian out front, two of your rangers on each flank, and one to the rear until we come to the first objective?"

"I kin see yer a man who knows his business," said Evans. "If you'll jest git my men into yer final briefin', so's they know what to expect, I'll use the time to renew my acquaintance with Toe-lee-ma. We'll be ready to start at yer signal."

Toe-lee-ma and Evans stepped away from the group and Sergeant Hargreaves, his mind so removed from the doubts occasioned by the arrival of the rangers that he now welcomed them heartily, turned to his men, determined to make his final preparations as brief as thoroughness would allow.

The exchange of information between Toe-lee-ma and Johnathan Evans was equally as brief. At no point in the ranger's narrative did the Mohegan show surprise, and, indeed, so accurate was his assessment of the characters of Bouchet and Satanis that he could almost anticipate the actions now being swiftly revealed.

"They are here," said the Indian as Evans finished his account. "They work together, Bouchet and Satanis with his St. Francis Abenakis, like wolves following the deer trail, watching for the young who are tired or the old who are weak and fall behind. It is said that they torture the children of the habitants who are slow to join in the hunting. I have myself read their sign in the village that lies to the east of this camp."

"I see the French ain't entire fools when it comes to pickin' the right man fer the job," replied the ranger fiercely. "Bouchet's an expert at stirrin' up trouble, and Satanis is an expert when it comes to liftin' scalps. But what of the girl? Hev ye heard nothin' at all about Sally?"

"No woman travels with them," was the Mohegan's direct answer.

"Well," said Evans, "it's certain Bouchet brought her with him. I thought that mebbe, with the exchange of prisoners and deserters bein' so frequent, some word of a girl as strikin' as Sally might have been passed. As far as that goes, he might even have put 'er in some kind o' disguise."

Evans's thoughts were interrupted by the sound of Sergeant Hargreave's voice readying his party of volunteers for the trail. The ranger noted with satisfaction that the men were in single file and every precaution had been taken. As he passed up the line toward the sergeant, he could see no shine from the muskets, and he realized that the preparations had been complete right down to the queue grease applied to the barrels.

"Place your men, Captain," said Sergeant Hargreaves, "and let us see what damage we can do to the enemy."

"Jed an' Charlie take the right flank, Owen and Tom the left. Chicken, you're the rear guard and Toe-lee-ma 'n me'll lead. It ain't a fit night fer bird nor beast to be out, but the rain is lettin' up considerable, so we'll use the owl fer signalin'. If he cries once, somethin' unnatural's been spotted. Twice means the enemy is close, but if he cries three times, git yer rifle ready an' find a tree."

The rangers went to their positions, word of the signals was passed from volunteer to volunteer as a precautionary measure, and Hargreaves gave the order to move out.

Out front, Toe-lee-ma and Johnathan Evans moved quickly, past an encampment of grenadiers, past the campfires of the Royal Americans and Bragg's Regiment, and into the dense woods through which the road to L'Ange Gardien had been cut. Toe-lee-ma began to move slower, keeping to the woods north of the road. Now they passed Howe's Light Infantry and moved into an area of guerilla warfare, a sort of no-man's-land, where bands of French Indians and Canadians, like pirate ships moving out of vast ocean mists down upon unsuspecting merchantmen, indulged their lust for blood and vengeance. The rain had stopped, but the arms of the waterlogged forest were waves of wetness that waited to drench the unwary voyager. Through the ocean of forest, without charts or reckonings to guide him, Toe-lee-ma moved unerringly toward the village of L'Ange Gardien.

Suddenly, the cry of an owl drifted back to the little party of volunteers. Though they had moved through the woods in constant expectancy of his call, the sound startled them, and they halted clumsily and noisily. Ahead, Toe-lee-ma mounted a rocky ledge and looked carefully down toward the village of the Guardian Angel. Then he retraced his steps and walked back to the Sergeant Hargreaves.

"There is a house burning near the village," he said. "The detachments sent to burn the fields and houses have rested from their afternoon's work. The weather has not dampened their spirit for destruction. When the rain stopped, they began again to light their torches. The countryside will be in arms, and the woods will hold those who watch and wait. We should go up the cliffs to avoid this village and come down when we are already east of Chateau Richer. There are houses and fields enough there to reward each man to his own satisfaction."

"It makes no difference where we burn," said the sergeant coolly. "Houses at Chateau Richer serve the general's purpose as well as houses at Guardian Angel. Take us across the heights, if you will."

The way to L'Ange Gardien had been difficult. The move toward Chateau Richer was, at best, perilous. A deer trail, narrow and winding, crossed with branches that would slap against chest and face, gave a short respite from the denser tangled obstructions of the untrodden forest, but Toe-lee-ma did not trust trails. He would move where even the deer did not move.

They all paid the full price for their security. The forest took vengeance upon the intruders who complicated its struggle for existence. It clawed and ripped clothing and flesh with its thorny nails and struck bruising blows with its twisted arms. It moaned and sighed until feet guided by fear tripped over roots they should have avoided and led their masters against the cruelest and heaviest weapons the trees carried, but the small group of volunteers struggled on until they had put the most dreadful of the forest's armaments behind them. Only then did they cease their efforts, and only then in obedience to the owl's signal.

Toe-lee-ma and Johnathan Evans stepped with Sergeant Hargreaves away from the exhausted men who sprawled on the forest floor. They stood on the edge of a cliff that rose two hundred feet above the St. Lawrence and looked down upon the river. The British batteries on Pointe de Levy exchanged their messengers with the French batteries at Quebec. The explosions lit up the night sky, so the three observers could read the message the British shells delivered to the city. The message was plain enough: "We shall obliterate your city. We shall explode and explode and continue to explode until even the rubble is in fragments." The French answer was plain enough too: "It is true. You can lay waste to our city, but we assure you that no British soldier will ever enter in at any of its gates."

Toe-lee-ma broke the silence. "You can see that the work continues at the Guardian Angel," he said. "Houses and fields are still on fire. Habitants will buzz around each burning hive, and they will sting somebody. Even here, the British bear has put his paw into the honey. It is not wise to walk near such a nest."

Displeasure wrinkled the brow of Sergeant Hargreaves. "There were no regular orders for Chateau Richer but mine," he said. "Look, only the house is on fire. There, sir," he said, turning toward Evans, "I think you see an example of colonial craftsmanship, as much a study in the art of looting as in the art of war. Well, well, it is only to be expected, after all, when the general order for scouring has gone out. I don't see it as any serious disadvantage to us. The house is one the western out-skirts, and we stand above the farms to the east. If you will take us straight down, Indian, we'll get on with our business. For too much of what grows in this parish ends up on Quebec tables, and too many of these farmers put on a different set of clothes when the sun goes down. Well, I intend to teach them some new manners as well as some new farming methods!" Harg-reaves strode back to his volunteers, already issuing orders for the descent.

Toe-lee-ma and Johnathan Evans led the party down. Finally, they stopped at the southeast edge of a huge cornfield that started some hundred yards from an old frame house and ran west for nearly a half mile. Sergeant Hargreaves called his men together and gave his final instruction.

"We'll get the field first," he said "The family shouldn't give us any trouble, but just in case one of 'em wakes up and starts poppin' at us, the rangers will cover the house from those trees in front. Allyn, you get some torches and take seven men down this side. Lyman, take the rest of the men and go down the other side. When the field's burnin' good, we'll go after the barn. Damn me if I don't wish they had enough people in there to have a go at us. That house has got a bad reputation as a gatherin' place for the resistance, and I intend to give any man in there who has a mind to, the chance to fight for his home. If the corn doesn't get to 'em, the barn may." He shook his head until his jowls bounced. "Not likely," he said to himself. "Not likely tonight, anyway. Any group of troublemakers would have to take leave of their senses to hole up on a frame house when the scourin's goin' on."

The rangers moved toward the trees scattered about the cornfield. They were silent out of habit as each picked his tree and merged with its trunk. They waited, listening to the sounds made by Allyn and Lyman working their way through the corn. They listened and relaxed until the cry of an owl, this time a barn owl, sounded somewhere out of the blackness ahead of them, between the trees and the house. They stayed with their trees until they were signaled, one by one, to return to the edge of the cornfield.

The report of Toe-lee-ma was delivered, as usual, without emotion. It was, as usual, brief and pointed. He had heard a sound that did not fit the night, and then another. He had moved toward the sounds until he began to see grotesque lumps of blackness. Soon the black lumps became a fence of large tree stumps that ran in front of the house and down its side. The sounds came from an ambush party hiding behind the fence. He thought the party was either Indian or Canadian or both. There was something he didn't understand behind the wall of stumps, but whatever it was, it was not worth the loss of time or the risk of discovery that closer surveillance would incur.

Sergeant Hargreaves was silent only for a moment after Toe-lee-ma concluded his report. Then he laughed quietly, almost inaudibly, with genuine pleasure.

"We have 'em now," he said "This is more than I hoped for. I thought we might get one, or maybe two, of the householders capable of bearin' arms if we could make 'em mad enough to fire at us, but this … this is almost too good to be true. With a little bit o' luck, we'll give 'em such a knock on the head here at Chateau Richer that they'll feel it in their toes down at St. Joachim."

Johnathan Evans certainly was not displeased with the turn of events, though he could not match the sergeant's pure delight.

"How many men do you reckon that wall o' stumps hides?" he asked Toe-lee-ma.

"I could not see many," replied the Mohegan, "but the ears are sometimes better than the eyes. The wall hides not less than twenty and not more than thirty, placed stupidly so close together that their line extends but halfway across the front of the house, and not more than thirty yards down the west side."

"Bring the men in, place 'em opposite the enemy, and move in as close as we can get until we're discovered. Then we'll give 'em a full volley from Brown Bess and with bayonets. There's no force of Indians or Canadians, habitants or militia, that can stand to a British charge, not even at fifty to one."

"You are no doubt right, Sergeant," said Evans, "except that they don't expect to stand to any charge. We're dealin' with either Indians or settlers er mebbe both, probably without even one regular to lead 'em. These are people who figgered this farm was a likely target fer some small scourin' party, such as ours, jest as soon as the burnin' started at L'Ange Gardien, so they set up their ambush much as a trapper sets his trap fer fur. If the trap don't work, they're gonna pick up an' move, jest like the trapper. Now, mind ye, I ain't sayin' they're gonna run blind. They'll most likely each pick a tree behind 'em jest as soon as they know we're out here. They'll let yer Brown Besses thunder; they'll let you run right up to the fence. Then, when ye're tangled up in the tree stumps, they'll pour it into you—an' not in a volley either. Each man will pick a target, fire, an' go to the next tree back. Now, I don't think you want to git into that kind o' fight when there's other ways o' doin' things."

Sergeant Hargreaves shook his head slowly, his chin moving between the angle formed by his left thumb and forefinger. "I'm afraid, Captain," he said soberly, "that I have been a little too anxious. I have my own reasons, you must understand, for wanting to get at these murd'rous, scalpin' devils, tho that's no proper excuse for stupidity. You are the one who is right. They will do exactly as you say. Damn! I have seen them fight that way more than once ... " He fell silent and let the full force of his blunder work inside him.

"Now, Sergeant," said Uncle John, "to my way o' thinkin', we ought to be countin' our blessin's. I can't pretend to understand the reason, but they've bunched themselves up in a very bad position. In fact, that worried me more'n anything else. If they was all Indians, er even if any sizeable amount 'em was Indians, they'd never bunch up like that; still, they got to be Indians, er Indians and Canadians. If they was French, er if there was more to the ambush than we know about, Toe-lee-ma would hev suspected it. No, Sergeant, this is a case where we can't allow too many suspicions to rob us of our good luck. The enemy hes jest been plain foolish is all, an' tho I can't figger out why, this is one gift horse I ain't gonna look in the mouth."

"I think, Captain Evans," said Hargreaves, "that you have been at this sort of thing long enough to have developed an instinct for it. Every minute we delay increases the possibility that the enemy may escape us, and I would rather trust to luck and charge 'em than let that happen. Whatever your tactic is, it is no doubt better than mine, so you'd best get on with it."

Uncle John did not hesitate. "The main thing is," he said, "to keep 'em where they are. As long as they're bunched up, they don't hev a chance. If me'n Toe-lee-ma was to git Allyn an' five of his men, we could git in behind 'em. We'd be lookin' right at their backs. There'd be eight o' 'em we could drop before they could turn around; there ain't probably more'n fifty yards on the east between the fence and the house. Ease my rangers in there to cut that off. You'll still hev plenty of men to place, like you planned to start with, right opposite the fence. When we're in position, Toe-lee-ma will give the signal fer everybody to start shootin'. It'll be as easy as spearin' fish in a barrel, jest as long as they sit there thinkin' we're still burnin' the cornfield. They're no doubt waiting for the light of the burnin' corn to outline us as we finish up on this edge and move toward the house. Now, if we'd been that foolish, we'd be in the barrel an' they'd be doin' the spearin'. We kin all be mighty thankful for the Mohegan's ears!"

"It's perfect," said Sergeant Hargreaves. "Unless one of my men blunders in the weeds, those hatchet throwers are as good as dead. But look, Allyn and Lyman are already more than half-way through the corn; we haven't time to waste congratulating ourselves."

"Owen," said Uncle John, "take the men and move 'em between the fence an' the house. You don't hev to git too close to 'em, jest close enough to keep 'em in."

The orders were more of a good-bye than orders. The rangers knew perfectly well what was expected of them. Evans and Toe-lee-ma moved quickly to find Allyn and Lyman. Lyman, who had been on several expeditions composed of elite troops selected from rangers, grenadiers, and light infantry, grasped the situation instantly and quietly moved his men back to Sergeant Hargreaves. Two of Allyn's men were detailed to continue on in the cornfield, making as much noise as possible, while Allyn and his five other men followed the ranger captain and the Indian to the north side of the field.

In order to preclude any chance of detection, Evans led his small party down the entire length of the field and into the woods at the far end. Once in the forest, he called a halt and reminded the men of the absolute necessity for silence.

"Walk single file in the footsteps of the man in front of you," he said. "Try to keep the line a pace apart, but watch yer feet. We can't have no twig-snappin' er branch brushin'. You all know what an Indian kin make of an unnatural sound in the woods. After we git through the fence, I want intervals of ten paces between each man. Look sharp, so you kin stop quietly when the man ahead of you stops. Kneel an' keep yer eyes right. If he moves forward, wait until he finishes his move. Then you move up, one at a time. That'll be the most important time fer us right there. We'll move up till every man kin git a fair shot. Keep yer mouth shut and breathe through yer nose, slow an' shallow. To an Indian like Toe-lee-ma here, a deep breath whistles over the teeth like a hurricane. Pick the middle o' the back fer yer target, if you kin. Nobody shoots till the owl calls. Then everybody shoots. With shots pourin' in on 'em from every side, them people in the stumps is goin' to want to run somewheres, but they won't know which way to turn, so don't fall back. Reload where you are and wait fer my order. Remember, we got the best crack at 'em. The sergeant's men ain't goin' to do much from the front, an' the curve o' the stumps is likely to give some problems to my men on the east. It's up to each man here to stay calm an' make his shot count. If there's somethin' you don't understand, speak up now."

Johnathan Evans paused briefly before entering the woods. "Better be sure you got it straight," he said, speaking very slowly and very carefully. "There's never two chances fer anybody in somethin' like this."

On the left flank, the rangers were already in position. Tom, on the end of the line farthest from the house, knelt behind the scant protection of a bush. He did not care for his evening's work at all. The battle at Ticonderoga took on new meaning for him. There, he had faced the enemy in open warfare. The whole affair had had an order; a form about it that suited his youthful idealism. Men of honor had performed honorably in the interests of cause and country. He recalled the spectacle of war and his enjoyment of it: the men at drill or at the target pits, the exchange of orders and salutes, the bayonets flashing in the sun. He recalled the majestic flow of the huge army over the waters of Lake George and the impressive array of brilliant red coats disembarking from the boats, bringing the color and the sound of glory to the untutored forest.

That, he thought, *is what war is supposed to be, but this— skulking in the night to shoot an' Indian in the back—and yet, the savages and the forest made the rules; we didn't.* He cherished the thought, for he knew it would make the killing easier; still, he couldn't help wondering what he would do if his rifle were zeroed in on another of his own kind. Suddenly an incomprehensible paradox of war occurred to him: a man of honor and integrity must always perform his duty, yet the actions involved in the performance need not be in themselves honorable. His thoughts flew back to the River Bend Tavern. He knelt in the dark forest, with murder in his hands, if not in his heart, and wished for some small particle of the wisdom of Robert Stevens.

No such doubts dwelled in the minds of Sergeant Hargreaves and his men. Their thoughts were as dark and primitive as the forest itself. Ghosts of dead comrades whispered in their ears, telling horrible tales of roasted and mutilated bodies. Hargreaves, staring intently into the darkness, hoping to see a head, an arm, a leg—anything definite to shoot at, instead saw the head of his nephew, blood and brains oozing out of the jagged chasm above the frontal lobe of the denuded skull. He squeezed his eyelids together hard, and the boy appeared again, smiling the innocent smile, the joy of life deep within kept nearly always on his lips. Hargreave's lids popped open, and the hairless, skinless skull reappeared. The blood rushed to his own head. He shook with the fever of hatred, and only the long, long years of discipline that made a British sergeant held him in his place.

Then everything changed. A gray, misty dawn began to break. The shades of night retired before the approach of the visible world. First, bushes and trees assumed distinct shapes. Fence and house took on normal outlines. An owl returning to his nest from the long night's hunt hooted dismally, and almost before his cry had faded on the wind, the thunder of rifles saluted the coming of day. Bullets ripped through leaves and bushes, making a sound that wind and rain could almost have duplicated. There were also the harder, heavier sounds of bullets that buried themselves in solid wood, and dull thuds followed by the sounds of humans crying out, first in fear, then in agony, and finally in terror and surrender.

"Hold yer fire, they're all done," shouted Captain Evans, but as he shouted, another volley erupted from Hargreaves's area, and new cries of panic and pain greeted the new day.

"Hold yer fire, I say, er I'll have every one o' you in front of a firin' squad," screamed the ranger as he ran forward, shaking his rifle furiously. "Can't you see us comin' in? Can't you see they're all done, Sergeant? Sergeant Hargreaves! Can't you keep yer men under control?"

Without waiting for an answer, Evans motioned Allyn's men and the rangers to pin the enemy against the fence. "Throw down yer weapons," he shouted. "Everything—knives and hatchets too. Throw everything down and turn this way with yer hands behind yer neck. Do it quick, er I won't be responsible fer what happens. Toe-lee-ma, tell 'em in Huron."

"French, not Indian," said Toe-lee-ma. "Canadians dressed and painted like Indians. Last night in the dark I could not be sure," he said apologetically.

"I'll bet that one understands English," said Johnathan Evans, "even tho he's the only one who ain't throwed his weapon down. There's a feller who likes hatin' too much to ever stop. Jest look at that face. He can't believe even now, with my rifle pointin' right down at his throat, that he's got to give the whole thing up."

Johnathan Evans jabbed the muzzle of his rifle hard into the Canadian's stomach, just below the breastbone. "I knew a feller that had his ribs cut away at the backbone, one at a time, and pulled out through his skin. Abenakis did it. Now, I ain't Abenaki, but I do know where to blow a hole in yer guts that won't kill you fer mebbe three days, if I put the bullet right, an' yer constitution's as strong as I think it is. I've been told that them three days would try the will of a saint. Now, put yer weapon down, so's I kin git a better look at you."

The man looked at Uncle John as if he thought he could actually burn him with the hatred in his soul, but he threw the rifle down, at the same time turning hips and shoulders, as if calculating the chances of breaking the circle that enclosed him. He began to speak rapidly and angrily in French, but another expertly delivered rifle stroke knocked the breath out of him.

"Speak English when yer talkin' to me, an' we'll git this thing settled a while lot faster—an' a whole lot easier," said Johnathan Evans, poking his rifle once more into the man's stomach. "Order yer men to make three lines an' stand at attention so we kin see what we got here."

The Canadian answered bitterly in broken English. "I can give no orders," he said. "We are habitants defending our homes and our fields, not soldiers. Our business is farming, not killing."

"You don't look much like farmers to me," replied Evans. "You made a bad mistake, dressin' like Indians. 'Sides that, you look like you've got every tribe east o' the Mississippi with you. There ain't no two o' these men dressed the same, er painted the same either. A dark night's a better disguise than all yer paint an' feathers."

Captain Evans peered through the gray down until he located Hargreaves. "Sergeant," he said, "this man ain't gonna give us no help, tho it's certain he's the leader here. Take your men and form the prisoners into three lines; git 'em to stand at attention, if you kin. Toe-lee-ma, Allyn—grab an arm. Twist this feller up straight so's we kin see what he really looks like."

The Canadian resisted silently, with a fierce, inner intensity, but Toe-lee-ma and Allyn grabbed his wrists and pulled his hands up behind his neck until he had to stand on his toes to keep his shoulders from being pulled out of their sockets. The pain was intense, and he stood with his face contorted and lips pulled severely back over his teeth, staring at the ranger captain with eyes that mirrored a soul so consumed with hatred that it did not recognize either pain or fear.

Evans reached out to grab the Canadian's hair. He pulled out two feathers, throwing them on the ground. "Was we supposed to think them feathers was attached to a scalp lock?" he asked scornfully. He continued to hold on to the hair with one hand, while the other energetically ground a mixture of wet leaves and grasses into the man's face. "Painted like a St. Francis Abenaki," he grunted. "I'll wager yer heart's as black as this stripe across yer nose."

Evans stepped back to survey the results of his efforts. "Sergeant," he called, "have a detail search those men. Strip 'em if you hev to." Then he reached out, ripping the Canadian's hunting shirt open. An early ray of the rising sun struck the man's chest. A flash of silver made Evans drop the shirt and stand back.

"A cross," he shouted. "By God, he's wearin' a cross. Seargeant! Sergeant, come over here an' hev a look. By God, I think we've got ourselves a priest."

Hargreaves came quickly to stand by Evans. Tom had not imagined that a man so broad could move with such speed. The sergeant stood staring at the Canadian. His eyes blazed brighter than either the new sun or the flashing cross. "Portneuf," he gasped. "Portneuf, Cure de St. Joachim." He closed his eyes against some inner vision of horror, shaking from a chill more severe and more penetrating than anything the cold forest dawn could produce.

"We've got you, you damned devil." His voice was a hoarse, shaking whisper. "I never really thought it would happen, not really. At first, right after you slaughtered poor, innocent Ned, I thought about what it would be like to get my hands around your throat. I thought about all the ways the Indians have of making a man die in agony, but I couldn't find one slow enough or terrible enough. I talked it over with the men—with Lyman, with Allyn—not one of us could come up with the one way to kill you that would satisfy the others. Well, priest, don't you worry. Now that we have you, we'll find a proper way to send you off to the devil."

Hargreaves turned toward the ranger. "You know what we've got here, don't you, Captain?" he said. "We've got the blackest devil in all the parishes on either side of the St. Lawrence. God knows how many soldiers he's murdered, scalped, and tortured, but I know of ten men from my own battalion, not counting my nephew, Ned, who was as promisin' a lad as England ever sent away to be mutilated in these damnable forests. What's more, we've got his whole cowardly crew, with the paint and feathers still on 'em. We'll see justice done this morning, Captain, right here on the spot, so there can't by any slipups. I know poor Ned will rest easier where we buried what was left of him, and every soldier garrisoned in the parish of St. Joachim will be able to walk his post without keepin' one hand on his rifle and the other on his hair; but day is breakin', so we'd better git at it. We've got the chief vulture and his flock, but there'll be other birds of prey, drawn by the night's scourin', roosting between us and the Montmorency. I know your rangers aren't used to this kind of work, Captain, so you can head back anytime you want to. My men know their business, Captain; we won't be far behind you." Johnathan Evans had stood quite still as he listened to the sergeant. No expression on his face or revealing change in position indicated that he had so much as heard Hargreaves speak, but his mind was busy evaluating the situation. The sergeant's words served as mirrors reflecting the broken bodies along the border and the black smoke curling above the Foster cabin, but the situation here was different, although the images did give Evans an understanding of the depth of Hargreaves's feelings and the near impossibility of changing the man's intentions.

"Sergeant," he said slowly, "my men understand the necessary evils of this kind o' war as well as yers do, mebbe even better, but look around you. There's thirty men over there, white men, an' it seems likely that some of 'em really are farmers, men pressured on the one side by the Catholic instinct to believe in a priest's words, an' on the other by French threats to turn Indians loose on their families. The least we kin do is look 'em over, one at a time. The way some of 'em reacted when we opened up, I'd bet they never fired a musket at anythin' but rabbits er squirrels, er mebbe deer. 'Sides that, this is a military expedition, not a turkey shoot. You're actin' under orders, Sergeant, which makes you personally responsible fer everything that happens. Now what you're fixin' to do don't fit my idea of the British soldier, an' I don't think it fits the gen'ral's either."

Hargreaves's reply was instant. "I'm afraid you're beyond your depth here, Captain," he said. "My orders make it quite clear that I am to do whatever is necessary to stop the settlers from siding with the French and terrorizin' the army. What I am going to do has been found necessary before and has been done before. As for the general, he intends to burn this country from Kamouraska to Pointe de Levy, and the only restrictions he places on scalps is that they come from Indians or Canadians dressed like Indians, but what is more important, you don't understand the nature of that priest. He isn't a true priest but spawn of the devil, materialized through some wretched woman's body and put on earth to do the devil's biddin'. Believe me, Captain, he has corrupted every last man you see over there beyond any hope of salvation!"

As he stood considering his reply, it occurred to Uncle John that Joseph Ely would probably have agreed with Hargreaves. Still, if he could only get the sergeant to agree to question the Canadians individually, there would be a good chance that the extra time would afford reason its chance to gain a foothold on the man's mind.

"Sergeant! Seargeant, look what we've found!" Evans and Hargreaves turned toward the sound of the voice. Allyn came running unevenly toward them, pumping harder with his right leg than the left. From his hand swung three scalps, the hair twisted and knotted together grotesquely by dirt and clotted blood.

"Found one in each line," Allyn said breathlessly. "They ain't fresh either. Can't tell how long they been carryin' 'em, but not long enough to find time to cash 'em in anyway, the bloomin' devils. One o' these could be Jess Leicester's, who was caught off post day before yesterday. If I knew fer sure, I'd ... I'd ... " Allyn could not continue. His face turned red and purple, and rage took his breath away.

Hargreaves shook uncontrollably, but his voice was calm, though raised to carry over the noise made by his troops as they herded the Canadians into a semicircle, swearing and jabbing at them incessantly with their muskets.

"I see you got 'em started," he said to Allyn. "Good, but don't let 'em know what's goin' to happen. We want this done right so we can get out of here. There's thirty of 'em, an' we don't have time to chase down strays now."

As for Hargreaves, he stopped and wrenched his head violently toward the sound of the musket shot that cracked sharply and reverberated through the open spaces. His glance flashed off the musket slowly being lowered and traveled beyond the small puff of smoke rising innocently toward the sky in time to see the Cure of St. Joachim jolt the ground with his knees, as if knocked down to pray, and then sprawl forward in a strange, final ritual of obeisance.

"The damn hellhound," he screamed. "He knew what was comin'. He cheated me. He cheated all of us." Suddenly he was running toward the fallen priest, still screaming. "What idiot let him get loose? Who fired that shot? Who ... "

Johnathan Evans wearily shut out the sergeant's voice. There was nothing he could do. Hargreaves was consumed by terrifying passion. Allyn ran after him livid with rage, and the men they ran toward were now hardly less intense in their hatred than their leader.

He motioned his rangers closer. At least he could save Tom from the dire spectacle that would follow the shooting of Portneuf.

"We might as well go home," he said. "Single file. Toe-lee-ma will lead. Then Charlie, Tom, an' Jed. I'll take the right flank; Owen, you take the left; Chicken'll trail. We'll change the owl fer a squirrel. Look sharp, now. Sun's up, an' every shadow in the woods between here an' Montmorency ain't jest a tree trunk."

Toe-lee-ma set out, running lightly, short-gaited and pigeon-toed, in a stride that could carry him all day and all night, if need be, without any loss of speed. The others followed automatically, but Owen Owens and Chicken Jones, commanders though they were of their feet, could control neither the thoughts of revenge that were akin to the sergeant's, nor the lust for scalps, valuable scalps, that was peculiarly their own. It would be sometime before either of the little Welshmen would regain the absolute concentration necessary to survival in the foreboding forest.

They ran swiftly over the flat farmlands of Chateau Richer, anxious to enter the forest labyrinth. Two volleys of synchronized shots sent synchronized echoes from the farmhouse, a series of undisciplined poppings followed, and then silence. Hargreaves was right. His men knew their work.

The rangers left by the same general route that had brought them in, but Toe-lee-ma was too wary to follow the same path. Anyone who had discovered any part of the earlier journey would lie in wait in vain. They moved steadily upward, turning west when the denuded cliff face offered neither foothold nor cover. The sun rose steadily in the sky, but the forest canopy turned its rays aside; still, the men sweated from their labors in the cool morning air.

The forest thinned out a little to let more light in. The way became easier and therefore more dangerous, but now the rangers could use all of their senses in the effort to escape detection. The device of the squirrel slipped to lower levels of concentration, for now no one figure was ever completely out of the sight of those who followed. Too, the forest offered enough space for silent movement, even seeming to contribute its own sounds as adequate cover for the minute errors that from time to time occurred. The rangers ran quickly, taking pleasure in the movement of their limbs and the swiftness of their progress, and then, so unexpectedly that its effect was paralytic, the squirrel chattered. For many seconds there was no other audible sound in the forest.

The rangers stood absolutely still, dominated by uncertainty, while Johnathan Evans used his almost magical skill to move invisible forward to meet the retreating form of Toe-lee-ma, who moved so slowly backward that he seemed not to move at all. The two did not come close enough to whisper, but the expressive hands of Toe-lee-ma told all that needed to be known. Uncle John communicated in the same manner, and the rangers spread out to form a thin, tree-protected line facing the forest in front of them just where it began to thicken.

Tom could see nothing strange about the forest except the forms of the rangers stretched out unnaturally behind the trees, like roots that had been penetrated by some hideous grub that had made them swell and twist in agony as it killed them. Nevertheless, for more than an hour he lay motionless, straining every fiber to detect by sound, sight, or smell the presence of the enemy, for the enemy was there. The hands of Uncle John and Toe-lee-ma had said so. At times he imagined he heard the grass part to let a hand or leg slide through, but the sound was never definite enough to have meaning.

Then suddenly, and, as usual, unexpectedly, the forest drama sprang into action. The defiant, blood-chilling death cry of an Abenaki warrior broke the silence, and Tom knew that the parting of the grass and the appearance of the feather had been real. He also knew that the death cry of the Abenaki had resulted from the successful interpretation by either Uncle John or Toe-lee-ma of similar partings and appearances. While the death cry was still trapped beneath the treetops, the sharp crack of a rifle was followed by a different howl of anguish, and Tom knew that another ranger had been at least partly successful. Then silence returned, for a time, to the forest.

Tom still lay motionless, the acuteness of his perception magnified by the brief action. Again, he heard the grass part, but this time he saw the hand that pushed it aside. A kind of horror ran up his spine. He wondered if it raised the hairs on his back the way a dog hackles rise in anger. The grass parted again, and again he saw the hand, and behind the hand appeared a face, and then a body, moving almost invisible until it disappeared behind a clump of bushes almost directly in front to Tom and not more than ten yards away. Then all form disappeared as the movement stopped. Wildly, Tom wondered at the skill of the Abenaki, at the same time shrinking from the thought that, motionless though he himself had been, the warrior knew exactly where he was and moved toward him with murderous intent.

Another rifle cracked sharply. Another death cry rose to shatter itself on the treetops, and Tom felt a sudden surge of anger at himself as he realized that his muscles had tensed revealingly at each sound. Before the anger could dissipate itself, Tom saw a gleam of metal from the bushes. He heard the snap of the flint against the firing pan, and then ... nothing. The Abenaki had misfired! As Tom triumphantly aimed his rifle at the bush, intending to make sure of his target before he shot, the Abenaki jumped up from behind his cover, tomahawk already drawn back past his ear, ready to risk everything on his speed and courage. He appeared to Tom like a demon straight from the depths of hell, grinning with the wickedness of the hell-born. The jagged bands of vermilion that ran from ear to ear across the eyes and the bridge of his nose could have found their inspiration in hellfire. Tom's rifle focused on the design of an officer's gorget painted in yellow on the demon's chest, and his finger pulled at the trigger as the Abenaki's hand moved into its throwing motion. Then Tom was suffused with feelings of helplessness and shame. Again, flint had aborted upon pan.

Oh, dear God, he thought, *Why didn't I change my priming powder when I had the chance? How many times has Uncle John told me that morning woods are damp woods?* The thought passed so quickly that no measurable time elapsed before Tom instinctively flattened himself against the forest floor, trying by sheer force of will to make the earth under him sink down. He felt a slight tug at his ear. Terror rose up from somewhere deep in his belly and moved him to frenzied action as he realized that the hatchet had pinned his ear to the outside of the tree. He wrenched the hatchet free, straining desperately to meet the Abenaki, whose falling body plummeted, knife poised at the shoulder, straight down upon him. Tom's shoulders turned and the hatchet blade turned with them, moving up and out, moving inside the knife that plunged down at his upturned chest, cutting through the arm thrown despairingly in its path, and biting deep into the Indian's face between the eyes, driving in until it obliterated the nose and reduced the mouth to four sagging folds of mutilated flesh. In the next instant, the point of the knife cut buckskin as the warrior's final reflex and the weight of the body, already devoid of its spirit, drove the knife through Tom's exposed chest. The force behind the blow rolled Tom over onto his back, and the dead Abenaki sprawled across his face. Tom closed his eyes in horror and ordered his muscles to push the Indian away, but no muscle responded. He struggled to open his eyes, but the lids would not move. A permanent blackness began to penetrate his body, seeming to shrink the tissues as it moved inward.

Then he was four again and in the smoke oven. He put what he had left of consciousness into an effort to scream, but he had waited too long. The blackness was too swift, and he succumbed to it.

8

THE PLAINS OF ABRAHAM

Young Tom Evans lay on his back, listening passively to distant sounds that seemed to have no point of origin and no destination. Some were sharp and some were muffled, but they were all a long way off. Occasionally, a tiny point of light would throb into existence somewhere in the deeper recesses of his consciousness, and shadow, indistinct and shapeless, would step before his mind's eye, only to fade away before it could materialize. Gradually the sounds came closer. The light began to flicker more frequently and move upward. Then the sounds moved into the center of the boy's existence, exploding into shrieks that created explosions of their own. Just as it seemed to Tom that his head would have to split to let the sounds out, they ceased instantly and entirely. In the frightening silence, Tom felt the weight of the dead Abenaki pressing down upon him. He felt his muscles contract in terror and expand in desperation, throwing the burden off. A sharp pain shook him from head to toe, and his eyes flew open, staring in hopeless confusion at the gray-green shape that bent over him.

"Well, now, Tom," said the gray-green shape, touching him with hands that proved both strong and gentle, "ye'd best let me help you ease back down on that pillow. You'll be sittin' up soon enough, lad, if you jest take it easy at the start an' do what of Jed tells you."

Tom remembered the touch of those hands. Over all the years, he still remembered those kind hands lifting him from the black fright of the smoke oven, and now he let them help him again, wondering at their incredible ability to express concern and affection.

Tom looked up at Jed Hawkins, in his confusion calling him Uncle Jed. "What happened, Uncle Jed?" he asked. "I don't seem to be able to remember what happened."

Tom lay still, beset by a series of images that never seemed to appear in the right place or at the right time.

"Why, Tom," said Hawkins, "you'll remember fine in jest a little bit. It's be downright unnatural if you wasn't a mite hazy 'bout what happened. It'll all come back soon enough, lad, an' a lot clearer too, after you've had a little more rest. Now me'n Charlie an' those feisty little Welshmen has been takin' turns sittin' here, jest waitin' fer you to sit up an take a little beef broth, made special to git you started on yer way outta here. A hospital ain't no place fer a ranger, anyhow."

Jed's face formed wrinkles of disgust. He moved to the curtains that boxed Tom's bed off from the rest of the ward. "This ain't gonna take no time at all," he said. "I'll be back before you kin figger out what ye're gonna ask me first." He parted the curtains and stepped out of sight before Tom could make a reply.

Jed was as good as his word. Before Tom could put his thoughts into any kind of order, Hawkins was back, carrying a bowl of steaming broth carefully in both hands. "Jest had to heat 'er up a little," he explained, drawing the chair over to the bedside and sitting down. "Now," he said, "we don't want to move that shoulder much jest yet. We don't want to start it bleedin' agin." He dipped a large spoon into the bowl and brought the broth up to his mouth. "Jest a little too hot," he said apologetically. "There, that oughtta do it. Yer gonna like this, Tom. Why, a man kin feel his strength comin' back with every swallow."

Tom allowed Hawkins to feed him the broth, although he did feel a little foolish as he adjusted his head to accept the first spoonful. Hawkins talked on cheerfully as the soup disappeared, answering Tom's questions and filling in the gaps in Tom's memory with expert comments of his own.

"No," he had said, "the wound ain't serious, leastways not anymore. It's a pretty good hole, but we kept the infection out, an they ain't nothing important got cut." "Yeah, it was a pretty hot little skirmish, but you were the only one who got unlucky." "No, we didn't have no trouble gittin' you back to Orleans." "Yeah, we're all here, but Toe-lee-ma and John. They come up with Satanis's footprint, scoutin' around after the shootin' stopped an' decided they'd best follow it. As fer as that goes," he said, "it ain't likely they'd find any other trail so apt to lead 'em to Bouchet and, sooner or later, to the girl."

Tom didn't want the last of the broth, but he ate it to keep Jed talking. He felt his eyes growing heavy, but he fought to deep them from blinking, fearful that Hawkins would leave before all his questions had been answered. Tom had an insatiable curiosity about the skirmish in the forest, about his part in it, and about its results, especially about the finding of the footprint. His questions came quickly, and Jed's answers were brief so that Tom had gained a reasonably accurate picture of what had happened by the time the last spoonful of broth had been taken, but, unaccountably, Jed's answers began to irritate him.

Why were they so short? Was the man deliberately trying to conceal the very details he wanted most to know? Had something happened that Hawkins was keeping from him?

Jed stood up and pushed the chair back. He took Tom's hand and held it in his own. Tom relaxed at the touch and fought harder to keep his eyes open. Suddenly he realized that he felt like crying.

"Tom, I got to go, an' you've got to git some rest. Mebbe I've stayed too long, as it is. You git some sleep, now. I'll come back later with Charlie Turner, an' that's a promise you kin count on."

Tom continued his efforts to keep his eyes open until the curtains parted and he was alone again. Then, with a sense of relief he had not expected to feel, he allowed them to close. Sleep came instantly.

Sleep became, indeed, the fundamental fact of Tom's hospital existence. At first it was natural and restorative, mending the torn tissues of both mind and body, but soon it became protective, offering relief from the total boredom of the hospital routine and the wearisome, irritating details of hospital life: the querulous demands of men well-along on the road to recovery; the fearful, wheedling questions of the seriously ill and badly wounded, seeking some kind of certainty which they could oppose to their fate; and the groans of mental anguish and cries of agony from the near dead and the dying. Tom developed a callousness that sent him in search of sleep whenever his nerves began to get the better of him. He would lie on his stomach and spin fanciful yarns about the future. Over and over again, he rescued Sally from Bouchet, inventing new situations for each rescue. He permitted the French to capture General Wolfe so he, Tom Evans, could cleverly rescue Wolfe, while at the same time capturing Montcalm. This daydream was a particularly effective one, usually bringing sleep before he could work out all the details of his numerous plans; hardly a day passed during which Tom did not work a series of miraculous escapes for the one general and captures for the other.

Still, Tom found hospital life unbearable. The rangers visited him whenever they could, enduring his vehement demands for release patiently. They listened quietly to each complaint, nodding sympathetically, and then proceeded to tell of their own activities. The war, Tom gathered, went on as it always had, with the British trying to keep the habitants peaceful and neutral, while the French tried to stir them up. The scalping and the scourings continued. Wolfe himself lay seriously ill in the loft of the farmhouse that served as his Montmorency headquarters, and the army was beginning to feel deeply that Quebec would never fall. The soldier wanted to go home before the cruel Canadian winter set in, and even the rangers seemed to have given up any hopes of success for the expedition. For Tom, personally, the most irritating point of all was the continued absence of Uncle John. Day after day passed without word of the ranger captain.

Surely, thought Tom, *the French could not capture Uncle John, especially when he has Toe-lee-ma with him, and yet, how could anybody prowl around behind their lines this long without being captured? And if he isn't a prisoner, or worse, dead, why hasn't he been able to locate Bouchet and Sally? He's certainly had enough time.*

Tom could see that the rangers were as much concerned about Uncle John's prolonged absence as he was, though they tried to deep their concern to themselves. They would not discuss the subject, except to mutter that it was only to be expected, but their reluctance had an adverse effect upon Tom. His anxiety merged with his hatred of the hospital into one fixation: he must find a way to free himself from this useless, unnecessary confinement and go in search of his uncle. If no alternative presented itself, he would simply run away. It would be easy enough to escape, and then the rangers would have to help him, but even if they refused, he would not stop. He would go alone. Sleep, which proved to be a jealous friend and would not come near Tom while he harbored this new companion in his bosom, left the boy to toss and turn and fret until daybreak.

Dawn came quietly enough to the hospital, bringing with it the dank river air that chills without killing. Tom drew his blanket up tightly around his neck to keep his limbs from shaking. Men who had passed the night in varying degrees of pain and discomfort clutched sleepily at their covers. Tom listened to the deep, half-conscious moaning of the fearfully injured striking the bass note of the chord of misery that would soon initiate the hospital's morning dirge. He had just begun to curse inwardly the cold that had prematurely touched the strings of agony when he noticed that the room had suddenly been filled by odd characters who appeared everywhere, like gray ghosts blown in on the river fog to materialize among the beds of the suffering soldiers, but their purposeful voices and movements soon dispelled any notions of occult visitation.

"Move 'em all down," said one of the voices, whose tone perfectly matched Tom's understanding of the word exasperation. "I said move 'em all down. Shove those beds up against the walls. Shove 'em up. Dammit, I don't care what's wrong with him. Shove the bed down there."

Tom's eyes focused on the shape that owned the voice. Its back was turned, but it wore a surgeon's garments.

"No, you rum-soaked fool," continued the voice. "Shove 'em together. No space between individual beds, dammit, just between lines. The closer they are, the warmer they'll die anyway. Where in the hell do they think I'm gonna get the supplies—not to mention the help—to take care of these men.

The voice came nearer and the shape turned. Tom could see the surgeon's face as gray as the dawn itself. A mouth that seemed too thin and short for the noise that came out of it was dominated by a huge, beaked nose that was swollen unnaturally and shot through with bulbous veins.

It almost seemed to Tom that the monstrous nose spoke and not the voice. "Now shove those beds on the north well over, right up ... no, no, no! You whiskey-fogged felon. Not that far. We have got to move between the lines, haven't we? By God, you must think we're stackin' bodies in a graveyard."

Rough, angry hands laid themselves on Tom's bed, tugging and pulling, lifting and pushing furiously. The bed jerked and bumped across the floor to the accompaniment of that irrascible, proboscidean satire.

"For the love of God, stop that," the voice trumpeted. "That man is nearly ready for duty. Are you tryin' to put him back on the casualty list? Damn me, if I don't think you're all bein' paid by the French."

The surgeon turned toward Tom's bed and glared malevolently at both Tom and the man who had moved him. The surgeon looked as if he had not slept much for a long, long time, and Tom could see that the wondrous nose owed at least a part of its grandeur to innumerable bouts with whiskey bottles.

"All right. All right. That's it in here," said the voice with a nasal inflection so pronounced that the sound seemed to issue from the promontory above the mouth. "Get those orderlies out in the hall and form 'em up. Sergeant. Have somebody help that grenadier in. I'll have a look at him while you put your scum in order. If any one of 'em causes trouble, I want him arrested. I haven't slept in at least twenty-hour hours ... probably won't for at least twenty-four more, and I'll not have my work held up by any sewer rat from the slums of London. By God, if they ever see the inside of a stockade, they'll wish they had stayed in Bartholomew Fair."

Tom sat up and rearranged his blanket, conscious of the dull throb of pain spreading out from the blue, puckered flesh that filled the hole in his chest. The confusion brought by the unexpected attack of the surgeon and his underlings was beginning to subside. The voice of the ward began to swell with anger, frustration, and curiosity.

Into the room stumbled a tall, gaunt soldier, one arm thrown loosely around the shoulders of the shorter man who helped him. The surgeon gestured impatiently, and the short soldier deposited the tall one on the bed next to Tom.

"Pull that shirt back," said the surgeon. "How do you expect me to fix what I can't see?" The next second his fingers were digging away at a mixture of rags, mud, and leaves stuck to the soldier's side. "Damn me," he said, "if I don't think half you men were physician's 'prentice to a squirrel." He leaned closer to the wound. "Small," he said. "Right place too, can't be much. Roll over, dammit. I have to see where it came out, don't I?"

The soldier dutifully rolled over, and the surgeon leaned even closer. "Never came out, did it?" he asked. "Hit a rib. Floating rib tho. Don't mean a damn, those floating ribs. Bullet's got to come out, tho. Infection. Might as well do it now. Sergeant! Get McNab and come in here."

The surgeon drew a flask from his black bag. "See this?" he asked the soldier. "It's precious. There's not much of it, but it's strong enough to blind you. You can have two swallows. Two swallows, mind you." He watched the soldier drink, gasp for breath, and drink again. He reclaimed his flask and signaled his men to hold the soldier down. Then he went to work.

It was over very quickly, really; there was a partially stifled shriek, a few moans, a few quick movements of the hand, and then the surgeon was speaking, flask again in hand. "Well," he said, "passed out, didn't he? Must lost a lot of blood before they stuffed that dirt in him."

He gazed pensively at his flask before tossing it back into the black bag. Then he picked up the bag and walked out of the room, leaving Tom, who had watched the operation with a concentration as intense as that of the man performing it, with a profound admiration of the surgeon's art. Not five minutes had elapsed between the original cut of the scalpel and the last wrapping of the bandage.

Tom flattened out on his back and thought of the events that had just passed so swiftly. The loud clamoring of the ward again irritated him; he tried to focus his attention on the grenadier, but the surgeon's visit had unleashed all the gossip of the past week, and Tom could not ignore the rumors and speculations that were being exchanged from bed to bed. The collective opinion of the ward was expressed by a grizzled private of the Royal Americans: "Wolfe got his ears pinned back when he tried to land on the Beauport Shore, an' he ain't had no luck above the city neither, not even way up at Pointe-aux-Trembles. He's spent the hull month of August lookin' fer a needle in a haystack, an he ain't found it. Why, they say he's spent so much time lookin' at the cliffs of Cape Diamond through his spyglass, it's a wonder he ain't bored a path. No, he's thrown the hull hand in, 'cause he can't do nothin' else."

"Either that, or he's getting ready fer one last big push, an' he figgers he's gonna need all the hospital space he kin get. Everybody knows he's burnin' up with fever an' ain't thinkin' straight. Even the other generals say so," replied a voice that Tom recognized as belonging to another Royal American.

"Now that ain't all possible, an' I'll tell you why," said the first voice. "This here is the first of September, that's why. Wolfe ain't had a word from Amherst, there's no way he kin git at Quebec by himself, an' it's the first of September. If we have to sit here another three weeks, we'll never git out. We'll be like ducks on a pond with their feet frozen in the ice. The winter'll do Montcalm's work for 'im, jest like he figgered all along. You an' I both know it's too late to start anythin', don't we? Now don't you figger a general's gonna be at least that smart? No, Bill, he's movin' all the sick an' wounded over to Orleans, an' we're gonna be the first ones shipped. I tell you, we'll be goin' downriver to Halifax afore the week's out."

The first voice, convinced either by the desire to go home or the logic of his friend's argument, now spoke up confidently and affirmatively. "Course yer right," it said. "Wolfe's been a mite disappointed, an' a mite sick, but he's still General Wolfe... an' one thing we all know fer sure, he ain't no fool!"

And so it went on. Tom began to feel the loss of the night's sleep. His thoughts began to divide, wandering first to the fate of Uncle John and Toe-lee-ma, then to Sally Williams, and back again to the hospital, unable to concentrate on any one train of thought, unwilling to exclude one sequence of events from another. His eyes closed and he fell into a shallow, restless sleep, only to be awakened by the groaning of the soldier next to him. He drifted off again and breakfast came, sending the ward into an uproar because the new arrangement of the beds caused such difficulty in serving. Then groups of men came in, filling up the remaining empty space with more beds. Soon the sick and wounded began to arrive. Some stumbled in alone and collapsed on the nearest unoccupied bed. Others, too weak to walk, were assisted by orderlies; few were carried in on hastily fashioned stretchers.

Several times during the day, the surgeon appeared. He would move quickly among the beds, occasionally turning to mutter something to the aidman who dogged his footsteps. His was the one figure that remained distinct in Tom's mind throughout the chaos of movement and sound that whirled through the room, turning the day into a nightmare. The surgeon never left the room alone. Always he was followed by the stretcher-bearers; always on the stretcher lay the shape of a body protected by a blanket from the merciless light of the world.

Dear God, thought Tom, *It's just like a lottery, except there aren't any winners, just losers, and it isn't even fair, because the odds don't pick the losers. The surgeon does!*

The image of the lottery faded before a stronger probability. *They were carried in dead,* he thought. *They died and nobody had time to notice it.* The idea overwhelmed him. He was still thinking about it when an oppressive night at last muffled the sounds of day, long enough to allow exhaustion to bring him release. He slept restlessly at first, but later peace came to him.

September second was a noisy, bustling day filled with movement, complaint, and endless discussion. Late in the day, the soldier who had been brought in on the first and bunked next to Tom had a visitor from his outfit, the Louisbourg Grenadiers. Listening intently to their conversation, Tom learned that the soldier had been shot while on picket duty at L'Ange Gardien. The next day, the Grenadiers had been sent back to the Montmorency campsite, and today, along with some other outfits, they had been ordered back to Orleans.

"But we won't stay here," the visitor said. "Rumor has it we're going to Pointe de Levy tomorrow or the next day, but nobody knows what for. Some of the boys say we're goin' home, but I don't know. Troop movements this large aren't that unusual.

We've been moved before. Still," Tom could see the man's head shaking doubtfully from side to side, "they did move all the women an' sick out yesterday. Maybe we are goin' home. I'd sure like to think so."

The two talked a long time. At last, the visitor got up to leave. "I'll be back tomorrow after evenin' mess," he said, "if we're still here an' I don't get caught for some extra duty. The boys will be glad to hear you're gettin' on so well. I don't mind tellin' you, when we saw where you was hit, we thought it was all up with you."

He moved away but turned back as if compelled to make just one more attempt to ease his friend's mind. The man's smile was both pleasant and genuine. "Why," he said, "the way you're comin', I better tell the sergeant not to worry about a replacement. You'll be back before we kin fit another man into your place."

The grenadier was as good as his word. He returned the following evening, full of news and bubbling over with good spirits. "It's pretty certain we're goin' home," he said. "Our outfit's bein' sent over to Levy tomorrow, probably to get ready to go on the troop ships. Wolfe has moved the whole Montmorency camp. Some outfits came here to Orleans, an' some went right over to Levy. Yes, sir, Wolfe's abandoned the intrenchments an' everythin'. He's gettin' the army together to take it home."

He kept his visit short. "I'd sure like to stay longer," he said, raising to leave in spite of the others' protests, "but I've got gear to repair and gear to pack, an if I was you," he winked broadly, "I'd stop layin' around pretendin' I wasn't fit fer duty. Yes, sir, if I was you, I'd get myself released tomorrow, pick up my gear, and go on over to Levy. Now, you do what I say, lad, 'less you want to be sent home on a hospital ship." He grinned good-naturedly and was gone.

Tom lay in the gathering dusk, knowing he could not leave Quebec without Sally. He saw himself standing on a cliff, watching the English fleet start its journey to the ocean. Behind him, he felt the eyes of the habitants and their Indian allies, watching from their forest cover the departure of the huge army that had ravaged their homes and fields. Soon they would creep out from behind their bushes and trees to take what vengeance they could upon the retreating British.

The night of September the third was very long. As soon as Tom slept, horrible nightmares besieged him until he awakened, sweating in sheer terror. When he was awake, his imagination ran wild, drowning him in a river of anguish made even more agonizing by the faint current of hope that ran beneath its tempestuous surface. Tom began to look to the east. Somewhere, way beyond the Basin of Quebec, far out on the ocean, the sun was already rising. It would come here, to the Basin of Quebec, even to this Godforsaken wilderness, and when it came the nightmares vanished. All he had to do was watch and wait. His vigil ended, as all vigils kept in faith eventually do, with the dawning of a new day and the promise of a new world. This time, the promise arrived, shortly after breakfast, in the very real form of Jed Hawkins, who brought with him a face that was one huge smile and a piece of paper that he waved joyously in his hand.

"Tom, Tom, we're gonna git you out o' here," were his first words. He shook the paper in front of Tom's eyes with one hand and threw a roll of clothing on the bed with the other. "Git yerself dressed so's I kin git rid o' this paper at the desk, an' we'll be gone. There's big doin's in the works, Tom," he said excitedly. "Big doin's! Well, c'mon boy, get a move on. We gotta git over to Pointe de Levy. Everybody's waitin' fer us."

Now the new morning sun shone brightly in Tom's mind, brightening and warming every corner where the images of the night lingered. He put his clothes on in no time at all, wondering why he had never realized before just how much fun it was to get dressed. He wanted to feel the sun shining right down on him. He walked past the desk where Jed presented the release and out into the sunshine. He walked toward the beach, watching the sunlight reflect off the buckles and muskets of the Louisbourg Grenadiers forming upon the Parade Ground.

"That's a good outfit," he heard Jed say. "Real fighters. They've been ordered over to Levy, along with the rest o' the army. Things are really movin' now. Wolfe's up an' movin' agin, an' when he moves, this army moves. Yesterday, I helped evacuate Montmorency. Wolfe wanted Montcalm to attack us, so he had several corps hide themselves during the night at their alarm posts. Then he put out a few guards with orders to look alert. I think Montcalm was fooled too. He sent a pretty big force right at the rear or the army, never suspectin' we was waitin' fer 'im. Then all of a sudden, he called 'em all back. Owen says he must've seen somethin' suspicious about the camp, but I heard some officers over at Levy say Monckton scared him off. Accordin' to them, Monckton, watchin' our withdrawal from the Point, saw what Montcalm was doin' an' sent two battalions in boats of the fleet to fake a landin' at Beauport. Accordin' to the reports, Montcalm fell for the fake and ordered his troops over there. Well, whatever happened, it sure saved the Frenchies a lot o' grief. I'll bet Wolfe was hoppin' mad about it anyway, 'cause he's in a fightin' mood." Jed laughed exultantly. "Yessir, you should have seen him yesterday. He's sure in a fightin' mood."

Tom pondered hard over Jed's words. Certainly Hawkins did not reflect the attitude of the men in the hospital. Tom's hopes began to soar. Jed had been out in the world; he had been in the middle of the action. He had even seen Wolfe. He must know what he was saying. Although Tom was still enjoying his freedom in the sun immensely, his thoughts now turned upon the hub of Jed's words.

"Listen, Jed," said Tom as Jed stepped upon the beach and headed for a line of canoes. "Everybody in the hospital said Wolfe had quit. I heard one of the Louisbourg Grenediers himself say his outfit was bein' sent to Pointe de Levy to git ready to ship home. Now that doesn't sound like Wolfe's in much of a fightin' mood, as far as I kin see."

"Well, now, Tom," replied Jed disdainfully, "you don't think the gen'ral's goin' to tell everybody in the army jest what he plans to do, do you? Why, he might jest as well send the French a written copy o' his plans. Still, anybody who kin read sign kin tell he's gonna fight."

"I ain't questionin' yer jedgment, Jed. You know that," the boy said seriously, "but it ain't the easiest thing in the world to read sign from a hospital bed."

Jed grinned good-naturedly, stepping into a canoe and picking up a paddle. "And that's fer sure," he said, punctuating his sentence by noisily but expertly spitting tobacco juice at the St. Lawrence. "But, look you," he said, thinking to himself that he had spent so much time with Owen and Chicken that he was starting to talk like them, "Wolfe called Murray, Monckton, and Townshend over fer a git together a few days ago, an' then things started happenin'. He didn't call them over jest to tell 'em he was goin' home. Fact is, I heard he told 'em he was goin' to go right up them cliffs under the Plains of Abraham, right under the Frenchies' noses. He probably told 'em that jest to make sure they understood he meant business without havin' to tell 'em where he really meant to fight, but he means to fight all right. Then we got orders to git out of Montmorency. Now he's givin' orders to git the whole damn army together at Pointe de Levy. He's causin' everybody a lot o' trouble that ain't necessary, if all he's goin' to do is go home. Not only that, but you look sharp when we pull into Levy. You'll see them ships ain't rigged fer no trip to the ocean. Fact, the way the fleet is movin' up an' down the river, you'd sooner guess they was goin' to start a ferry service. You look at all them flat-bottomed boats too, bein' loaded up with baggage an' stores. Must be thirty or more. My guess is they're takin' the stuff upriver."

Jed interrupted himself to place a thumb and forefinger's worth of tobacco in his mouth, rolling it up behind his lips and shoving it over into his left cheek with his tongue. He rested his paddle on his knee, watching Tom work, half expecting the boy to offer some comment. After another second of silence, Jed continued both his paddling and his talking.

"All right," he said, "here's the clincher. Me'n the boys has been ordered up to Goreham's Post to join his company fer special duty, an' it ain't scourin' duty either, tho' lots o' rangers hev been given orders to burn everythin' left standin'. We got to be there this afternoon too, to help git things ready. Somebody's gonna ford that river right where it's only fifty feet across, right where the French batteries at Sillery kin lay it on 'em. Now, do you think Wolfe's goin' to all this trouble jest to embark the army above Quebec out o' gun range? No sir, Wolfe's gonna hit 'em good somewheres, an' to me it sure looks like the north shore between Cape Rouge an' Cape Diamond, an' he's so damn smart he'll manage it. He'll drive the French army crazy tryin' to figger out what he's goin' to do. You kin see, Tom, that every move he's making' could mean he's gettin' ready to go home, er it could mean he's gearin' up fer one last win er go-to-hell push. The French are gonna want to think he's quit, an' they're gonna say he has to quit, because the cold weather hes come and he can't expect no help from Amherst now, but they can't be sure. They'll be watchin' the ships go up an' down the river, watchin' every move, tellin' themselves that if he is damn fool enough to attack, they'll be waitin' fer 'im, but all the time they'll be thinkin' he's goin' home 'cause that's what they'd do if they was him."

Tom listened silently. He wanted to agree with Jed, but he couldn't escape the fear that the men in the hospital had been right. As they drew into Pointe de Levy to beach the canoe, Tom tried to fix every detail of the scene in his memory: the number and types of ships, their disposition and appearance, the flat-bottomed boats and the baggage strewn along the shore, the regiments represented by the men swarming along the shore; he even studied the faces and attitudes of the soldiers they passed, trying to read in their expressions and actions the determined excitement of men preparing to fight, but his efforts were in vain. He had seen nothing that would either confirm or deny Jed's opinion.

There's nothin' I kin do but string along with Jed an' see what happens, Tom thought. *There might not be anythin' to prove he's right, but there ain't nothing to prove he's wrong either.*

Tom's face brightened as he spotted the other rangers, who stood at the edge of a small drill field, watching a squad of light infantry practicing brush tactics. They were too absorbed in drinking their bottles of spruce beer and cheering the sweating infantrymen on, interspersing their cheers with advice that was as caustic as it was vulgar, to notice Tom and Jed's approach, but the warmth of their greeting more than made up for its tardiness. For the first time in weeks, Tom felt the joy of life pulsing in him as these hardened men of the forest revealed the softer side of their nature. For a moment, he felt almost as good as he had that day at the River Bend Tavern, when Uncle John had made it clear to everyone that his nephew, Tom Evans, was a full-fledged ranger, entitled to all the respect and privileges the title conveyed. He pictured his own pewter mug, standing on the shelf behind the bar, right next to Uncle John's. He felt strong and secure, and he wondered how he could have so seriously doubted the providence of God. Surely men like these, with leaders like General Wolfe and his Uncle John, could never fail when right was on their side. Suddenly, he became absolutely certain that the fall of Quebec and the rescue of Sally Williams were as inevitable as God's final triumph over Satan on the Day of Judgment.

Tom took his happiness with him down the road that led away from the Pointe de Levy encampment. He took comfort in the fact that two rangers ran before and two behind him, welcoming as he ran the pains in his chest and the weakness in his legs as proof that he would quickly regain the strength that the days of convalescence had taken from him. He was content to wait in silence outside Goreham's Post while Jed checked out the details of their orders, and he willingly ran after Jed over the half-mile that separated them from the River Etchemin. When they stopped at the river's bank, he listened intently.

"It's work we can afford to git sloppy at either. General Murray's goin' to ford the Etchemin tomorrow with four battalions, probably better'n two thousand men, if they're anywheres near up to strength, an' then he's gotta march 'em eight miles upriver. Our job is to scout them eight miles tonight–an' that's all night, boys–an' report everythin' we see in the mornin'. Now, that don't mean jest lookin' out fer an ambush, tho that's possible, seein' as he's only got two thousand troops an' they's plenty o' habitants an' Indians runnin' round loose. No, the job's harder than that. They want to know everythin' and anythin' we find. If there's French watchin' the path, they want to know that right away, 'specially if we think there's an officer with 'em. If there's one Indian in the woods, they want to know what he's doin' there an' what tribe he belongs to. If we don't see no people, they want to know what sign we see, even if it's a day-old mocassin print. As I already told Tom, I think Wolfe's plannin' to take one more crack at Quebec, an' if he's goin' to have any chance o' success, he's got to hit 'em when they ain't lookin'. Well, he knows they're watchin', but he's got to find out jest where they're watchin' an' how close. Then he'll let 'em look all right, but he'll arrange things so they can't understand what they're seein', er mebbe he'll trick 'em into lookin' too hard in one direction so's he kin whack 'em in another. We probably never will know what use he makes o' what we find out, but every man here has got to understand how important this job is."

Jed paused to study each ranger's face, trying to read in their expression the impact of his words. Tom, doing a little studying of his own, saw that Jed was satisfied with his reading.

"The general don't make mistakes," said Owen. "I've had a talk er two with 'im, personal, an' it's only natural he'd pick Owen Owens and the rangers fer a chore like this one. If I ain't done nothin' else fer 'em, I've taught him that he kin depend on the rangers when he's got somethin' important to do that he ain't got the time to do hisself."

A variety of expressions appeared on the rangers' faces as they stared at Owen, but no one cared to endure the torrent of abusive boasting that any objection to his pretensions would bring forth.

"I'm fer settin' up camp right here," said Hawkins. "We kin git ourselves a good meal an' plenty o' sleep to start out on. You never kin tell when you set out on a job like this jest how long it's gonna last."

The rangers found themselves in agreement, and each set about his allotted task expertly and efficiently. Still, the afternoon shadows had lengthened considerable before the men were ready to turn in. Tom was surprised to find just how much the day's activities had exhausted him, but a deep, healthy, refreshing sleep began its restorative work almost as soon as he closed his eyes. Sleep filled him from hair root to toenail, pushing out every care, relaxing all the fibers of mind and body, curing him with nature's own prescription. When he finally awoke under the gentle pressure of Charlie Turner's hand, he felt renewed. The hope inspired by the experiences of the day surged in each wave of returning consciousness. Tom jumped to his feet. He was ready for whatever the night might bring.

The darkness was overwhelming. Tom knew even before they forded the Etchemin that the night would be very, very long. Going upriver, they stayed close to the path which, though hardly more than an indentation in the tangled forest floor, was the route intended for Murray's battalions. Aided by the impenetrable blackness, the forest obstructions were able to defeat the most cautious and skilled efforts of the rangers to avoid them. Finally, they stumbled out upon the path at the western boundary of their scout. As if by mutual consent, they walked to the cliff's edge and stared down at the St. Lawrence.

Charlie Turner broke the silence. "The water's angry enough," he said, "but I'd sure like to take a canoe back down to the Etchemin. We didn't find nothin' on the way up, an' we ain't gonna find nothin' on the way back. Hell, we scouted the area from St. Nicholas on down pretty well anyway. 'Sides that, what good would it do the French, er anybody fer that matter, to come prowlin' around here. We ain't got no camps er outposts er nothin' in here. Why, they couldn't even git a scalp, 'less they took it off some hair-brained idiots like us, who ain't got nothin' better to do than stumble around in the dark runnin' into trees."

"Well, Charlie," replied Jed, "that's sure a hard argument to answer, but you know as well as the rest of us that we've got to go back the way we come. Only thing is, we got to go back a little deeper an' a little slower. Mebbe if we don't hit the last mile er two till daybreak, we'll turn somethin' up." Jed held up his hand. "Now, wait a minute," he continued. "I got my share o' bumps and cuts too, but they ain't no use complainin'. We all know what has to be done, so we might as well git started."

"Look here, all of you," said Owen. "Didn't any o' you swamp rats ever stop to think that what we don't see might mean jest as much to a man like the gen'ral as what we do see? Swear, sometimes I believe you think the whole world's jest as ignorant as you are." He took time to let his head shake disgustedly from side to side. "Now, let's git back in them woods an' do what we're supposed to do, an' I don't want nobody slackin' off 'cause he thinks he knows more than the gen'ral either." The rangers' sense of duty forced them to agree with Owen. They recrossed the path and again entered the woods, each man determined that, should any sign be overlooked, the fault would not be his. The hours passed slowly and uneventfully. Dawn broke, but its early rays could not penetrate the forest canopy. The rangers struggled on until they could hear the Echemin ahead of them. Soon, the trees thinned, and they stood on the bank of the river, nerves and clothing frayed by the indefatigable claws of the forest. They had nothing to report, and the sense of frustration was deep in each man—too deep to be eased by the usual consolation found in thoughts of a difficult task well-done.

"Might as well go right on in an' tell 'em what happened," said Hawkins unhappily. "Owen, why don't you do it; the rest of us kin go over to the tent an' git a good breakfast started."

Owen hadn't wanted to make the report either, but he had accepted the task without argument, stepping disconsolately into the water, heading for the opposite bank and Goreham's headquarters with head and shoulders bowed, as if he bore a burden too great for his small frame to carry. Now, as the rangers watched him approach their tent, they could see that the act of delivering the report had not lightened his burden. Tom was quick to interrupt his own breakfast to hand Owen a trencher, as the wiry little man came over and hunkered down, Indian fashion, by the fire.

"Well, Owen," Jed asked, "how did it go? How did they take it?"

"Never said a word," Owen replied. "Some fancy dude wrote down everythin' I said on a piece o' paper, an' then he made me sign it. But the worst part o' the whole thing is that we got to do the job over again. That's right," he said, anticipating the incredulity that appeared on his comrades' faces, "we got to do it over. Seems like Monkcton and Townshend are takin' three more battalions across the ford tomorrow, so they want us to run them eight miles all over again."

"Well," said Jed, "it's gotta be necessary, er we wouldn't hev to do it. Like you said, Owen, what we don't see probably means jest as much as what we do see. I guess we better get what rest we kin agin' the night, 'cause there ain't nothin' more wearin' on a man than a tough miserable job that don't seem to hev no point to it."

Hawkins cleaned his trencher and his cup and strode toward the tent. The rest were not long in following. Sleep appeared to them not only as the replenisher of their vitality, but also as the only possible release from their anxieties. As they both needed and wanted sleep, no man among them had to search very long to find it.

It was, in fact, very fortunate for the rangers that they had taken to their blankets so early in the morning, for the events of the day made sleep impossible. First, Howe and his light infantry came marching right past their tent and began setting up a temporary encampment. The forest resounded with the sounds of a busy army. Men shouted orders and cursed vehemently, axes thudded into trees, hatchets pounded on tent stakes. The rangers hid inside their blankets and turned left and right, trying to turn away from the noise, but there was no escape.

Then the forest shook with a new sound, deeper and more pervasive than the others. The very ground under the rangers seemed to shake, forcing them out of their quarters. The battalions of Murray, over two thousand strong, were marching to the Etchemin.

"We sure as hell can't git any rest with all this goin' on," Charlie Turner shouted. "We might as well go down to the river an' see how they plan to git all them soldiers across without losin' any of 'em."

"Well now, you boys kin go down an' watch the redcoats swim in the river,' said Chicken Jones, "but I believe I'll jest go over an' talk to some of them light infantrymen. You never kin tell what kind o' useful information I might pick up. Them light infantry soldiers is real fightin' men, fer Britishers, an' I've gotten real fond of 'em, I have."

"You mean you've gotten real fond of somethin' you saw one of 'em carryin'," hooted Owen. "What was it Chicken?"

"Some trinket they took off a French officer, er somethin' more substantial, like mebbe a barrel o' rum? Oh, you'll pick up somethin', all right, but it won't be information!"

"Why Owen," replied Chicken Jones, "it's downright unfair, not to mention ungrateful, o' you to say things like that. Now, I've been known to do a little tradin', it's true, an' I have been known to come out ahead, once or twice, but…"

The rest of Chicken's remark was lost in the thunder of cannon. In the distance, the guns of Pointe de Levy opened up in earnest; out on the river the frigates began blasting away at the north shore. The French were not long in replying, and soon the batteries at Sillery began to rain death and destruction upon the banks of the Etchemin.

"C'mon, we'd better git to the river," shouted Jed Hawkins, "them men down there are catchin' hell." Jed ran swiftly, but Owen Owens was the first to reach the ford. There really wasn't much the rangers could do to help. The British troops were superb. The discipline Wolfe had instilled in them was superior to the savage roar of the cannon. The lines moved across the ford quickly and competently. When a man was hit, he was picked up so quickly by the men before and behind him that there was no break in the lifelines that moved through the cannon fire, as if they had been doing that sort of thing all their lives. The entire action was over much more quickly than Tom had imagined possible, and the youth found himself cheering and shouting wildly as the last line of troops left the water and moved toward the protection of the forest.

Tom stood in the water, almost hypnotized by the quiet courage of the British columns, while a hand pulled roughly at his elbow. "C'mon, you young fool. Get out o' there," screamed the voice of Owen Owens. "Do you think I want to tell Johnathan Evans I let his nephew stand out in a thunder storm o' cannon an' git his head blown off?"

Tom obeyed Owen's urging, at the same time unaccountably resenting it. On the way back, scenes of glory filled his mind. In the tent, while the other rangers grabbed their blankets to store up sleep for the night's scout, Tom lay wide awake. Files of British troops kept marching through his mind, moving in rhythm to the booming cannon of the enemy without a single break in the order of their lines. In his mind's eye, he saw those same files marching straight up the unscalable cliffs that protected Quebec City, forming up on the Plains of Abraham and facing the French with the same, almost automatic, determination that had carried them across the Etchemin. Then Tom's thoughts ran wild. Three times he fought the battle of Quebec, each time, though severely wounded, leading his troops to victory, before he finally drifted off into a restless slumber. Inexperienced as he was, Tom could not play the waiting game the way his comrades did, but as the days passed, he came to understand that a large part of the soldier's life, even in war, consisted of just waiting. He marvelled at the way active men like Jed Hawkins and Charlie Turner could sit, hour after hour, and do absolutely nothing but eat and drink and talk. Tom thought the eighth day of September would never end. Dark storm clouds blackened out the sky over the Quebec Basin, unleashing a hard rain that beat the St. Lawrence into and angry torrent and pelted the forest mercilessly. The war had to stop while nature proved to these beings, who made her waters ugly with warships and wantonly cut down her forests with no purpose except to exterminate one another, that the ultimate power in the world was not theirs, but hers.

The following day brought no relief. The rain continued to come down in torrents, and Tom's mood grew as dark as the skies above. The arguments between Owen and Chicken no longer amused him. *Owen's just a braggart and Chicken's just a thief,* he thought bitterly. *Why, when everybody else was down to the river doin' what they could to help, Chicken was looting Howe's camp. No wonder Uncle John warned me against them.*

In fact, nothing that occurred could please Tom now. He was sick and tired of the continual re-hashing of each night's scout. Why did they have to deep going over them, proposing this and suggesting that? One was just as fat a failure as another, just as the sixth of September had been like that fifth. The only difference was that four battalions had forded the Etchemin instead of three, and Monckton and Townshend had led them over instead of Murray. So what if the soldiers did have orders to take just one shirt and one pair of stockings, besides what they were wearing? And why was Jed so fascinated by the embarkation of the troops? "Yep," he would say, always shaking his head wisely, "they marched 'em eight miles upriver, put 'em on the flat-bottoms, and took 'em out to the ships." Then, obviously taking delight in this, he would say, "I heard the forty-third's quartered on the Sea Horse, yes sir, quartered on the Sea Horse!"

Good Lord, thought Tom, *what did he think they were going to do with the troops when they got up there, drown 'em?* And then, after Jed Hawkins, Owen Owens would always enter the conversation—always Owen, never anybody else. Tom thought that the peculiar predictability of these men was beginning to irritate him even more than the emptiness of what they said.

"Ain't he the one," Owen would say softly, like a woman trying to hush up a child at meetingtime. Then again, slapping his thigh smartly, bent over in laughter, loudly this time, "Ain't he the one! He's got the French dizzier than a half-broke hound on the trail o' a granddaddy fox. Why, he's got Bougainville runnin' thirty miles up an' down the river on foot tryin' to keep up with every ship that drifts down with the tide. Then, when he got tired o' runnin' him up an' down till his coat was full o' briars an' he was trippin' over his tongue, he headed right at 'em. I'll bet Bougainville jumped right out o' his skin fer joy. Imagine how good he must have felt, after runnin' hisself an' his men right into the ground, when he thought Wolfe was gonna hit 'im at his own headquarters. Course, he put his call out soon as he saw Holmes takin' his part o' the fleet upriver. He had plenty o' time to get all his men together, 'cause the ships didn't open fire till the afternoon. Bourgainville must have said to himself, 'Let 'em come. I'll put an end to this foolish thing right here an' now. When I git through with 'em, they'll be glad enough to git back on them ships an' sail straight fer home, an' that'll be the end o' this eternal runnin' up an' down the St. Lawrence, night and day, tryin' to keep up with a bunch o' bastards that're jest sittin' on a boat smokin' a pipe an' laughin' their fool heads off at us!'"

No one ever interrupted. No one ever added a comment, although every man knew the story of the seventh as well as

Owen. Always, they sat and listened appreciatively, nodding their heads and tapping their feet in a kind of silent applause that sent the blood rushing furiously to Tom's head. He, in turn, always just sat there, face burning, angry at Owen because he kept talking, angry at the others for listening, angry at himself for not shouting out that they were acting like a bunch of old women spreading gossip at a sewing circle. *Why*, he wondered, *don't I just tell them all to shut up and go away?*

But he couldn't. So Owen always kept right on talking. "The best part of all was putting the troops in the boats an' rowin' up an' down like they was lookin' fer a landin' place. Bougainville must have thought, My God, here they go again, runnin' our tails off, but this is the end of it. We'll git 'em now, soon as they put in, then we'll shoot their tails off, an' that'll put an end to this damn runnin'."

Owen slapped his thigh again and bent over double, clutching his ribs, body and features contorted with mirth. He choked and snorted, unable to control himself, laughing shrilly until Tom was nearly ready to reach over and clout him. The spasm passed, and Owen continued, "An' then, jest as smart as you please, they rowed back to the ship an' sailed off. Bougainville must have felt like somebody hit him right between the eyes with a hickory cudgel. I'd like to of been there when he come to, when he finally realized how he'd been had." Another spasm started, shaking Owen from head to toe. "I'll bet he broke every record the French ever had fer cussin'," he gasped, and then he completely gave way to the fit of laughter that seized him. As always, the others joined him, forming a wild chorus of antiphonal laughter.

Tom got the feeling that the whole world was dominated by chaos. He saw again the French cannon shot smashing into trees, breaking them off and flinging their tops fiercely to the ground. Shells thudded into the riverbank, tearing out huge chunks of sod and throwing up geysers of mud and rocks. Bombs burst in the air, hurling their fragments in a thousand directions, so that no bit of space was secure from their penetration—but through the wild confusion, he saw the lines of British troops moving unflinchingly, their order and precision impervious to the destruction that whirled around them. He concentrated on the image of the troops, following them one by one across the river and into the forest, until very suddenly his feelings and his experiences magically came together, generating the hot, white heat of understanding. He knew now what held those lines together. Under Wolfe's discipline, these men had made duty a habit, and upon that habit, the traditions of the regiments had worked a miraculous change. These men marched magnificently through the chaos of war because their regiments had marched through all the wars of their history in just this manner. Each soldier knew that his sergeant fully expected it, and they could not fall below those expectations. They walked straight past fear and terror, past all the basic instincts that pulled at their footsteps and tugged upon their hearts, because they had learned to follow that one glorious point on the compass of civilization to which men have given the exalted name of honor.

Tom's spirits rose, buoyed up by the new truth that he cradled preciously in his bosom. The rain lifted, bringing renewed life and activity to Wolfe's army. September tenth was a busy day for the regulars, but just another day of watching and waiting for the rangers. Starting from a point above Cap Rouge, Holmes's fleet drifted down river with the ebb tide all the way to Quebec. The weary Bougainville and his exhausted troops could do nothing but follow them until the flood tide moved the ships back upriver. Again, Bougainville had no choice. He turned and led his men back across the high cliffs, back to Cap Rouge.

About midday, Owen and Chicken, having nothing else to do, went up to headquarters, "jest to hang around and see what's goin' on," as Owen put it. It was late in the afternoon when they returned with exciting news.

"Well, first off," said Owen in reply to a question from Jed Hawkins, "they've pulled about half the troops off the transports upriver and quartered 'em at St. Nicholas. Good thing too. It ain't no picnic to set out a storm in a troop ship. This way they kin git their equipment dried out, 'specially the clothing, knapsacks, 'n blankets, but wait'll you hear the big news. Me'n Chicken heard somethin' that'll knock you right off the stool ye're sittin' on, tho I can't say as how it came as any big surprise to me."

"Owen," said Charlie Turner impatiently, "sometimes you kin be as exasperatin' as a dog that keeps runnin' off a bear track to chase squirrels. Now, I ain't gonna listen to no long-winded speech tellin' me how much smarter you are than the rest of us when it comes to figgerin' out jest what this here army's goin' to do. If you got somethin' to say, jest come right out an' say it."

"You ain't got no stories 'bout a coon dog bellerin' up an empty tree trunk, hev you, Charlie?" asked Owen innocently. "I've heard some o' them stories that'd make a grown man cry."

Owen disdainfully turned his back on Charlie and spoke again to Jed. "Now, as I was sayin'," he continued, "seems like Admiral Saunders had a meetin' with all his commanders an' told 'em he figgered it was time to go home 'cause he didn't want his ships to git froze in the river, an' ice floes was already beginnin' to form in the Gulf of St. Lawrence. Naturally, bein' sailors, they all agreed, includin' Holmes, so they sent word to Wolfe, tellin' him what they had decided. Well sir, the gen'ral, he rushed over to Saunders's flagship an' told him he'd found a secret path that led right up to the Plains of Abraham. If a hundred an' fifty good men could git up there an' overpower the guard posted at the top, why the rest of the army could walk right up like they was goin' on a picnic. Now, Saunders, he ain't no fool; fact is, I b'lieve he's about the smartest sailor I ever did see, so he didn't give Wolfe no more trouble 'bout goin' home."

"That's good news all right," broke in Charlie Turner, who was still angry at Owen, "but I don't see nobody faintin' away in surprise. Fact is, it jest proves what we all been sayin' right along, an' it don't change our situation either. We still got to sit around this stinkin' tent dodgin' flies an' skeeters till Wolfe's ready to move. By God," he said, "I've have a bellyfull o' hangin' around this sweatbox doin' nothin'."

"Charlie, if I was you I'd quit complainin'," said Chicken. "They got some duty rosters posted up at the orderly room that'd make you turn green if you saw yer name on 'em. 'Sides, not that the weather's cleared they're sendin' out scourin' parties to every point on the compass. Matter o' fact, there's one rumor that says all the ranger companies are gonna be joined together under Colonel Scott, beefed up with handpicked regulars, an' sent out to destroy everythin' that's either built er growin'. They're sup- posed to burn this whole damn miserable country right down to the ground. There's gonna be plenty o' action passed 'round, an' you kin be sure we'll have more'n our share after everythin's said an' done."

Chicken's right fer sure, thought Tom. *When Wolfe attacks Quebec, every outfit's gonna have its own job to do.* Throughout the twilight and evening hours, Tom remained virtually silent, not wanting his own private thoughts limited by the garrulous and often quarrelsome speculations of the rangers. Even after the others had finally taken, still grumbling, to their blankets, Tom could not sleep. Over and over again he considered the possibilities opened up by the news Owen and Chicken had brought from Goreham's Post, but he could not decide which course of actions offered the best chance of rescuing Sally. If his orders took him with Wolfe's army to the Plains of Abraham, they would still have to win the battle on the Plains before they could besiege the city, and the time lapse between the engage- ment and the surrender of the city could offer the crafty Bouchet innumerable opportunities to slip away. On the other hand, if his orders sent him on a scouring expedition, even to the north shore below Quebec, he would have very little chance of find- ing Sally. In the first place, Bouchet might never have brought her east of the city, and in the second place, if he had, Tom still would have no idea where to look. The longer Tom thought, the more he came to feel that his particular orders really would make no difference. He would have to wait for the fall of Quebec. Once the city fell, all Canada could not hide Bouchet from him. He fell asleep picturing himself tracking Bouchet through the snow-covered Canadian forests.

The rangers stayed late in their blankets on the following morning, their desire to shorten the waiting period of the day struggling against the habit of getting up with the morning sun. Finally, sick of their blankets and themselves, they began poking around at fixing breakfast, confining their comments to the necessities of the task. Each man felt that everything that could be said about their situation had been said the day before. Breakfast, with its function reduced to the mere consumption of time, was tasteless and unsatisfying. They ate in morose silence, weary with the peculiar weariness that inactivity brings to active men. So deep was their languor that the noisy, inept approach of the British lieutenant who clumsily threaded his way through the forest obstacles aroused in them neither curiosity, annoyance, nor laughter.

"I say," said the lieutenant, irritably freeing his coattails from the clutches of a small sapling, "do you chaps know where I can find a ranger called Thomas Evans? The major said he was tenting just over the hill, an' damn me if I haven't had to walk a good half mile in these beastly woods, wearing my last clean uniform. Well, the old gent will hear about this, they can be sure. Paid damn good money for my commission, he did too." He stopped to take out a lace handkerchief and dab delicately at his perspiring brow. "Well, well," he continued, "what's the matter with you chaps? Can't you understand the king's English? Do you know this fellow Evans, or don't you?"

There was silence as the rangers studied the strange young officer who fidgeted nervously in front of them. At last, Tom placed his trencher on the ground and stood up. "I'm Tom

Evans," he said, wondering in amazement what possible business this effeminate fool could have with him.

The officer stepped back a pace, bringing his hand up to grab his chin. Tom wondered if the action was designed to keep his face from twitching right off his head. "Damn me if it doesn't speak," the officer said in mock amazement. "If I hed you in London, many's the gentlemen who'd put up his pence to see such a strange sight."

The rangers had heard enough to activate their sensibilities. They stood up and moved toward the lieutenant.

The Britisher moved back another pace, limbs and features twitching furiously. "Here now," he said, "don't you fellows try to interfere with a king's officer carryin' out his orders. Hev you all thrown in irons, I will. General Wolfe himself sent for this man, and I warn you he'll brook no interference from scum like you."

The rangers moved another step closer, a meaningful step that boded ill for the fatuous lieutenant.

"Wait jest a second," said Tom. "If the general wants to see me, he must have news of Uncle John. I'd best go with him ... with this ... " Tom flung his arm at the officer helplessly and started over. "I'd best go see what this is all about as quick as I kin."

Tom moved quickly to the officer's side. "You'd better git goin'," he said urgently, "because if you say one more word, I don't think you'll ever see England again."

Fear seized the lieutenant, twitched him around, and sent him off in the direction of Goreham's Post. Tom followed, intent on the purpose of Wolfe's summons, while the lieutenant complained bitterly to himself about the injustices of service in an uncivilized wilderness.

The man's ineptness in the forest was truly unique. Somehow or other, he managed to get lost, and Tom was forced to step by him and lead the way back to the post. A corporal met them at the orderly room door and turned the officer away. Tom could hear his furious complaints as he stamped off, but in the next moment all that was past ceased to be, for Tom found himself looking straight into the eyes of Johnathan Evans. As soon as the first shock receded, a million doubts and questions came flooding into the boy's mind. These, in turn, gave way to the observation that two generals flanked Uncle John: one was James Wolfe; the other he did not know. Then he heard his uncle's voice gently telling him to sit down. It sounded like an echo reverberating from a far-off mountaintop. Tom strained to separate one succession of sounds from another. His efforts were not entirely successful, but he understood that all he had to do was sit and wait. Soon Uncle John would be free, and then all his questions would be answered. He sat silently while other echoes from equally distant mountains surrounded him.

The "mountaintops" sat at a small table upon which was spread out a newly drawn map. "Yes, sir," said Brigadier General Robert Monkcton, drawing his finger along the north shore of the St. Lawrence, "I fully understand the disposition of the French troops between the Montmorency and Cap Rouge. I think it is safe to say that every officer at the command level understands the impossibility of a frontal assault upon the cliffs of the city itself, and your own fiasco of July thirty-first upon the Beauport Shore proved the futility of any effort below the city. Remember, General, we brigadiers met in consultation two weeks ago, as you requested, to consider your plans of attack. We knew then that no possibility of success existed unless a footing could be obtained on the north shore above the town, as we stated in our recommendations, but this ... "

Brigadier Monckton's finger moved down the map to rest on the Anse du Foulon. "This," he continued, "offers very little chance of success, even if everything you and this ranger say is true. This path admits but one man at a time, and he would have to be half mountain goat to climb up it. Besides, the top is still guarded. We can see the tents up there. Maybe a coward like Vergor is in command, but didn't Captain Evans report that Montcalm himself had spotted this path, as he has every other access to the heights? What was it Montcalm said to Vaudreuil, Captain? Something about not needing to suppose the enemy have wings and then swearing that a hundred men posted there would stop our entire army? Have you considered, General, that we have already made several attempts above the city in force in spots where landings indeed might have been affected, without any success whatsoever? You asked my opinion, sir, and my opinion is still that a landing here would be folly."

The brigadier removed his finger from the map with a quick, abrasive action, as if he meant to remove the Anse du Foulon from the map. "Of course," he continued, smiling, "I appreciate the confidence you have shown in me personally in pointing out the place you intend to attack. Just the other day, Brigadiers Townshend and Murray expressed the wish that you would show this same sort of trust in their abilities, and in truth, sir, I think they warrant it."

The eyes of General James Wolfe contained pieces of cold, blue steel that the fiery furnace his face had become could not melt. He turned toward Johnathan Evans, unwilling to trust himself to answer the brigadier directly.

"I believe, Captain Evans," he said, so severely and distinctly that all echoes stopped in the ears of the boy who listened to this strange council of war, "you had better repeat those fortunate discoveries which led us to choose Anse du Foulon. The brigadier doesn't have to agree with our interpretation of the facts, tho staff agreement is normally conducive to success, but it is necessary that he understand clearly what the facts are … " He turned chair, body, and head, until he looked directly in the eyes of Monckton, "because the landing at Foulon will go on. I'll not see opportunity squandered by a bunch of mathematicians who prefer adding probabilities to walking in the paths of glory."

"Well, sir," answered Johnathan Evans, "any attack on Quebec is goin' to look hopeless if you figger the French are gonna anticipate our every move, but there's no real reason to think that, while there's good reason to think we kin fool 'em. Everybody knows that Quebec is a sewer, Sodom on the cliffs of the St. Lawrence. The intendant, Bigot, is as crooked as a hound dog's hind leg, an' he's got the ear o' Vaudreuil, who's so jealous of Montcalm that he insults him in public. Bigot's got his hand so deep in the king's purse that he might jest see defeat as a way to cover up his crimes. It was Bigot's advice that got Vaudreuil to move the *Guienne Rigiment* off the Plains of Abraham, where Montcalm had 'em stationed, all the way back to the St. Charles, and who would you guess had Captain Martin replaced as commander of the guard at the top of Foulon? Martin was a regular officer, handpicked by Montcalm for the duty. You know who commands there now? The Chevalier Duchambon de Vergor, tried for misconduct and cowardice in the surrender of Beausejour in '55, only to be saved by his crony Bigot and the protection of Vaudreuil. That's the man we got to git by. Not only that, but all he's got is a hundred men, mostly Canadians from Lorette, an' he's givin' forty of them leave to go home to harvest their crops, providin' they also work on his farm. Like I said, New France has been a cesspool fer years. Now the sewage had floated to the top an' the stench is gonna stifle 'em. You give me a handful of good New England rangers, an' we'll throw Vergor off the cliff before he kin git out o' his night shirt."

"Natrually," said Brigadier Monckton, "I know about the quarrel between Montcalm and Vaudreuil, and the character of Vergor is no secret to me. After all, I commanded at the capture of Beasusejour, but you seem to forget that the French have a post at Samos, with some seventy men and four cannon, just beyond the one at Foulon, and another beyond that at Sillery, with something like a hundred and thirty men and more cannon. Minutes would bring Vergor the help he needed, even if we could surprise him. Besides, the cliffs between Cap Rouge and Foulon are patrolled every night by a force under Captain de Remigny. Suppose de Remigny should spot our troops and report to Bougainville? Montcalm doesn't take any chances. He's increased Bougainville's force to three thousand men. The

French watch us day and night, above and below the city. No, I must still insist that the plan is foolhardy."

"Vergor will not have minutes, if we have any luck at all," replied Evans, "and once we're on the heights, we kin hold position till some o' the army gits up. As for Bougainville, he's sick near to death o' following Holmes up an' down the river. He longs for the company of Madame de Vienne, up at Jacques Cartier. If things work out right, I don't think we're gonna hev to worry about Bougainville. As for patrols … well, I got a hunch there's gonna be a perticular night when men on patrol would be better off stickin' in their blankets. I got a friend still on the north shore who swears that on this particlar night the patrols won't hev no luck at all. Somebody's even gonna steal them three horses de Remigny takes such good care of."

Johnathan Evans had relaxed as he had spoken. His features betrayed a strange, almost religious excitement. He spoke emphatically, puncturing the air with his finger and sweeping the fragments aside with the back of his hand. "This is the best chance we've had at Quebec, as well as the last one we're gonna git," he said confidently. "Like the gen'ral says, we've been given the opportunity, now all we've got tuh provide is the faith an' determination."

Brigadier Monckton sat on the edge of his chair, hope and doubt chasing one another across his face. "Probably there is some chance," he said, "especially with Vergor in command at the top of Foulon … yet, if anything at all goes wrong for us, we are exposed, and if anything at all goes right for them, they will see us. I don't like the odds. Not only that, but the odds don't get much better even if we do get troops up the path. How many men would you say we could reasonably get up there before the French hit us? Three thousand? Four? And without artillery, at that! Montcalm shouldn't have trouble getting seven or eight thousand troops between us and the city, and Bougainville would be at the rear with another three thousand. We could find ourselves outflanked, encircled, and out-numbered three to one. Montcalm could blow our army to ribbons and sweep the pieces off the cliffs into the river." Hope retreated as Monckton marshalled the probabilities of failure. The brigadier sat back in his chair and sighed.

"There is simply too much against this plan," he said unhappily. "The brigadiers would never accept it."

General Wolfe, too, leaned against the back of his chair and sighed. "You still do not understand," he said. "The French are divided, not simply because their troops are posted above and below the town, but because they must obey two commanders. We have reduced the countryside to ashes and Quebec to rubble. They are starving to death, and there is universal discontent among their Canadiens. Montcalm has a numerous body of armed men, not an army. Only his five regular battalions could face British steel. I would relish a fight with the rest of that rubble at ten to one odds. If you really understood the situation, you would know that circumstances have been slowly working in our favor."

Wolfe pushed himself up out of his chair and looked down at Monckton. "Well, sir," he said quietly, "I suppose the theory does not matter that much to you after all. Suffice it to say that the moment has arrived. The blow will be struck. In the meantime, there are details that I must work out and orders that you must carry out. I think we'd best get on about our business."

Johnathan Evans knew that the conference was over. He rose with Wolfe, standing at attention until the general had finished with Monckton. Then he saluted as Wolfe turned toward him. "There's not a whole lot of time left to me now, Gen'ral," he said. "I'd like to git on over to the tent with the boy here, if it's all right with you."

Wolfe returned the salute gravely, wishing that he had the time to understand what had shaped the intense competency of this colonial whose fierce earnestness had won first his admiration and then his compassion. "Your time is your own until tomorrow, Captain," he replied. "You know what is to be done as well as I." Wolfe began to turn away, but a compulsion he could not explain stopped him. "I have come to feel," he said slowly, "that you and I share the same fate here before Quebec. 'Tis a bothersome feeling, for it tells me that I shall never see England again," Then he did turn away, but not before Tom could see the bright sun of victory that shone in Wolfe's eyes, contrasting strangely with the dark shadows of death that lengthened along the lines in his face.

The walk back to the tent had been a happy, exciting experience for young Tom Evans. The forest became a being; a father who offered inexpressible joy and contentment to his children. The quick eye of Johnathan Evans caught a squirrel industriously making his last preparations for winter, and the ranger's heart wished the little creature well. The brightest birds exposed their brilliance briefly then disappeared, striking for man and boy the mysterious chord that turns experience into intuition. Among ferns touched at the tips by death, they stopped to wonder at a fragile wildflower, awed by the delicate perfection of the petals, hushed by its pastel beauties, and if the pulse of creation surged most fiercely in the heart of the forest priest, yet its softer beat brought to his acolyte a deeper comfort.

They walked together, almost hand in hand, the one moved by a foreboding sense of imminent destiny to hear eternal chords beneath the forests evanescent melodies, the other content to be a simple sharer in the joy of each moment. Tom, in fact, discovered as much delight in the perilous adventures of Uncle John and Toe-lee-ma had traced Bouchet through the French encampments. As his uncle talked on, he began to feel that the exposure of the weakness in the French defense must have been providential, and then, at the end of this forest interlude, came the most wonderful revelation of all. Sally had been found, hidden away among Madame de Vienne's entourage at Jacques Cartier. Tom's heart pounded exultantly. Visions of victory for Wolfe, rescue for Sally, and punishment for Emile Bouchet descended upon him with prophetic certainty.

Tom's spirits were buoyant for the rest of the day. The exhuberance of the rangers could be contained by neither camp nor forest. They sat around the tent drinking Chicken's stolen rum, they rushed outside to throw their hatchets at the unoffending trees, and their laughter ran out raucously, rising above the leafy arch overhead. They asked Johnathan Evans a hundred questions, and then asked them all over again. Could not quench their curiosity and they could not quench their thirst. In the Canadian wilderness, a pagan festival was held. The season of waning and wasting had ended. The god had been reborn. Soon the fruit of Quebec would fall at their feet. Exhausted, and yet in some mysterious way revitalized, the revellers sought the warmth and comfort of their blankets.

For hours, a sleep that partook of the grave reigned over the cot of the ranger captain, but as dawn approached, slumber's rule was disturbed by forces of its own creation. Fantastic apparitions began to leap and bound through Johnathan Evans's darkened soul. There, in the shadows of guilt, they began to assume the shapes of day. Outlines of arms and legs became visible. Hats and feathers came to rest upon immaterial heads. A strange new light suddenly appeared. The young Johnathan Evans could see that it emanated from a luminous hatchet, which whirled round and round, hacking silhouettes of men out of the darkness and placing them in low relief against a background of forest growth. The forest frieze came to life as a silhouette detached itself from a tree, became an Indian, and crept toward an indistinct figure dressed in the uniform of a New England ranger.

Sergeant Evans raised his rifle. *My God,* he thought, *Matt doesn't even see him!* Evans judged the distance and the difficulty of the shot with a calmness that belied his youth. In his heart, a prayer of thanksgiving arose. He had never broken his covenant with God, and God would not now break covenant with him. His finger tightened confidently on the trigger.

Then, in the blackness behind him, a twig snapped and a violent motion disturbed the air. Something older and deeper than his covenant spun him around. He pulled the trigger all the way back. As the rifle recoiled against his shoulder, a vast feeling of satisfaction spread over him, and he looked down upon the Indian who had fallen at his feet.

The power that had betrayed him went as quickly as it had come, freeing him to turn back to the task at hand. He watched helplessly, branded by the same horror that Cain must have felt when he slew Abel, as the Abenaki hatchet bit into Matthew Evans's skull. Johnathan Evans knew that the strands of discipline which bound him to the anchor of his faith were yet too weak. He ran through the lengthening shadows toward Matthew's fallen figure. "Oh, Lord," he cried, "abide with me. Oh Lord, with me abide!" The darkness deepened, and he gratefully slept again the sleep of the grave.

The dawn of September 12, 1759, broke over the Basin of Quebec slowly, mingling its grayness with the fog that rolled heavily across the waters of the St. Lawrence and blanketed the forest floor. In front of the ranger tent, Johnathan Evans squatted stolidly, mechanically feeding logs to his morning fire. He looked at the glowing bed of coals that lined the bottom of the firepit and turned to the task of readying his men for the day's work. He touched each man upon the shoulder and returned to the fire. No commands were necessary. Long-ingrained habits moved the men through their own rituals, making speech both unnecessary and undesired. Long before the sun could disperse the early morning vapors, the rangers sat around the remains of their breakfast fire, waiting for the order to move out.

Johnathan Evans sat with his back against a tree, silently appraising his men. The ordered and yet individual efficiency with which each ranger had prepared for the trail had stirred in his heart an intuitive sense of beauty. He wanted to simply stand up and lead them out, without saying a word, knowing that they would follow. He pushed away from the tree and stood up, noting with pride that the rangers, to a man, stood up with him. He stood before them, a man bewitched, until the sound of his own voice broke the spell.

"Boys," he heard himself saying, "we're gonna take a little walk through the woods to the river an' canoe out to the Sutherland to spend the day with the navy, but I kin promise you this: the next time yer feet hit dry land, it'll be to scale the cliffs of Quebec. By this time tomorrow, you'll all stand with Wolfe on the Plains of Abraham."

The rangers stood in silent confusion. Johnathan Evans's fingers tapped three times at his jacket. "In here," he said, "are the orders assigning you to a special assault force that's gonna lead the way. When we git on the Sutherland, I'll introduce you to Colonel Howe and Captain Delaune. You'll git yer orders from them."

Owen spoke for the rangers, reducing all their questions to one statement. "If the colonel's got no objections," he said quietly, "I'd jest as soon git my orders from you, John."

"I appreciate that, Owen, but I've got work to do with Toe-lee-ma on the north shore—work that might decide whether or not you git up them cliffs. There ain't no use talkin' about it. I jest can't say no more than I've already said."

A great acceptance settled over the rangers. The numbness of the final waiting period that precedes attack prematurely enveloped them. Unthinking feet took them to the St. Lawrence and the hands of habit paddled them out to the flagship. They stepped forward stolidly to acknowledge their names and mutely withstood the scrutiny of the British officers. Only the last remark of Johnathan Evans registered on their consciousness: "Take keer of Tom, if you kin, Jed. I know it might not be possible, the way things go, but if you kin … ⨍"

And so they sat on the timbers of the ship, rocking with the current, cultivating sleep, layer upon layer, like so many oysters cultivating pearls. Later in the day, they were joined by twenty-four men who turned out to be the rest of the assault party, and the quiet time was over. Tom noticed that most of the new arrivals were light infantrymen. At first, their conversation annoyed him, but soon he found himself listening intently to their every word.

"You heard Colonel Howe, Cameron. If any of us survive we can depend on being recommended to the general."

"Well, now, Mr. McPherson," said a voice sarcastically, "I'd have to say that the survivin' comes before the recommendin,' an' it's small comfort a wife will take from knowin' they sewed an extra stripe on yer corpse before they planted it in this god-forsaken land."

"This is a volunteer force," replied the other angrily. "If you didn't want to come along, you should have kept your mouth shut."

"I never said I didn't want to go," answered Cameron, "but any man who'd take a chance like this just for the sake of an extra stripe is a damn fool."

"We all know why we volunteered," interrupted a third voice. "There ain't no point in arguin' about that. What any one man does, we'll all do. You'd both best spend yer time asking the good Lord to help us all get up to the top of that cliff."

The infantryman's words broke up the argument, and the volunteers began to form naturally into groups of two and three. Their conversation turned from the war back to England, back to the home and hearth that suddenly becomes so precious to soldiers on the eve of battle, and then turned again to the unknown perils that lay before them. Tom got up and moved over beside Jed. Soon, the others moved over, forming a small, tight circle, as if in obedience to some ancient instinct. They herded together, finding a false security in numbers, listening to the St. Lawrence slap against the hull of the Sutherland as the ship pulled against its anchor. Then they became conscious of new sounds and new movements. Voices began to give orders, and all over the ship they heard the shuffling of moving feet and the click of bayonets snapping onto rifles. In the confusion, the watch called the midnight hour, and Captain Delaune appeared before them.

"We're going to move out now, rangers first and then the light infantry. You have five minutes to check your gear. Once you're in the boat, there will be no noise of any kind. Keep still and keep quiet. Don't move until I give the order to land. Then follow me and McDonald to the path up the cliff. From there you will be on your own, but stick as close together as you can. If a sentry challenges us, McDonald will answer him. Once you get to the top, you'll see the tents of the outpost. Charge 'em and drive the French out. If they run, don't follow them. Our job is to secure the top until the troops behind us can get up. Now, does anybody have a question?"

There was no reply. Delaune waited as the men completed their preparations. Then he motioned them forward. "All right, rangers first, and remember, if you want to see Quebec in the morning, you won't make any noise tonight."

They followed Delaune down the corridor and over to the ship's rail. Around them they could see the other ships of the fleet, and below them they could see the *bateaux* moored alongside the vessels. Down the ladder they went to take their positions near the bow of the *bateaux*. The night began to speak of war with a thousand tongues: oarlocks creaked as sailors steadied the landing craft, feet thudded dully into the boats and, directed by restrained curses and urgent vulgarities, made their way clumsily forward and aft until the first assault wave was loaded. Now they all waited, Howe's Light Infantry; the regiments of Bragg, Anstruther, Kennedy, and Lascelles; and Frazier's detachment of Highlanders and American Grenadiers; they all waited for the tide to ebb and the order to cast off. To Tom, the scurrying sounds became ominous, and he could not keep away the image of rats deserting a sinking ship.

Tom heard behind him one final soft thud, and he wondered idly where they would put the new man in the crowded boat. He looked up as the footstep approached. The tall, thin figure that moved past him was hidden by the darkness and a large, heavy cloak, but there could be no mistake about the identity. The late arrival was General Wolfe.

Before Tom could form any other thought, the order to cast off had been given, and the *bateaux* drifted free on the ebb tide. Across the river six miles downstream lay the Anse du Foulon, and the path that would lead James Wolfe to glory and to the grave.

The silence and the darkness began to work on Tom's nerves. He began to feel like a shadow in the mist. He could not believe that the ship was real or that the guns, which gaped ominously at him, were made of iron and not darkened patches of fog. It struck him as ridiculous that General Wolfe should now be urgently calling out to this phantom of the St. Lawrence.

"Ahoy, the sloop. Ahoy, the Hunter," he heard Wolfe shout. "Don't fire those guns. This is General Wolfe speaking. Is Captain Smith on deck?"

"Right here, General," came the answer. "Right here on deck interrogating these two deserters."

"All right, Captain," replied Wolfe. "I didn't want to call out, but I couldn't have you blowing us out of the river. What do the deserters say?"

"They claim the French are sending provision boats down from Cap Rouge tonight. They say it's Bougainville's orders."

"That's fine," replied Wolfe. "As long as we're ahead of them, that'll make it easier for us to get by the sentries posted near the shore. Keep a sharp watch, Captain. The boats carrying the second wave are close behind, and the rest of the ships and troops will follow them."

"That's all right, General," Smith said in a loud, hoarse whisper as the *bateaux* began to move past the Hunter. "You can depend on me, an' Gen'ral, I sure hope you give 'em hell!"

Wolfe made no reply. As the boats neared the north bank, the need for silence became essential. As the tide bore them even closer to the shore, Tom peered intently at the mighty wall of rack and forest that towered in darkness on their left, but he could see nothing. Then, suddenly, Tom felt his back stiffen. His heart seemed to take one gigantic leap in his chest and stop its beating. The sharp *"Qui Vive!"* of a French sentry had infused the chill wind of the river with the touch of death.

"France! Et vive le roil," answered a voice from a nearby boat.

"A qual rigiment?"

"De la reine," came the reply

"Pourquoi est-ce-que vous ne parlex pas plus haut? Tas-toi! Nous serons entendue."

The boats swept by, and the silence returned. Tom peered again at the shore, wishing they wouldn't come as close to the Heights of Samos, for surely any sentry who wasn't half deaf would hear the terrible thumping of his heart. His worst fears were soon realized. Out of the darkness, another sentry came running at them. *"Qui vive! Qui vive!"*

Again, a French-speaking highlander gave the answer from a nearby boat. "Provision boats. Don't make so much noise. Do you want the English to hear us?"

The sentry waved them on. Tom could see the gray of his cuff against the black of the cliff behind him. Before Tom could recover from this second challenge, they had rounded the headland above the Anse du Foulon. The current ran fiercely, and they were being swept past their intended landing place. Tom grasped his rifle hard and waited. It suddenly occurred to him that he was very much afraid.

"All right. Out of the boat. Get out. It's now or never. C'mon, you can't be afraid of getting your feet wet." McDonald and Fraser were already out of their boats. Captain Delaune was racing for the foot of the cliffs, and the rangers followed him, leaping over rocks and surf to the narrow strand that stood below the steepest hill Tom had ever seen. *How,* the boy thought, *How in the name of God will we climb these heights without wings?*

The rangers slung their rifles at their backs and worked to keep up with Delaune and McDonald. In the depths of the great ravine that cleft the heights, they could hear the Ruisseau St. Denis splashing in the stillness, and they hoped vainly that its sounds would conceal the noise of their struggle upward. Tom found himself clinging to the face of the cliff, all progress seemingly forever halted. His feet, struggling frantically for purchase, dislodged stones and dirt and split his terror between the fear of falling and the fear of discovery. At last, one foot struck a stone that gave but held, and Tom was able to see in the darkness above a small bush growing out of the rock itself. He let go of the cliff with his right hand and pushed hard with his foot. As his body shot upward, he dug in with his left hand and pushed again, only dimly aware of the pain the jagged stone had inflicted. Miraculously, he hooked his fingers at the second joint around the bush and hung suspended in space. The bush wiggled its roots in protest, and Tom quickly pulled down with his right hand and swung his left hand up to close around the branch. His feet kicked against the cliff, taking weight away from the yielding bush. For a moment he hung there, a humpbacked, rootless monstrosity.

Then he swung up upon the outcropping that had given the bush, and him, the chance to struggle for survival. Above him, he could hear the others struggling up the cliff face.

For the third time that night, the *"Qui Vive!"* of a French sentry challenged the volunteers. McDonald was ready.

"Post relief," he hissed in his hoarse whisper. "I know it's after four, but I'm not that much late. I'll take care to give a good account of the English if they land."

The sentry hesitated, thinking how nice it would be to get out of the dampness and crawl into his blankets. He hesitated too long. Shadowy figures surrounded him, and then the volunteers charged with blazing muskets.

Suddenly, from sky to shoreline, the basin of Quebec became a gigantic, blinding holocaust. The ships of Saunders, carrying out the feint that kept Montcalm at Beauport, illuminated the sky with candles of destruction. The British batteries at Levy and on Orleans joined in, and the French guns responded. To the left of the volunteers, the French batteries at Samos opened fire on the boats in the rear and the vessels coming down from Cap Rouge, and the battery at Sillery voiced its full-throated defiance.

At the foot of Foulon, Wolfe ordered in the second wave, and men were busily clearing the narrow, slanting path that led to the Plains of Abraham. In the gray of morning, the long file of redcoated soldiers moved quickly upward and formed in order on the plateau above.

For young Tom Evans, the early morning world of the plateau was a world without pattern. Behind him, he heard bushes shaking, involuntary grunts, and muttered curses as a detachment of light infantry struggled toward the top of the cliff. Ahead of him he heard Vergor, shot in the heel, screaming like a stuck pig. The drizzling rain dampened his soul. Then, out of the gray mist, Jed Hawkins appeared at his side.

"C'mon, Tom. We've got to git out across the plains and git the lay o' the land. When Montcalm gits here, we'd all better be in the right spot er we'll never git inside the walls o' the town."

Tom and Jed, followed by Owen, Chicken, and Charlie Turner, made their way across the Plains of Abraham. They crossed the Sillery Road, and Tom subconsciously noted that the folds of uneven ground would provide excellent cover for fighting. They moved over scrublands and through cornfields, until Jed halted them in a clump of Hawthorne trees at the edge of the St. Foye Road. Across the road, they could see several houses and a mill.

"We can't go no further," said Jed. "Wolfe ain't hardly got enough troops to reach this far as it is, but we've got to hev them houses; otherwise our left flank is in fer a terrible poundin'. We'll jest wait here and watch till them light infantry ketch up with us."

They stood in the rain among the Hawthorne trees, watching the houses. The minutes revealed no movement, no sign of life. Jed Hawkins carefully broke the silence. "No use waitin' any longer," he said. "There ain't nobody in them houses, 'less it's a settler. We'll move up on that big one, by itself there, an' if nothin' happens, why, we'll jest move in."

They followed Jed across the road, through chokecherry and alder, until they faced the front door.

Jed held up his hand and they halted. "All right," he whispered, "let's see if anyone's home."

They ran swiftly. Crouching low at the door, Jed grasped the handle and swung the door open. Tom's breath caught in his throat and he stopped still, his body tightening to receive the shock of whatever might come. Then he plunged after Jed into the house.

Tom was halfway across the room when he realized that nothing had happened, that nothing would happen. The tension left him so abruptly that his knees buckled just as if he had taken a rifle butt at the base of the skull.

"Have a chair," he heard Jed saying. "Pretty soon company'll be here, an' we'll have a housewarmin'."

While the rangers rested in the house of Borgia and waited for relief, the British troops were busily occupying their positions. Across the St. Foye Road on the left flank were the light infantry and Amherst's fifteenth regiment. Anstruther's fifty-eighth, Fraser's seventy-eighth, and Lascelle's forty-seventh stretched across the plain to the Sillery Road. To the right of the Sillery, which ran through the British center, were Kennedy's forty-third, Bragg's twenty-eighth, the Louisbourg Grenadiers, and Otway's thirty-fifth. In reserve were the 260th, the Royal Americans, and Webb's forty-eighth. Murray commanded on the left and Monckton on the right, but Wolfe, determined to leave no detail to chance, was everywhere. If any general ever held an army together through the perilous and awesome circumstances that precede the moment of truth when main battle lines are joined, that general was James Wolfe.

A light rain still fell on the British troops, who persevered against the harassment of the Canadians and Indians who fusilladed them in front and on the flank. Squatting behind bushes and knolls, kneeling at the edges of cornfields and thickets, the enemy poured their venomous fire into the British ranks. Wolfe, dressed in an immaculate new uniform, strode amongst his men. That thin red line of heroes, stretching nearly a mile across the plain, could see him as he restored the courage of a young private who stood, half-crazed with fright, in harm's way. At his general's touch, discipline returned and the boy sought shelter on the grass from the shot breaking around him, or he could see him stoop to press the hand of a captain, shot through the lungs, providing comfort he could with words of praise and the promise of a promotion for gallantry. Now he was on the left flank with the fifty-eighth, where the struggle to control the houses raged. Not far from the house of Borgia, where the rangers now fought to defend that protecting edifice, a Canadian in the bushes south of the St. Foye Road touched off a lucky shot. Wolfe paid no attention to the bullet that shattered his wrist, other than to wrap a handkerchief around the wound. He had other things to occupy his mind, for Montcalm was ready. The decisive hour was near at hand.

Joseph Louis, Marquis de Montcalm-Gozon, had arrived upon the scene. With him were the finest troops of New France, some of them veterans of the incredible victory at Ticonderoga, but all together numbering only five battalions. He had expected to see a detachment of British troops; instead, he looked with despair upon an army. *Mon Dieu,* he thought, *I could have corrected all Vaudreuil's error's, if only he had Guienne on the plains and St. Martin at the top of Foulon.* Still, he might yet save New France if he acted quickly. He had little confidence in the irregulars, but perhaps his veterans could perform one final miracle. He threw his Canadians and Indians out on the flanks and wheeled his veterans into position. On his right, nearest the St. Foye Road, he placed the regiment of LaSarre, then Languedoc and Bearn. The British could see a mass of white linen gaiters, light gray breeches and coats, and small, black three-cornered hats trimmed with yellow. A closer look contrasted the red coat and collar facings of Bearn with the blue of Languedoc and LaSarre. On the other side of the Sillery Road, they could see the Guienne regiment, their uniforms matching those of Bearn, and the Roy Rousillon, their blue facings, red vests, and yellow buttons matching the colors of Lanuedoc and LaSarre.

Montcalm and his officers decided that they could wait no longer. The British might be fortifying themselves and waiting for reinforcements. The forces from the left wing of the army had not come. No doubt Vaudreuil had detained them. Ramesay had sent only three of the twenty-five fieldpieces from the palace battery. If they waited for Bougainville to bring up his troops at the English rear, Vaudreuil might appear and hamstring all their efforts. Two fieldpieces blasted the British ranks with grapeshot, and the order to attack went down the line. The French troops moved off the ridge, shouting their battle cries. It was nearly 10:00 a.m.

The British rose from the ground to receive the enemy. Whatever their personal thoughts were, they had been trained by Wolfe and they would not betray his faith. They stood still as the French came on. Bullets began to thud into the thin red line. Soldiers fell to the ground, but the line did not break. The French were forty yards away when the command rang out. The British volley sounded like a cannon shot. Another volley followed. Smoke from the muskets still enshrouded the battlefield as the red line moved forward twenty paces, according to the frill book, and fired again. When the smoke lifted, New France had been deflowered. The battalions who had fought brilliantly from Fort Necessity to William Henry were only so much light gray litter on the Plains of Abraham.

A tremendous cheer rose from the British ranks. Lascelle's forty-seventh broke in upon the remains of the French center with fixed bayonets. Four hundred and fifty kilted highlanders, screaming their ancient battle call, decapitated the fleeing French with single strokes of their flashing broadswords. Wolfe led the Louisbourg Grenadiers on the right. His troops thought him invincible, unaware that he had taken a piece of metal in his belly just below the navel. He was hemmorrhaging seriously inside, but the giant spirit that moved his frail body would not stop short of victory; he pressed on toward destiny. Ahead of him, hidden by a clump of bushes, dressed in the clothing of a Canadian sharpshooter, knelt an English sergeant, reduced to the ranks by Wolfe, who had deserted to the French in the vicious hope that the wanton and cruel workings of fate would give him an opportunity to murder the man who had forced justice upon him. Now suddenly, unbelievably, he had Wolfe in his sights.

He squeezed the trigger. Wolfe staggered and sat down as the bullet struck his breast. His last act was an order to Colonel Burton to cut off the French retreat from the bridge. Then secure in his men's reports of victory, he turned on his side. "Now, God be praised, I will die in peace!" he murmured. Moments later, he was immortal.

9

RESCUE

Everywhere the French ran, and the British ran after them. On the left flank, the house of Borgia had as its sole occupants the men of the First Independent Company of New England Rangers, who were engaged in a very serious argument.

"I say we hed to fight too hard to keep this place to go runnin' off after them French. They ain't gonna do nothing but run into the town er over the bridge of boats anyhow," said Charlie Turner. "What's the point o' runnin' after 'em an' mebbe takin' a stray bullet in the head?"

"Well, it's a good point you have, Charlie," replied Owen. "There's plenty o' English to do the moppin' up, an' I can't see as how we're gonna miss anythin' by settin' here a spell."

"It's a matter o' how long ye're gonna set," said Hawkins. "Pretty soon someone's gonna come along an' kick our tails outta here, an' when they do, they might jest have a detail for us that we ain't gonna be partial to."

"Why then, we'll jest leave," answered Owen. "They kin yell all they want to. We don't have to do nothin'. We're rangers— unattached rangers, at that. Fact is, we're volunteers, an' we done what we volunteered to do. Kin you see some bloody lobsterback makin' us do something we don't have a mind to do?"

"'Course," interrupted Chicken, "there is a thing er two we got to think about. Fer one, there's apt to be a whole lot of unpleasant work in front o' Quebec, diggin' in an army this size on a battlefield. I surely don't want to git sucked into any o' that! Fer another, well, I don't like to mention it, but war's war, as you all know, an' right now them English is stuffin' French watches into their breeches. Now, jest suppose we can't git inside the gates an' have to set siege agin' the city till the snow starts flying. Where we gonna git our extry rations, er boards fer our floor, without somethin' to trade? A man's got to do a certain amount o' lookin' out fer himself if he wants to survive in this old world, I say ... "

"Chicken," interrupted Jed, spitting a stream of tobacco juice on the floor, "we ain't worried about yer future. If wust comes'to wust, you'll grab a pick axe and dig bodies right out o' the frozen ground. The thing is, we ain't seen hide nor hair o' John, an' I say we ought to set right here an' let him find us. 'Sides that, I'm gittin' a mite worried 'bout him. There ain't nothin' he had to do over here that wouldn't be done by the time we hit the top o' Foulon. Where in hell can he be anyway?"

"Now, Jed," said Chicken, "I don't mind none if it helps you to cuss me out, but jest remember how you'd all be livin' if you didn't have ole Chicken to do yer dirty work fer ya."

"Oh, shet up Chicken," said Charlie as he turned to face Hawkins. "Jed, did John say he was goin' to meet us here?"

"Not exactly," replied Jed. "He said if the landin' was successful he'd find us before the real shootin' started, an' jest before he left, he told me to keet an eye on Tom as best I could till he got here." Jed looked self-consciously over at Tom, who sat dozing by the stove, letting the warmth of the fire draw the misery out of his body.

"Well, that settles it," said Owen. "If John said he'd find us, he meant us to stay put. There ain't nothing else to do but set here till he shows up er we git word from him." Owen picked up his chair and moved over to the stove beside Tom. He turned the chair around and let the heat hit him in the back.

Charlie and Chicken shoved the wood box over to the stove and sat down on the floor, leaning their backs against the box. The issue was settled. They sought, as soldiers who know they have nothing to do but wait usually do, the relief offered by sleep, while Jed stood guard at the window.

The moments passed slowly and painfully for Jed Hawkins. They crawled into minutes, and the minutes became an hour. His bones began to ache, and occasionally his eyelids blinked shut. Sleep became a beautiful thought, but he would not wake the others. He felt as if he had been given a special trust that somehow he would betray unless he performed it alone.

The ridges along Jed's eyes deepened and seeped permanently into his features as he doggedly watched. The eyes themselves squinted into oblong slits that blinked open and shut. Gradually he became aware of something that jumped erratically into view. Then the figure became two figures, and Jed clawed across his eyes with fingers and thumb, pinching the bridge of his nose hard at the end of the stroke. He concentrated his energy into a fierce, final squint that shut his eyes tightly and tingled along the muscles of his shoulders. Then his eyes popped open, and very clearly he saw Johnathan Evans and Toe-lee-ma moving away from a clump of chokecherry trees, moving quickly but not hurriedly toward Borgia's house. He turned his head toward the dozing rangers to shout, "John's here, an' Toe-lee-ma's with 'im." He threw open the door and stepped out to meet them.

Johnathan Evans grabbed Jed's outstretched hand and squeezed hard. "Everything go all right here?" he said.

Jed knew what he meant. "Yep," he said. "Nobody so much as got scratched."

Toe-lee-ma nodded and followed the men into the house. The rangers left the stove and surrounded Evans and his companion. They wept their question in their eyes.

"Well," said Johnathan Evans, "I guess we kept you boys waitin' a mite longer than I expected, but we had some trouble we didn't look for. First, we hed a devil of a time stealing de Remigny's last horse, an' after that, a couple of sentries along the cliff were a little harder to git rid of than we figured, but everythin' considered, the hull affair couldn't hev worked out much better. Only thing is, them delays put a detachment of Bougainville's men between us an' Wolfe's line. We tried to go around 'em too fast, and some Abenaki scouts spotted us. They was dog-determined to get us too. Figured they would, I suspect. There ain't much chance o' hiding on the plains. It was touch an' go there for a while, but we finally got a pretty good lead an' lost 'em in the hardwoods north of Old Lorette. By the time we got back, the big show was over."

Johnathan Evans paused to look at his comrades. In the silence, he moved over and put an arm around Tom's shoulder. "Well," he continued, "it don't really matter none what held us up. We hev Toe-lee-ma to thank for discoverin' what counts. We was comin' back toward Wolfe's left when he heard them three volleys that did the French in. We stepped up our pace, an' in a few minutes we were nearly opposite this house, tho a good deal to the north, so we left the woods and crossed the Old Lorette Road. I was already across the road an' goin' into the scrubland when Toe-lee-ma called me back. Down the road he'd seen something unusual he thought we ought to take a look at. I was in such a hurry to git over here, I nearly didn't go. Wouldn't hev, if jest one time I'd known his intuition to be wrong."

He turned to the Indian. "You saw it, Toe-lee-ma. You tell 'em about it."

"Silver flashed in the sun. The sign was bad," said Toe-lee-ma simply.

Evans knew his companion had spoken all that he thought necessary. "It was a bad sign, all right," he said. "Bad for Bouchet. That flash as an officer's gorget dropped by some Abenaki who already had too many 'souveniers' to worry about losin' what he looked upon as jest another trinket. Toe-lee-ma did some trackin' an' figured out that Abenaki was one of a bank of ten comin' from the plains an' headin' northwest on the Lorette Road. He knew what he was lookin' for then, an' it wasn't long before he found it: that unmistakable devil's print of Satanis. The tracks stopped on the next bend. It was certain Satanis was waitin' for somebody, an' sure enough, again comin' up from the plains was the print of Emile Bouchet. He knows it's all over for the French, so he's hightailin' it to Jacques Cartier to pick up Sally an' disappear into the interior. He got more'n an hour an' a half's start, an' he don't hev no particular reason to hurry. Jacques Cartier is near thirty miles. He don't want to wear himself out before he gits there. He's got too far to go afterward."

"I guess we better git started then," said Hawkins, picking up his rifle. "Even if Bouchet loafs a little, like you say, he's bound to make thirty miles in less than five hours. We gotta make it in three to be sure we beat 'em, and that ain't gonna be easy."

Johnathan Evans watched the other rangers grab their rifles. Though he had been certain of their help, this silent, unquestioning demonstration of loyalty moved him profoundly. He would honor them with an acceptance as silent and as rudely gracious as the offer.

"Toe-lee-ma will lead," he said. "He's surer of the way than I am."

They followed Toe-lee-ma out the door and onto the St. Foye Road. Almost immediately, Toe-lee-ma took them into the woods to avoid Bougainville, whose forces were still to the British rear, as well as any other refugees from the battle who might be fleeing toward Jacques Cartier. They ran mostly parallel to the road, marveling at the Indian's ability to find unimpeded paths that allowed them to pursue a direct and speedy route westward. For several miles, Tom tried to measure time by counting his paces, but then the strain of keeping up with Toe-lee-ma began increasingly to absorb his powers of concentration.

The pain of the long run began to set in, turning his thoughts to the night he and Uncle John had conquered the darkness, the forest, and the Mooserack Trail to warn Number Four, only to be too late to save the Foster housewarming from Satanis. The simple act of breathing became a struggle of the will, and Tom felt the pain moving up and down his throat between his heart and his head. He ran in a sort of numbness, penetrated only by half-formed images of the brutal trip from the Foster massacre over the mountains and down to Lake Champlain in the vain attempt to catch Bouchet and rescue Sally. Then everything went blank, and he ran the last few miles from habit, running on and on until Uncle John's hand on his shoulder slowed him down and brought him to a stop.

They stood on a little knoll looking down at the house of Madame de Vienne. "We'll wait here, Tom," he heard Uncle John say, "while Toe-lee-ma goes down an' has a look. None of us kin do much anyway till we git our legs back."

Tom's fatigue was so deep that his anxiety over Sally could only flicker momentarily. He sank down on the grass and flattened his back against the ground. Toe-lee-ma returned before any of the rangers were ready to move.

"The sun moved faster for Bouchet than it did for us," he said. "They have taken the girl to the river. The grass still springs back from their tracks. We will take them when they come out for the canoe."

Johnathan Evans was on his feet instantly. "This might git delicate," he said, "because we got to make sure no harm comes to the girl, but we ain't got many choices. Bouchet's on a path that comes out into a clearin' about a mile from here an' then runs down to the river. We're gonna beat him to that clearin' an' hit him when he steps into it. Don't step on a single twig or brush by any branches. We won't be more'n a hundred yards away when we pass him, an' them Abenaki's has all got ears as good as Toe-lee-ma's. Take cover across the clearin' an' face the path. Tom, you stay with me. Remember, the important thing is to save the girl. If we don't do this right, they'll tomahawk her for sure. Bouchet might do it himself, jest out o' spite. Follow Toe-lee-ma, an' if you kin, step where he steps."

Toe-lee-ma led them down the gentle slope and into the woods beyond the house. He followed a path so narrow that Tom had to twist his shoulders, at times running almost side-ways, to keep from hitting the branches on either side. Once or twice his clothing actually touched a branch, and the whisper of its movement sounded in his ears like a cannon shot. Then they were across the clearing and invisible behind bushes. Tom was not satisfied with his cover, but there was no time to change it. Already he could hear the sounds of Bouchet's party. He imag-ined he heard soft, short whisperings. There was a moment of absolute silence, and then the glistening, painted head of an Abenaki appeared behind a bush at the edge of the path. The head barely moved, but the eyes in it moved everywhere. Tom's heart skipped a beat. *They're suspicious,* he thought. *They heard the branch I touched. They know we're here!*

The Abenaki came half-erect and moved a few steps into the clearing. Another warrior rose from the other side of the path and joined him. They stood silently, sniffing the air like dogs. Tom half-expected to see their jaws drop open and their tongues hang out. Suddenly, they whirled and leaped for the woods, stretching their bodies down and out. Two shots rang out. The Abenakis hit the ground, but they did not roll. They lay still, one with his head and shoulders hidden by the cover they had so desperately sought.

"Keep their heads down," yelled Uncle John. "Tom, follow me. Everything depends upon how quiet we are."

Timing their dash to the crack of the ranger rifles, Tom and his uncle leaped across the clearing and ran down the narrow path they had just left. They ran furiously, paying no attention to the protesting woods. Up ahead, they heard a scream.

"Sally," shouted Uncle John. "Pray God we're not too late. I knew that damned Bouchet would make one last attempt to get the girl away safely. He heard us comin' after him, and he's done whatever he planned to do to stop us." Uncle John tore into the woods and smashed his way through.

When they broke out onto Bouchet's path, Tom's heart stopped again. Ahead, a narrow trail, no larger than the one that had carried them to the clearing, led off to the north, forming a fork with the path on which they stood; and on that trail lay the body of Sally Williams, limp and crumpled, like a rag doll with broken limbs cast aside by a petulant child.

Johnathan Evans stood immobilized as the alembic formed by twenty years of border warfare distilled away the horror and despair, reducing the situation to its barest facts. Stood watching Tom running down the path toward the fallen figure until his intuition put the facts together. Then he raised his rifle to his shoulder and moved after his nephew, concentrating all his energies upon the bushes and scrub trees that flanked the trail beyond the body of Sally Williams. His eyes photographed every horizontal line of the woods, seeking the one vertical that did not belong. Not until Tom knelt in the path beside Sally did Evans find what he was looking for. Farther back than he had suspected, a few small shrubs reached up to touch the barren branches of a dying tree, and behind them was the vertical that did not belong. There was a movement, almost imperceptible, but obviously unnatural, behind the middle shrub. He knew that Bouchet had zeroed in. Half an instant's delay would see Bouchet's bullet plowing into Tom's head. There could be no thought. Only habit could act swiftly and accurately enough to place a bullet just above and to the right of that strange movement in the woods in time to save Tom.

But there was yet another force at work in the wilderness. Even as his rifle moved automatically to execute its work, Evans heard the footstep of destiny behind him and felt the wind of its instrument descending upon him. The old instinct was yet alive, but this time, the bonds of duty, fifteen deliberate years in the forging, held fast. It occurred to Johnathan Evans that the recoil of his rifle had driven him back and up into the cutting edge of Satanis's hatchet, and then, in the deepening darkness, he saw Bouchet's rifle fall onto the ground and the demon himself pitch out of the brush to lie on top of it.

Up ahead, Tom whirled toward the sound of the shot in time to see Satanis place his foot on his uncle's neck and jerk the hatchet free. An uncontrollable, desperate rage shook the boy. "Devil," he screamed. "Devil." The answering cry of defiance that rose in Satanis's black soul never passed his lips. Tom's shot pounded into his forehead and dropped the Abenaki to his knees. His body bent back, arms outstretched, until his head rested on his heels. He could have been a sun worshipper awaiting the morning appearance of his god.

Tom turned back to Sally. Upon the numbness of his mind, the faint rise and fall of her breast made its impression. He realized that Bouchet had brutally struck Sally to make her the bait for his trap. After the trap was sprung, Bouchet intended to carry her off, probably to St. Francis. Tom sat down on the path and gently placed the girl's head in his lap. He sat there rubbing her wrists, listening to the battle that still went on at the clearing, almost unaware of the tears that rolled down his face.

Tom sat there until Sally began to stir. Something like panic struck him as her eyes fluttered open, and he read there the terror that she had lived with daily. As carefully as he had ever done anything in his life, he raised her up and let her sink against his chest. A strange, quiet comfort flowed between them. Finally, Tom turned aside, and leaving his arm around her waist, he led Sally through the woods back to the clearing.

Once they were safely behind the ranger line, Tom turned to meet Jed, who came to them with mixed emotions chasing one another across his lean features.

Tom spoke first. "He's dead. Uncle John is dead." It wasn't what he had intended to say or wanted to say, but suddenly it was the only thing he could say.

Disbelief was written in every muscle of Jed Hawkins's body. "No," he said, "no, that can't be. You're mistaken, Tom. That can't be."

"He's dead." Tears filled Tom's eyes. "I saw him. He's jest dead, that's all." Hawkins looked at the boy closely, and compassion restored the man's composure. "All right, Tom," he said quietly. "You stay here an' do what you kin for the girl. We'll take keer o' what's left o' the Abenaki. Toe-lee-ma is out on their left flank, an' he must have got two of 'em, 'cause there's only five guns still firin' an' none on the left. We been jest keepin' their heads down mostly, but now we'll roll 'em up fast."

Sally put her hand in Tom's. She sat down slowly, and Tom, responding to the slight pressure of her fingers, sat down beside her. They waited together, hand in hand, for the return of Jed Hawkins.

They did not wait long. There was a short silence, the thunder of guns, Toe-lee-ma's victory cry, and the death wail of an Abenaki. Another short silence followed, and then the rangers stood before them.

"We left Charlie and Chicken shootin'," said Hawkins. "Owen went behind 'em, an' I took the right. When they heard us comin', they took off. Two of 'em didn't make it fer sure, an' I think I got lead in another one."

Jed stood there, shifting his weight from one foot to the other, not knowing how to ask what he had to ask. Finally, the hesitation became too burdensome to hear. "Tom," he said, "you're gonna hafta show us what happened. I think you owe us all that much."

Tom gently disengaged his hand from Sally's and got to his feet. He knew that he must do what Jed asked, but he would do it absolutely without thought, and more than anything, he knew he would not look again at the lifeless body lying on the path. He moved past the rangers, but he no longer moved in their world.

Somehow, he got through the ordeal. In his memory, he recorded only the quiet acceptance of Toe-lee-ma, who seemed somehow to know everything that had happened before Tom said a word. An overwhelming urge grew in him to have the Indian share with him the miraculous understanding that both foretells and surpasses event and circumstance, just as Uncle John had communicated to him that day on their walk back to the tent the fierce joy of life felt by men who sense that they are soon to lose it.

Toe-lee-ma and Tom walked down the path ahead of the others. They stood by themselves at the edge of the clearing, while the rangers gathered around Sally. The red man looked at the white boy and reached his arm out toward the clearing.

"The summer flowers are gone," he said, "but they will grow again in the spring, just as the lilies of France, uprooted here by the English, will grow again in some other soil. It is the law of nature and the seasons."

The boy looked at his companion's stern face. "There ain't no other soil that concerns me," he said. "And I had no uncle but my Uncle John." For a moment, he wondered if the Indian's acceptance of death represented no more than the essentially pitiless nature of the savage, yet in his heart, he knew the thought was unworthy.

"War is not only here," replied Toe-lee-ma, raising his arm and sweeping it outward in a circular motion. "Spirits struggle in the earth below and in the skies above us. War is everywhere. The Indian, too, calls for help to the spirits of the earth or sky, and they do not hear him. That is also the law. Then the Indian's heart is a hollow drum that beats out the sounds of grief and sorrow, but the Indian remembers that beneath the winter snows sleep the seeds of spring. What is dead will be reborn in kind, and that is the law of life."

Tom found no consolation in the words. The war had torn something out of his heart which philosophy could not replace. Johnathan Evans was dead, as dead as if he had died with Matthew Evans at Louisbourg, and what shrivelled the boy's soul was the thought that all the hopes that had carried them over the long, hard trail meant no more now to the uncle than they did to the father in the grave these fourteen years. The boy turned expressionless eyes upon the Indian.

"What good are laws like that?" he asked. "Why should we struggle and suffer just to stay alive till something kills us? If your laws really rule the earth, any critter in the forest is better off than we are. What's the use o' havin' sense in a senseless world?"

The Indian's answer was slow in coming. "My brother knew of another law, beyond the law of nature, a law given by the Great Spirit in his Book to all men. My brother said that the man who kept this law would not be bound by the law of nature but would become like the Great Spirit himself. Then, my brother let the law of nature tempt him to break his agreement to follow the Law of the Book, and the Great Spirit turned his face away from him. When we came back from Louisbourg, he said to me, 'Toe-lee-ma, I must prove to my God that I can keep my covenant with Him and with my people, or He will not look upon me again.' On all the trails that led us from Louisbourg to Quebec, he carried this burden. Now he has thrown it down, just as he hoped to throw it down, according to his own law; no man can do more. If we are sad, it is because our hearts cannot stand their own emptiness."

There was no answer. Toe-lee-ma could see in the boy's eyes the grief that had stricken mind and spirit.

"Your uncle told me that few men could understand the thing he called 'covenant,' and fewer yet could keep it, but the few were enough. I did not understand either. I thought my brother came to love this 'covenant' too much, so that neither earth nor sky pleased him anymore, but I felt the power of your uncle's law, and it would have been foolish to move against it." The Indian paused to gaze intently at the boy, seeing in Tom's eyes a mute despair that caused his own stoic heart to feel the boy's pain.

"There is still for us the law of nature," he said. "Look to the forest. The old trees will fall, even as the new growth begins. The young fox will bring his first mate to the den. The seasons will turn, and the earth will flower with life as we follow the old trails. You will say, 'There is the meadow where the fat, fall deer grazed, and there the oak on the hillside where I stood watching, and I will say, 'Yes, but the forest grows in.' See, the aspen and pine have new brothers. Before this season turns five times, we will not hunt here again. We will become a part of the forest, and its laws will be our laws."

Deep within Tom's breast, a pulse began to beat again. His eyes reflected the new life, faint though its flame was. "If you are going back to the border, Toe-lee-ma, I will go with you," he said. "There doesn't seem to be anything else to do."

"We will tell Jed Hawkins," replied Toe-lee-ma. "He will look after the girl and whatever concerns you here."

The parting was as brief as Toe-lee-ma's explanation. Tom shook hands silently with each ranger. Unaccountably, the past overwhelmed him. First, he was trapped in the smoke oven at Number Four. Then, the darkness became the smoke clouds hovering over the Foster cabin, before changing into the angry black puffs of the cannon of Quebec. He turned, at last, as if alerted by some ancient instinct, to grasp the outstretched hands of Sally before she could wrap her arms about him. He felt the rhythm of the generations that survives the centuries pulse in those hands, and he thought of Toe-lee-ma's law of life. Grief had broken the bond that united mind and heart in the deepest understanding of sorrow, and again he felt that his life had been more senseless than the life of the creatures of the forest, and all that had made living meaningful was gone. He would join the cycle of the seasons and the life of the forest, where all things are permanently repeated until they simply cease to be.

Still, as he held the girl's hands, another law, a part of Toe-lee-ma's law but yet above, directed him to draw Sally close and give comfort to a feeling that was as much within him as it was within the girl. The mystery of the spirit that is man's real reason for existing conquered him. The covenant, not yet fully understood, but all-powerful nevertheless, made the final decision. He could not leave this suffering girl in the midst of strangers, no matter how caring they might be. He would lead her back to Number Four, gladly guiding her through the dangers that would come. This task was the fountain of all his faith and all his responsibilities. Only when it was completed would he be fit to join Toe-lee-ma in the life where the laws of nature and the forest prevail.

Only then could he hope to walk in the footsteps of Johnathan Evans as the protector and guardian of his people.

HISTORIC NAMES, PLACES, AND OBJECTS MENTIONED IN *THE BORDER COVENANT*

Sir William Johnson

Sir William Johnson is noted for establishing strong relations with the native tribes, in particular the Mohawks, one of the five founding Nations of the Iroquois League. He learned their languages, dressed in their clothing, welcomed them into his home, and labored to preserve their lands from encroachment. He also provided them with educational opportunities and religious instruction. In 1744, Johnson was appointed Superintendent of Indian Affairs for the Six Nations by the governor of New York.

Governor William Shirley

William Shirley was a noted British colonial administrator and military leader. In 1733, he became an advocate general, a position that enabled him to travel widely throughout New England. During these journeys, he became acquainted with the plight of frontiersmen living in the shadow of the French and their Indian allies. From this time forward, he became a hated enemy of the French.

Shirley was named to succeed General Braddock as commander-in-chief of British forces in North America during the French and Indian War. He quickly fell into disfavor, however, when he failed to capture Fort Niagra. In 1756, he was recalled to England and faced treason charges over his poor decisions and performance. He was later cleared and resumed his career, serving as governor of the Bahamas in the 1760s.

General Jeffrey Amherst

Amherst led the British assault on Louisbourg. Amherst, newly promoted to major general, captured the key French *bastion* on Cape Breton Island, Canada, on July 27, 1758. This victory opened the St. Lawrence River to future British invasions, and Amherst was named commander-in-chief in North America. He planned a three-pronged attack against French Canada in 1759: a westward push up the St. Lawrence to Quebec, a northward invasion from Albany by way of lakes George and Champlain, and the quelling of French strength in the west at Fort Niagra. All major objectives were met during the "Year of Victories," with Amherst playing a direct role in occupying former French positions at Fort Ticonderoga and Crown Point. He completed his triumph with the capture of Montreal in September 1760.

General Montcalm

Louis-Joseph de Montcalm-Grozon was born at Château de Candiac, France, the son of a nobleman.

Montcalm accomplished great military success in the early fighting in the French and Indian War. In 1756, his forces captured Fort Oswego, which assured French control of Lake Ontario. The following year, the French captured Fort William Henry and its two thousand soldiers; Montcalm risked his life to prevent the slaughter of English captives by enraged Indian allies.

Montcalm's brightest moment came at Fort Ticonderoga in July 1758. The French managed to hold their position despite the assault by vastly superior English forces under General James Abercrombie.

In 1759 at Quebec, Montcalm prudently refused to be lured out of his defensive position, facing the army of James Wolfe along the St. Lawrence River. However, in a masterstroke, Wolfe sailed around Montcalm, scaled the heights to the Plains of Abraham, and had his army prepared for storming Quebec. Montcalm was forced to confront the English in a momentous battle that claimed the lives of both Montcalm and Wolfe. Following the fall of Montreal in 1760, the era of New France was ended.

General James Abercrombie

General James Abercrombie headed a combined army of nearly fourteen thousand British and Colonial men in an attempt to take Fort Ticonderoga (Fort Carillon) from the French, headed by General Montcalm, in 1758. He failed, and more than two thousand of his men were killed or wounded. Eventually, his force panicked and fled, and he retreated to his fortified camp south of Lake George. This disaster caused his replacement by General Jeffrey Amherst and his recall to England in 1759. Many rangers were lost in this first attempt at the fort.

Major Robert Rogers

Robert Rogers was a popular military leader during the French and Indian War, who developed and maintained many frontier-style practices of warfare and whose forces are regarded by some as the model for later ranger activities, including todays U.S. Army Rangers.

Rogers was born in Methuen, Massachusetts, but received his experience as a frontiersman in New Hampshire. In 1756, Rogers formed a group that came to be known as Rogers' Rangers a six hundred man force of frontiersmen who had been personally recruited by Rogers himself. In *Rogers' Ranging Rules,* he set down more than two-dozen no-nonsense rules for frontier warfare. He insisted on the intensive training of his men, including exposure to live-fire exercises. The result of his efforts was to create the first special operations force on the early American Frontier, assigned to counter terrorist-style raids by the Indians on behalf of the French on the colonists.

In 1758, Rogers was given command of all colonial ranger forces in North America. The rangers used unconventional techniques, evident in the "Battle on Showshoes" (1758), when Rogers's forces struck an unsuspecting enemy near Lake George by trekking across snow and ice on snowshoes, skates, and sleds. Most armies of the day simply closed down operations during the cold weather months, but not the rangers, who even skated on the ice under the guns of Fort Ticonderoga at night while scouting the fort.

The Rangers staged their most celebrated exploit in 1759. The fierce Abenaki (Abnaki) Indians in the St. Francis River basin, now southeastern Québec and New Brunswick, had launched devastating attacks against English settlements to the south. Hundreds of lives had been lost, and public furor was further aroused by the tribe's attack on a British army retreating under a white flag of truce. Rogers assembled two hundred rangers then struck deep into enemy territory, surprised the Abenaki, killed many of them, and destroyed their village. Later that same year, Rogers served with James Wolfe at Québec, and in the following year with Jeffrey Amherst at Montreal.

General James Wolfe

General James Wolfe was commissioned in the Royal Marines at age fourteen, not an unusual age for that era. He saw action in the War of the Austrian Succession and the Jacobite Rebellion in Scotland, rising to lieutenant colonel by 1750. William Pitt, the secretary of state, hoped to capitalize on Wolfe's aggressive spirit and named him second in command to Jeffrey Amherst; the duo quickly repaired British fortunes in the French and Indian War in North America.

Wolfe's triumph on the Plains of Abraham is legendary. He was wounded three times in the short encounter, the third shot striking his lungs; he died shortly after receiving word of the British victory. The fall of the French capital in North America ended their empire, leaving Britain and Spain to vie for control of the continent.

Captain Louis-Philippe Le Dossu D'Hebecourt

Known as "Hebecourt" in *The Border Covenant*, the captain was the French commander of Fort Carillon (Fort Ticonderoga) in 1759, who sabatoged the fort with massive explosive charges and abandoned the fort at night with four hundred of his men before the British mounted an attack. The British were warned of the trap by deserting French soldiers and did not get caught in the horrific blast when the powder magazines exploded the next night, but General Amherst could not bribe anyone to go into the fort to find and douse the fuse before it exploded. The fort caught fire but remained essentially intact.

Pierre Francois de Rigaud, Marquis de Vaudreuil-Cavagnal

Known as Rigaud and Vaudreuil in *The Border Covenant*, he was a Canadian-born French colonial governor in North America. He often clashed with his General Montcalm over the plans of war. He was also Governor of French Louisiana. He lived from 1698 to 1778.

Hon. Robert Monckton

A soldier in command of the expedition against the French at Fort Beausejour in 1755. In 1759 he was senior brigadier-general under Wolfe at Quebec, and was severely wounded at the battle of the Plains of Abraham. He was appointed Governor of New York in 1761.

Joseph Goreham

Born in Massachusetts. Goreham was an officer in the Rangers assigned to protect British settlements in New England from Indian and French attacks. In 1757 Goreham and some of his rangers were dispatched to reconnoitre Louisbourg and in 1758 he served with General Amherst at the successful siege of the Fortress. In 1759 his company formed part of General Wolfe's assault on Quebec.

François-Charles de Bourlamaque

Bourlamaque was a French military leader. After entering the French army, Bourlamaque was promoted to the rank of Colonel in 1756. He was sent to Canada in 1756 as third in command of the regular troops and served with distinction throughout the subsequent campaign in Canada. In the Battle of Carillon in 1758 he commanded the French left and in 1759 led the French forces at Ticonderoga. He was made a Brigadier-General in the same year, becoming a Major-General in 1762.

OTHER TERMS OF BATTLE

Abatis (a French word meaning a heap of material thrown) is a term in field fortification for an obstacle formed of the branches of trees laid in a row, with the sharpened tops directed outward toward the enemy. The trees are usually interlaced or tied with wire. Abatis are used alone or in combination with wire entanglements and other obstacles. They are formidable to cross without aid of cannon.

Bateaux, Bateau, or *Battoe* is a rough-hewn boat out of wood with a flat bottom, raked bow, and flared ribs. At Ticonderoga in 1759, they were about thirty feet long and were capable of holding perhaps twenty men, and hundreds of them were used at a time in battles on the lakes. There are *bateaux* from the French and Indian war still sunk in the bottom of Lake George. A larger craft, the *radeau,* is not mentioned in *The Border Covenant,* but recently, a large *radeau* was recovered from Lake George, 107 feet down and largely preserved. It was a larger boat, fifty or more feet long, and carried cannons. *Fort Carillon* is the French name for Fort Ticonderoga, which was situated between Lake George and Lake Champlain on the waterway connecting the Hudson Valley in New York with the St. Lawrence Seaway and Canada.

Wobi Madaondo is an Algonquin tribal name meaning White Devil—a nickname for Major Robert Rogers given by the French Indians.

Onontio is a general Algonquin Indian term for the Governor of New France, or by extension the King of France.

Brown Bess is a nickname of uncertain origin for the British Army's Land Pattern Musket and its derivatives. It was a .75 caliber flintlock musket, and was the standard long gun of the British Empire's land forces from 1722 until 1838 when they were superseded by a percussion cap smoothbore musket.

The Fort at Number Four is a small fortification at Charlestown, New Hampshire, that was built in 1743 to protect the local inhabitants from French and Indian Raids on the Frontier Border during disputes over territory that eventually led to the French and Indian War. It was attacked repeatedly during the time of *The Border Covenant* and it is a key location in the story. Today, a reproduction of the fort stands at the original location and is open to the public.

A BRIEF TIMELINE OF THE WAR

May 17, 1756

The British formally declare war on the French. Fighting spreads to the West Indies, India, and Europe.

August 9–10, 1757

The French take Fort William Henry. However, there is a miscommunication with their Indian allies, who are angered by the terms of surrender, and the next day, they capture or kill hundreds of British. James Fenimore Cooper's book offers a fictionalized version of this story in his book *The Last of the Mohicans.*

July 8, 1758

Despite having many more troops, the British Commander Abercrombie cannot take Fort Ticonderoga. He suffers major losses and retreats. Rogers' Rangers are at the battle, and it greatly affects their thinking in the second battle for "Fort Ti," which is called Fort Carillon by the French.

June 8-July 26, 1758

The British Generals Amherst and Wolfe take the fortress at Louisbourg. This opens the St. Lawrence River and the water route to Canada.

July 26, 1759

The French army retreats, and the British capture Fort Ticonderoga and Crown Point. This battle is prominent in the first
part of *The Border Covenant.*

September 13, 1759

The French surrender the city of Quebec after the British defeat
them in an early morning battle just outside the city. Rogers'
Rangers make a surprise journey up the trails through Indian
Territory in bitter weather to meet up with General Wolfe, who
dies in the battle, along with his French counterpart, General
Montcalm. The story of *The Border Covenant* culminates in the
battle for Quebec on the Plains of Abraham.

September 8, 1760

The British capture Montreal. Fighting ends between the
French and the British in North America. The British and
French are still fighting in other parts of the world.

ROGERS' RULES OF RANGING, 1759

1. All rangers are to be subject to the rules and articles of war; to appear at roll call every evening, on their own parade, equipped, each with a firelock, sixty rounds of powder and ball, and a hatchet, at which time an officer from each company is to inspect the same, to see they are in order, so as to be ready on any emergency to march at a minute's warning; and before they are dismissed, the necessary guards are to be draughted, and scouts for the next day appointed.

2. Whenever you are ordered out to the enemies forts or frontiers for discoveries, if your number be small, march in a single file, keeping at such a distance from each other as to prevent one shot from killing two men, sending one man, or more, forward, and the like on each side, at the distance of twenty yards from the main body. If the ground you march over will admit of it, to give the signal to the officer of the approach of an enemy, and of their number, etc.

3. If you march over marshes or soft ground, change your position and march abreast of each other to prevent the enemy from tracking you (as they would do if you marched in a single file) till you get over such ground, and then resume your former order, and march till it is quite dark before you encamp, which do, if possible, on a piece of ground which that may afford your sentries the advantage of seeing or hearing the enemy some considerable distance, keeping one half of your whole party awake alternately through the night.

4. Sometime before you come to the place you would reconnoitre, make a stand, and send one or two men in whom
you can confide to look out the best ground for making your
observations.

5. If you have the good fortune to take any prisoners, keep
them separate till they are examined, and in your return,
take a different route from that in which you went out, that
you may the better discover any party in your rear, and have
an opportunity, if their strength be superior to yours, to
alter your course, or disperse, as circumstances may require.

6. If you march in a large body of three or four hundred with
a design to attack the enemy, divide your party into three
columns, each headed by a proper officer, and let those columns march in single files, the columns to the right and left
keeping at twenty yards distance or more from that of the
center, if the ground will admit, and let proper guards be
kept in the front and rear, and suitable flanking parties at
a due distance as before directed, with orders to halt on all
eminences, to take a view of the surrounding ground, to prevent your being ambuscaded, and to notify the approach or
retreat of the enemy, that proper dispositions may be made
for attacking, defending, etc. And if the enemy approach
in your front on level ground, form a front of your three
columns or main body with the advanced guard, keeping
out your flanking parties, as if you were marching under
the command of trusty officers, to prevent the enemy from
pressing hard on either of your wings, or surrounding you,
which is the usual method of the savages, if their number will admit of it, and be careful likewise to support and
strengthen your rear guard.

7. If you are obliged to receive the enemy's fire, fall or squat
down till it is over, then rise and discharge at them. If their
main body is equal to yours, extend yourselves occasionally,
but if superior, be careful to support and strengthen your

flanking parties, to make them equal to theirs, that if possible you may repulse them to their main body, in which case push upon them with the greatest resolution with equal force in each flank and in the center, observing to keep at a due distance from each other, and advance from tree to tree, with one half of the party before the other ten or twelve yards. If the enemy push upon you, let your front fire and fall down, and then let your rear advance thro' them and do the like, by which time those who before were in front will be ready to discharge again, and repeat the same alternately, as occasion shall require; by this means you, will keep up such a constant fire, that the enemy will not be able easily to break your order or gain your ground.

8. If you oblige the enemy to retreat, be careful in your pursuit of them, to keep out your flanking parties, and prevent them from gaining eminences, or rising grounds, in which case they would perhaps be able to rally and repulse you in their turn.

9. If you are obliged to retreat, let the front of your whole party fire and fall back till the rear hath done the same, making for the best ground you can; by this means, you will oblige the enemy to pursue you, if they do it at all, in the face of a constant fire.

10. If the enemy is so superior that you are in danger of being surrounded by them, let the whole body disperse, and every one take a different road to the place of rendezvous appointed for that evening, which must every morning be altered and fixed for the evening ensuing, in order to bring the whole party, or as many of them as possible, together, after any separation that may happen in the day; but if you should happen to be actually surrounded, form yourselves into a square, or if in the woods, a circle is best, and if possible, make a stand till the darkness of the night favors your escape.

11. If your rear is attacked, the main body and flankers must face about to the right or left, as occasion shall require, and form themselves to oppose the enemy, as before directed; and the same method must be observed, if attacked in either of your flanks, by which means you will always make a rear of one of your flank-guards.

12. If you determine to rally after a retreat, in order to make a fresh stand against the enemy, by all means endeavor to do it on the most rising ground you come at, which will give you greatly the advantage in point of situation and enable you to repulse superior numbers.

13. In general, when pushed upon by the enemy, reserve your fire till they approach very near, which will then put them into the greatest surprise and consternation, and give you an opportunity of rushing upon them with your hatchets and cutlasses to the better advantage.

14. When you encamp at night, fix your sentries in such a manner as not to be relieved from the main body till morning; profound secrecy and silence being often of the last importance in these cases. Each sentry, therefore, should consist of six men, two of whom must be constantly alert, and when relieved by their fellows, it should be done without noise; and in case those on duty see or hear anything which alarms them, they are not to speak, but one of them is silently to retreat and acquaint the commanding officer thereof, that proper dispositions may be made, and all occasional sentries should be fixed in like manner.

15. At the first dawn of day, awake your whole detachment; that being the time when the savages choose to fall upon their enemies, you should by all means be in readiness to receive them.

16. If the enemy should be discovered by your detachments in the morning and their numbers are superior to yours and a

victory doubtful, you should not attack them till the evening, as then they will not know your numbers and, if you are repulsed, your retreat will be favoured by the darkness of the night.

17. Before you leave your encampment, send out small parties to scout round it to see if there be any appearance or track of an enemy that might have been near you during the night.

18. When you stop for refreshment, choose some spring or rivulet, if you can, and dispose your party so as not to be surprised, posting proper guards and sentries at a due distance, and let a small party waylay the path you came in, lest the enemy should be pursuing.

19. If, in your return, you have to cross rivers, avoid the usual fords as much as possible, lest the enemy should have discovered and be there expecting you.

20. If you have to pass by lakes, keep at some distance from the edge of the water, lest, in case of an ambuscade or an attack from the enemy, when in that situation, your retreat should be cut off.

21. If the enemy pursue your rear, take a circle till you come to your own tracks, and there form an ambush to receive them and give them the first fire.

22. When you return from a scout, and come near our forts, avoid the usual roads, and avenues thereto, lest the enemy should have headed you and lay in ambush to receive you when almost exhausted with fatigues.

23. When you pursue any party that has been near our forts or encampments, follow not directly in their tracks, lest they should be discovered by their rear guards, who, at such a time, would be most alert; but endeavor, by a different route, to head and meet them in some narrow pass, or lay in ambush to receive them when and where they least expect it.

24. If you are to embark in canoes, battoes, or otherwise, by water, choose the evening for the time of your embarkation, as you will then have the whole night before you to pass undiscovered by any parties of the enemy, on hills, or other places, which command a prospect of the lake or river you are upon.

25. In paddling or rowing, give orders that the boat or canoe next the sternmost wait for her, and the third for the second, and the fourth for the third, and so on, to prevent separation, and that you may be ready to assist each other on any emergency.

26. Appoint one man in each boat to look out for fires on the adjacent shores, from the numbers and size of which you may form some judgment of the number that kindled them, and whether you are able to attack them or not.

27. If you find the enemy encamped near the banks of a river or lake, which you imagine they will attempt to cross for their security upon being attacked, leave a detachment of your party on the opposite shore to receive them, while, with the remainder, you surprise them, having them between you and the lake or river.

28. If you cannot satisfy yourself as to the enemy's number and strength, from their fire, etc., conceal your boats at some distance and ascertain their number by a reconnoitering party when they embark, or march, in the morning, marking the course they steer, etc., when you may pursue, ambush, and attack them, or let them pass, as prudence shall direct you. In general, however, that you may not be discovered by the enemy upon the lakes and rivers at a great distance, it is safest to lay by, with your boats and party concealed all day, without noise or shew; and to pursue your intended route by night; and whether you go by land or water, give out parole and countersigns, in order to know one another in the dark, and likewise, appoint a station every man to repair to, in case of any accident that may separate you.

Lightning Source UK Ltd.
Milton Keynes UK
UKOW02f2155060115

244100UK00017B/1153/P